A SEAL'S VOW

By Cora Seton

Author's Note

A SEAL's Vow is the second volume in the SEALs of Chance Creek series, set in the fictional town of Chance Creek, Montana. To find out more about Boone, Clay, Jericho and Walker, look for the rest of the books in the series, including:

A SEAL's Oath
A SEAL's Pledge
A SEAL's Consent

Also, don't miss Cora Seton's other Chance Creek series, the Cowboys of Chance Creek and the Heroes of Chance Creek

The Cowboys of Chance Creek Series:
The Cowboy Inherits a Bride (Volume 0)
The Cowboy's E-Mail Order Bride (Volume 1)
The Cowboy Wins a Bride (Volume 2)
The Cowboy Imports a Bride (Volume 3)
The Cowgirl Ropes a Billionaire (Volume 4)
The Sheriff Catches a Bride (Volume 5)
The Cowboy Lassos a Bride (Volume 6)
The Cowboy Rescues a Bride (Volume 7)
The Cowboy Earns a Bride (Volume 8)
The Cowboy's Christmas Bride (Volume 9)

The Heroes of Chance Creek Series:

The Navy SEAL's E-Mail Order Bride (Volume 1)
The Soldier's E-Mail Order Bride (Volume 2)
The Marine's E-Mail Order Bride (Volume 3)
The Navy SEAL's Christmas Bride (Volume 4)
The Airman's E-Mail Order Bride (Volume 5)

Visit Cora's website at www.coraseton.com
Find Cora on Facebook at facebook.com/CoraSeton
Sign up for my newsletter HERE.
www.coraseton.com/sign-up-for-my-newsletter

CHAPTER ONE

C LAY PICKETT SNAPPED awake with an alertness
born of long years of active duty as a Navy SEAL.
But he wasn't in the hills of Afghanistan, the deserts of
Iraq or any of the other exotic locales he'd visited
during his years of service. He was thirty feet from the
bunkhouse at Westfield, a large, once-prosperous ranch
in Chance Creek, Montana, where he'd come with
several of his oldest friends to build a sustainable
community and show the world a better way to live.

There shouldn't be any danger here, but Clay was as
alert as if he'd been sleeping in a minefield. You never
knew where trouble would spring from. He found it
best to expect the worst and be pleasantly surprised
when disaster didn't strike. Holding his breath, he
listened for the noise that had jolted him out of his
dreams, but all he heard was the normal early morning
sounds in Base Camp—the assortment of tents and
outbuildings that formed the headquarters of the
community for now. Someone was snoring. Someone
else rolled over and settled back into sleep.

Clay quickly pulled on boxer briefs, a pair of sweat-pants, socks, shoes and a T-shirt, and eased the zipper of his tent open. As he stepped out into the cool pre-dawn air, the familiar scents of the countryside made him inhale deeply.

Home.

He was back where he belonged. Where there was good work to be done and a future for him. As he scanned the quiet tents, the nearby fire pit, bunkhouse and barns, and the farther off pastures that rolled down to the distant mountains, Clay relaxed.

There was nothing out of order that he could see. Just his destiny spread out before him. Life was good. Real good.

Something snapped in a row of bushes lining the dirt lane that ran from the bunkhouse out to the highway. Clay, alert again, moved quickly to investigate, and laughed when a wren darted out of the foliage and flew so close by his head he heard the whirr of its wings. There was nothing to fear here in Chance Creek.

Except failure.

Clay tried to ignore that thought, but it wound its way into his mind with the tenacity of a serpent entering paradise. He and his friends had a number of tough challenges ahead of them, but only one of them gave him pause.

He needed a wife.

Soon.

Clay turned around to face the large, three-story stone house perched on a rise of ground a quarter mile away. Nicknamed the manor for its grandiose style, it had sheltered Westfield's owners for over a hundred years. Now it housed Nora Ridgeway and her friends, who'd come to Chance Creek on a mission of their own. They'd left their jobs, apartments and city life behind to come to Westfield, and had promised each other they'd spend six months devoting themselves to the artistic endeavors they had studied back in college. In order to stretch their budget, they'd sold most of their possessions. Like the men of Base Camp, they practiced a frugal way of life, but where Clay and his friends relied on the latest technology to make their community sustainable, the women had gone in an entirely different direction. Instead of focusing on the future, they had turned to the past.

"A Jane Austen life is a beautiful life," Nora had explained to him in the early days of their acquaintance, back when he'd thought she was falling for him as fast as he was falling for her. "By living the way her characters did—without modern distractions—we have more time for our art, music and writing. When we wear Regency clothing, it's a constant reminder of our goals—and, as Avery puts it, we're less likely to go gallivanting into town all the time. People stare."

Clay had quickly grown to like those Regency dresses. They set off Nora's figure in a wonderful way. In fact, he had to concentrate when she was around not to let his gaze drop too often—and linger too long—on her cleavage. Whatever she wore underneath those clothes did wonderful things to lift and plump up her breasts. More than that, Nora in one of those old-fashioned gowns revved him up in some primal way he couldn't quite put into words. Her looking so womanly made him feel like a man. He'd never say that out loud, but it was true.

The simple, peaceful rhythm of the women's days appealed to Clay, too. He thought the two groups had goals that weren't mutually exclusive, but that didn't mean all went smoothly between them.

Far from it.

Clay missed the days when talking to Nora was simple. They'd ended as soon as the women had heard about the reality TV show being filmed about Base Camp. Once Nora knew the rules Clay had to live by, she'd backed off fast and Clay had promised not to pursue her. That had been a big mistake, one Clay regretted the moment he'd made it.

Still, who could blame her? He knew what had scared her off. It wasn't that the homes they built had to consume less than ten percent of the energy normal houses used. It wasn't that their energy grid had to run exclusively on renewable resources. It wasn't that they needed to create a closed-loop gardening system and grow all the food they'd need to last through the winter.

It was that their financial backer—eccentric billionaire Martin Fulsom—had dictated all ten men living in Base Camp had to marry within six months, and three of their wives had to be pregnant with the next generation, or they'd lose the ranch.

Nora refused point blank to consider marrying anyone in such a short period of time. Clay had tried to be a gentleman. He'd tried to back off. But it hadn't worked. He couldn't cure himself of the desire to make Nora his wife.

Somehow he had to convince Nora he was the man for her—despite her reservations. He didn't know how. Didn't know if she could be convinced.

But he sure as hell was going to try.

Starting today.

SOMEONE WAS WATCHING her.

Nora came fully awake and sat up in bed, listening to the silence. She'd been on edge for months now, ever since she'd started getting disturbing phone messages from one of her students. But she'd left all that behind her when she'd come to Chance Creek. No one outside her family and a couple of friends had her address or new phone number. She hadn't heard a word from her stalker in the two months since she'd arrived.

Dust motes danced in a beam of early morning light that pierced through the curtains of her third-story bedroom. The old-fashioned furnishings and pretty curtains were the same as ever. Nora loved this room, but something had woken her. A sound.

A click.

She turned to the door but it was shut as tight as always when she went to bed. She didn't lock herself in at night—she was paranoid about fires in this large, old house, and mindful of the two-story drop outside her window should she ever have to escape one. Had one of her friends opened the door, looked inside to see if she was awake, then shut it again?

"Riley?" Nora whispered.

If anyone was awake this early it would be her. It was only two days to Riley's wedding, and Nora knew her friend was nervous about it. She slid out of bed, threw her robe around her and went to the door. She opened it carefully, looked out into the empty hall and padded over to the staircase. "Riley?" she called softly again.

No answer.

She must have been imagining things. Or maybe the house had settled. This old pile of stone did that a lot.

Nora returned to her room, but although the bed looked warm and comfortable, the quiet countryside she could see through her windows beckoned to her. She seldom got time alone these days, and if she hurried, she could get a little writing in before breakfast and morning chores. She'd head down to Pittance Creek, bring her notebook and a pen. Maybe the setting would inspire her and she'd finally make some headway.

She moved to the window, surveyed the cluster of tents down by the bunkhouse and picked out Clay's. There was nothing to distinguish it from the others, but she knew exactly where it was. She'd seen the handsome SEAL enter and exit it a hundred times.

Nora knew she shouldn't watch him like this.

She couldn't seem to stop.

Clay Pickett. Strong. Rugged. Six feet plus of muscles, piercing eyes and a smile that did things to her insides. A coil of energy waiting to spring most of the time. She'd met him the day he'd flown into Chance Creek. The day she'd been trying to fly out of it, trying to run back to Baltimore, back to her old life. She'd changed her mind almost the second Riley's fiancé, Boone Rudman, had spotted her, crossed the terminal to intercept her and introduced her to Clay. She was sure Clay had felt something, too. He'd taken her hand, caught her gaze and the next thing she knew she was headed back to Westfield. She'd never admitted it to any of her friends, but on that very first day, right there in the airport, she'd seen Clay decide she was the one. She'd read it in his eyes. The answering heat that had rushed through her when he held her hand had almost convinced her he was right. That was her weakness: the way Clay touched her. Carefully. Confidently. She melted every time. Two strangers shouldn't know they were meant for each other.

Couldn't know, Nora reminded herself. Who was to say her parents hadn't felt a similar heat when they met? Attraction like that flared hot, then quickly burned itself out, leaving everyone involved nursing wounds—especially the children. She'd seen it all firsthand when she was young and her father had walked out on her family, leaving her mother to struggle to make ends meet for the rest of her short life. Nora wanted no part of it.

Still, her gaze slid in Clay's direction whenever he was near. But he was out of bounds, determined to marry within a time period so short it was ridiculous, because he had to for the reality television show he was starring in. Maybe that made him a man of honor since he'd vowed to do whatever it took to make Base Camp succeed, but in Nora's eyes it made him a fool. Love took time to grow. Lots of time. Her parents were a classic example of what happened when a man and woman leaped before they looked. She wouldn't repeat their mistakes.

Not even with a man like Clay.

Time to write, she told herself firmly and began to dress, struggling with her old-fashioned clothes. Several months back, she and her friends had each been saddled with dead-end jobs, high rent and low pay in their various cities. They'd met at Riley's apartment for a girls' weekend, and realized they all needed to make a change. Savannah Edwards, a lovely blonde and an expert classical pianist, had been the first to suggest they pool their resources, cut way back on their expenses and take six months to pursue their artistic goals.

Riley Eaton, a pretty brunette with a passion for painting, who'd believed her family still owned West-field, suggested they make use of the empty house and live rent free. When Nora told the others they were fooling themselves if they thought they had the discipline to pull it off, Avery Lightfoot, a talkative redhead, suggested an unusual way to make sure they kept close to home. She pointed out that since they meant to live a Jane Austen–style existence for six months, they should dress like Jane Austen heroines, too. They'd spend their mornings doing chores, and leave their afternoons free for creative pursuits. Riley would paint, Savannah practice her piano, Nora write her novel and Avery produce a screenplay.

In the end, they'd all agreed to the plan—even Nora—and their Regency outfits became a physical representation of the oath they'd taken to see the full six months through. Each morning when she dressed it was like renewing her promise to herself to give writing a real go. To her surprise, Nora found she loved it. Putting on a Regency gown was like stepping out of time. She wasn't the only one who felt that way. When Savannah's cousin found out what they were doing, she asked to hold her wedding at the manor. That sparked an idea for a Jane Austen–style bed-and-breakfast—and wedding venue—that would allow them to stay at Westfield past the initial six months.

Nora had come to love the pace of life at the manor. Here at Westfield it was easy to imagine herself in those long-ago days—until she looked out her window and saw the encampment of nylon tents down by the outbuildings. Base Camp—the only fly in the ointment. Once she and her friends had arrived at Westfield, they'd quickly learned Riley's uncle had sold the ranch. Luckily Boone—Riley's husband-to-be—would own it with his friends—if and when they fulfilled the requirements of the reality television show they were part of.

Unfortunately, while Nora and her friends viewed their purpose for being here as a chance to pursue the arts, the men of Base Camp seemed to view them as wife fodder—conveniently placed single women who should be happy to marry them at the drop of a hat. She hadn't come here to marry, though.

Nora had come here to write—and, if she was honest, to get away from the student who'd made her life a living hell back in Baltimore. But she didn't want to think of the increasingly disturbing and violent messages he'd recorded on her voice mail before she'd left—not when a beautiful morning was dawning outside her window. All that was behind her now, and if she'd had to leave the teaching job she loved to get away from his harassment, that was just life.

A light rap on her door startled her. "Nora? Do you need help with your clothes?"

Nora took a deep breath, willing her heart to start beating again. Damn her stalker and the way he'd made her into this nervous wreck. She went to open it and found Riley in the hall, hair tousled, looking far younger than her years in the voluminous, old-fashioned night-gown she wore.

"Did I wake you?" Nora asked her to cover her overreaction.

"I'm not sure. Something did. Where are you off to so early?"

"Down to the creek. I'm looking for inspiration."

A smile curved Riley's mouth. "Pittance Creek can be inspiring."

Nora wondered what memory inspired that smile, but she finished pulling on her underthings and slipped her stays on over her chemise. Riley moved behind her and began to tug the laces tight. Getting into Regency clothing was not a solitary pursuit. Several minutes later, Nora was dressed.

"What about you?" she asked Riley.

"Go on. I want to shower. I'll wait for Savannah or Avery to help me."

Five minutes later, Nora struck out down the track that led past Base Camp toward the creek. She wondered if Clay was awake. The camp seemed quiet as she walked past.

It didn't matter, she told herself. That wasn't why she was here.

But she was disappointed when she didn't see him.

As CLAY JOGGED down the two-lane country highway that led to town, his earlier disquiet slipped away. These daily runs were a lifesaver to him. Always had been. Like his father before him, Clay was wound as tight as a watch. His endless energy had gotten him kicked out of more grade-school classrooms than he could count when his bouncing knee jostled a desk for the third time in thirty minutes and knocked pencils and papers flying, or his endlessly tapping fingers finally drove a teacher to lose her cool and start screaming.

He didn't mean to be disruptive. He was never even aware of what he was doing. The Navy had finally taught him that eight miles before breakfast took the edge off his overflow of energy.

Four miles in he hit the mid-point and turned toward home, his mind on Boone's upcoming wedding, so when a man launched himself out of the bushes and nearly bowled Clay over, Clay shouted and lashed out, stumbling before he regained his balance and stopped short.

"What the hell, Walker?" He shoved the larger man away, struggled to regain his composure and began to jog again, unwilling to let his friend know his heart was pounding with shock.

"Thought I'd join you," Walker Norton said with a shrug. The large man jogged after him. "Kinda slow today, aren't you?"

"Jesus—" Clay bit back a string of curses. He hated it when his friend did shit like this. A man of Walker's size shouldn't be able to sneak up on anyone, which was why the Native American had so much fun doing it. Walker was always quiet, and in natural settings it was like he could disappear in plain view, something that had helped him excel as a Navy SEAL. Clay didn't begrudge him the way he'd managed to climb the ranks, but it infuriated him when Walker caught him off guard.

"You're getting predictable." Walker picked up speed and jogged past him.

Pissed, Clay ran after him. He knew Walker meant he kept taking the same route. Where the heck else was he supposed to go? Clay wondered. It's not like there were a lot of choices out here in ranch country. He caught up to his friend and elbowed past him. He wasn't about to let Walker set the pace.

"You're getting soft," Walker continued, easily keeping stride. "I followed you all the way from Base Camp. You didn't even notice."

"I wasn't expecting to be followed."

"Which is exactly when you should be vigilant."

Clay did his best to ignore his friend's presence and return to his previous train of thought. He was proud of the tiny homes he'd designed for Base Camp and he'd be prouder still to build them. Back in high school, he'd thought he might attend Montana State and study architecture. His father's response still rang in his ears as his feet hit the pavement in steady beats.

"Architecture? And who's going to pay for that? Your rich uncle?"

Walker, still running at Clay's rapid pace, reached out and snapped off a handful of small twigs from a bush at the side of the road. He discarded all but two, stripped those of leaves as they ran, fooled around with them a bit and then held out a fist toward Clay. The two twigs protruded an equal distance from his meaty fingers. Clay eyed them suspiciously.

"What's that?"

"Pick."

"Fuck, no." He'd had enough of Walker's tricks this morning. He'd been feeling upbeat—almost relaxed—when the other man jumped out of the hedgerow. Now he'd bet his life he was about to be ambushed again.

Architecture. He could use that degree today, but stung by the fury in his father's tone, Clay had never brought it up again after the first time. He knew his father had attended two years of school following the same passion before his family's ranch had gone bust and Dell had left school to help support his mother and father. He'd never gone back, and had nothing good to say about higher education now. "We've raised a prima donna," he'd heard Dell say to Lizette, Clay's mother, in the kitchen later that night. "Sooner that boy learns what life's about, the better." Clay hadn't heard his mother's response—he didn't need to. He understood once and for all that higher education wasn't for him. He'd joined the Navy with his friends within the year and had never looked back.

Now he cursed himself for his short-sightedness. Ever since they'd decided to found Base Camp, he'd studied everything he could find on building sustainably, but what if he made a mistake in front of thousands of television viewers?

"Pick," Walker insisted, shaking his fist near Clay's face as they ran on.

"What am I supposed to be picking for?"

"Who's up next—after Boone."

Clay's stride faltered, but he caught himself and kept going. Walker was talking about marriage.

"Boone's getting hitched," Walker continued. "One of us has got to go next. Could be you." He shook his hand in front of Clay again.

Clay had been trying to forget about that part. It was going to take time to convince Nora to change her mind.

"What about Jericho?" he hedged. He, Boone, Walker and Jericho had all pledged to marry fast and start working toward those pregnancies. Even though the other men who had signed on knew they needed to marry by the deadline, Clay and his friends figured as founding members it was up to them to lead the way.

"He already picked. Drew a long one. It's just you and me."

"I didn't see him do it."

"I did."

Walker wasn't backing down and Clay had a feeling if he didn't pick one of the damn twigs soon, that fist he was waving would connect with Clay's face. Not that Walker was a violent man.

But he was an insistent one from time to time.

"Come on." Walker shook the twigs again. Clay ran faster.

Walker put on a burst of speed, got ahead of Clay and turned around, jogging backward in front of him. He held out the twigs. "Get it over with."

Clay tried to get past him. Walker blocked his way.

Clay veered to the other side. He couldn't be next to marry. Not until he could convince Nora that he was serious about her. Walker followed, blocked him again, came to an abrupt halt and forced Clay to do the same.

"Pick."

Clay sighed. There was nothing for it; he was only putting off the inevitable. He surveyed the two sticks in Walker's hand, knowing that if his turn came next he'd never have enough time to change Nora's mind.

"Here's an idea," he said. "I'll hold the sticks. You pick."

The shift in Walker's expression was so subtle, only someone who'd known him as long as Clay had would notice it. This wasn't his friend anymore. This was the man who'd been his superior officer in the SEALs. And he was at the end of his patience.

With a nod to acknowledge he got the message, Clay reached out and hesitated, trying to divine which stick was longer.

Time to bite the bullet. He chose one and pulled it free of Walker's fist.

Walker held up the other one—twice as long as the stubby twig in Clay's hand.

Clay's heart sank.

A grin tugged at Walker's mouth and he stepped aside. "Better get going. You don't have much time to find a bride."

Clay couldn't move. He could only stare at the twig in his hand. After a long moment, Walker jogged off, leaving Clay to slowly walk the rest of the way home, wondering how the hell he could convince Nora to marry him.

Fast.

By the time he reached Base Camp, he had decided to grab the bull by the horns. He could pussyfoot around the problem and hope for a miracle, or he could confront Nora, tell her how he felt, lay out all the reasons why they'd be good together and hope she agreed with him. Maybe all this time he'd spent thinking about her, she'd been thinking about him, too. He'd noticed her watching him a time or two when she thought he wasn't looking. Maybe underneath all those Regency clothes beat a heart that wanted him as much as he wanted her. What if she'd been waiting for him to make the first move?

"Where you off to?" Jericho called on his way to the bunkhouse as Clay walked past. A tall, muscular blond, he was one of the other founding members of Base Camp, and an old friend.

"I'll be back soon. Just want a word with Nora first," Clay told him. He turned toward the manor.

"I saw her heading down to the creek," Jericho said.

"Thanks." Changing direction, Clay strode off on the dirt track that led to Pittance Creek, then broke into a jog. No sense wasting time. Today was the day he'd convince Nora to be his wife. In fact, he'd flat out ask her. Maybe she'd say yes. Maybe he'd been overthinking things all this time.

He broke into a run.

NORA SAT ON her flat stone gazing at the creek, her thoughts too tangled to get any writing done, although her notebook sat in her lap, a pen clipped to its pages.

She kept thinking of Riley's upcoming marriage to Boone, which inevitably led to thoughts of Clay. It was hard not to wish their circumstances were different. Living so close together, they should have had lots of chances to meet up, talk and get to know one another. Without a deadline, they could have discovered their areas of common interest. Maybe they would have gone for long walks. Maybe they'd have swum in the creek in the summer. Eventually they might have dated, kissed and...more. The thought of a long, slow courtship with the SEAL made her veins sizzle. She couldn't pretend she hadn't dreamed of how it would go—how Clay would seduce her over time.

But Clay needed a wife far too soon for them to experience anything like that. She'd explained that to him. He'd said he didn't have a choice. Someday soon he'd marry.

And she'd still be alone.

As much as she tried to enjoy the beautiful setting and the soft morning air, that thought kept intruding, along with memories of Baltimore. The last few years hadn't been easy. After her mother's death following a long illness, Nora had been lonely and vulnerable, an easy mark for a teenager with a grudge.

It had been several weeks since she'd really thought about her stalker, and she wished he wasn't on her mind now. She had an unsettled feeling, the same one she always got when the wind shifted around to herald an oncoming storm. As she watched the creek roll past, she allowed memories of her stalker's messages to seep through her defenses. She shut her eyes when his voice—his awful, mechanically distorted, gritty voice—filled her mind instantly with echoes of his violently sexual messages. He was always harping on the relationship between them. That she'd been the teacher, but now she'd be his student.

I'll teach you so many things you don't know. You'll like it when I touch you. You'll get wet for me. You'll beg for more.

She hated the way his words had twisted her insides around with shame and fear.

I'll tease you until you're shaking, until you open for me, hoping I fill you full. I know you like it rough and it'll get rough—I promise you that, Nora.

She hated the way he'd used her name over and over again until she'd thought about changing it legally when she left Baltimore. How unfair that someone could take something so personal and make it so ugly—as if he owned more of her than she did.

None of that was what kept her up at night, though. It was the violence in his later messages. The detailed descriptions of how he'd kill her. The way he'd twisted it together with sexual images until her flesh crawled with the dread of his hands on her skin.

I'll fuck you long and hard. Until your screams leave your throat hoarse. Until you can't scream anymore. And that's when the real fun—

"Nora! There you are!"

Nora shrieked when someone hurtled at her out of the woods, scooped her up and swung her around in a circle. Adrenaline sliced through her as she kicked out her feet and pummeled her fists against her attacker. She screamed again, fought to shake him off, but he had her in such a tight hold she couldn't move.

"Nora!"

She flailed and kicked and thrashed but she couldn't get free. She couldn't—

"Nora, it's me! It's Clay! Baby, you're all right." He set her back down on the stone and circled quickly around to crouch before her.

Nora couldn't breathe. Hyperventilating, she scrambled to her knees to ward him off. "No…no!"

Clay backed away, his hands held out to appease her. "It's just me. Calm down! I'm sorry I scared you."

She sat down again on the rock with a thump, wrapped her arms around her stomach and bent over, trying to catch her breath. Her heart was racing, her pulse tripping and catching in her veins. Tears pricked her eyes but she refused to let them fall. Damn it, what had Clay been thinking, sneaking up on her like that?

"Are you okay?"

She straightened. "No… I'm not… okay." She wasn't, not even close. Her heart wouldn't stop and she pressed a hand to her chest, willing it to slow down. It was hard to breathe, too. She tried to suck in air but somehow it wouldn't reach her lungs. Clay's expression changed from worry to outright concern.

"Nora, look at me." She did so. "Count. One, two, three…" He led her up to ten, back down again and repeated the exercise. Nora did her best count with him. Was her heart slowing? Maybe.

They did it again. Bit by bit, the air reached her lungs.

Finally she was able to let her shoulders relax, and the world stopped spinning. She felt like she'd woken from a nightmare, shreds of the dream still flapping around her.

"I'm sorry." Clay's gaze searched hers. "I won't do that again."

Nora could only nod.

Clay sat down beside her. "So much for impressing

you with my romantic fervor."

Despite everything, she laughed, a funny little gulp that was almost a sob. "Yeah. So much for that." She fought for composure. "I was thinking about Baltimore. About that kid..."

"The one who stalked you?" Clay raked a hand through his hair. "Shit, I didn't even think..."

"It's okay," she assured him, embarrassed by her overreaction.

"Can we start over?"

"I guess so." She couldn't help but notice the way the sunlight brought out the color of his eyes. He was so close to her she could see faint traces of laugh lines radiating out from the corners of them. His concern was plain and she relaxed a little more. The SEAL was so damn handsome.

And such an ass for scaring her like that.

He took a deep breath. "Nora, there's something I want to ask you. Something really important—" He cut off and frowned as if he'd changed his mind. "You know what? I'd probably better walk you back to camp. It's getting late and we've got a lot to do to prepare for the wedding."

She nodded, gathering herself together, but she wondered what he'd really wanted to say. Had he been about to ask her out?

No. She'd made it perfectly clear she wouldn't date him.

He reached out to help her up, then snatched his hand back quickly, probably afraid she'd decline after his botched attempt to sweep her off her feet. What had he been thinking when he'd scooped her up like that? He'd said it was a romantic gesture, but they'd agreed he would leave her alone.

Had he changed his mind?

It didn't matter, she told herself, because no matter what, he was out of bounds. He'd sworn to marry quickly. She'd sworn to only wed when she really and truly could say she knew her fiancé through and through.

But as she stood up and matched her steps to his as they turned their backs on the creek, she wished once again that things were different.

CHAPTER TWO

ON A MOONLIT evening several days later, Nora stood arm in arm with Savannah and Avery, and watched Riley and Boone ride off on Behemoth, a large black stallion, to their honeymoon tent on the far side of the ranch. Their wedding had gone off without a hitch, and Nora was thrilled for Riley. Her friend had positively glowed at the altar as she exchanged vows with her husband-to-be. It was almost enough to make Nora believe in marriage again.

Almost.

The champagne she'd drunk toasting the happy couple had gone to her head and she swayed a little on her feet as they watched Boone and Riley go.

"That was so romantic," Avery sighed as the horse disappeared in the dark night.

"Riley is so lucky," Savannah agreed.

"Nora, how about another dance?" Clay appeared suddenly by her side and Nora blinked up at the tall SEAL, wondering not for the first time how he could possibly look so good dressed as he was in the old-fashioned uniform of a British redcoat. All the men of Base Camp were dressed in the same way—the closest equivalent to the ladies' Regency wear they'd been able to come up with on short notice. Riley had wanted a Jane Austen wedding, and the men had done everything they could to accommodate her. A local seamstress, Alice Reed, had the uniforms on hand. Nora's heart was full when she thought of how hard these hardened warriors had worked to give Riley a wedding she'd remember all her life.

"Okay," she said, although she knew she shouldn't. She was finding Clay difficult to resist tonight, though. She'd danced with him half a dozen times already. He'd held her carefully in his arms during the slow numbers, and executed the complicated steps of the Regency dances perfectly. Nora couldn't help but feel she'd been transported into a fairy tale, and for once she decided to kick common sense to the curb. It wasn't like Riley would ever marry again. This night would never be repeated.

Besides, Clay was intelligent, thoughtful, and she was... well... tipsy, at the very least. "You did good tonight," she told him as he led her back into the barn where the reception was being held. The men had cleaned it top to bottom and strung fairy lights all around the rafters. It was a magical space, and the music and champagne combined to make Nora feel relaxed and happy. She placed her hands on his shoulders and he rested his briefly at her hips before he pulled her close and wrapped his arms around her. Pressed against him, Nora tingled all over, all too aware of his body.

"Jericho and I snuck out to their tent earlier today. Made sure they'd have champagne on ice and everything else a couple of lovebirds might want."

"You didn't play any tricks on them, did you?" Nora pulled back. If they had, Riley would laugh it off, but Nora knew she wouldn't like it.

"Nothing like that," Clay assured her. "Boone and Riley deserve more respect than that. They've worked hard to be together despite everything Fulsom threw their way. I know it wasn't easy for either of them."

His serious tone squeezed her heart. Most men she knew treated anything akin to romance as a big joke. Clay was different. Maybe his time with the SEALs had taught him to value any true emotion wherever he might find it. The hardships in her life had taught her to feel that way. That's why her friendship with Riley, Savannah and Avery was so important. No one else came as close to knowing her as they did. Was it the same for Clay, Boone, Jericho and Walker?

They swayed in time to the slow ballad the live band was playing, and Nora revelled in Clay's comforting smell, the beat of his heart and the careful way he held her. "No, it wasn't," she agreed. "But Riley loves Boone, and I think he loves her, too."

"He definitely does," Clay assured her. "I think the two of them are proof that any problems between people can be worked out if they both make an effort. Don't you?"

Nora was too smart to walk into that trap, but she

couldn't entirely disagree with him, either. Too many times she'd seen relationships in which one person made the effort and the other person didn't. "If two people are willing to do whatever it takes, maybe, but that's rare, don't you think?"

"Rare, but not unknown," he countered. As he guided her gently around the dance floor, Nora felt the play of his muscles under her hands. Clay was doing it again—holding her with such confidence she felt absolutely safe with him. Did he have any idea how often she dreamed about his hands on her bare skin?

A girl could fall for a guy like him.

Even if she knew she shouldn't.

"When I set my mind on a goal, I give it my all," he said lightly.

Nora glanced up at him and found him looking back down at her. She was finding it difficult to breathe again, her ribs hemmed in by the boning of her corset, but unlike down at the creek, this had nothing to do with fear and everything to do with the man who was holding her. "Have you set your mind on a goal?" Her throat was dry, the words hard to form.

His arms tightened around her. "Yeah. I have."

A wild hope fluttered inside her chest that he'd decided to renew his attempts to be with her. Immediately she shut it down. Clay was off limits. He needed to stay that way.

"What do you think about that?" he asked when she remained silent, their two bodies moving rhythmically together in a way that didn't satisfy her cravings at all.

Nora wanted to be closer to Clay. She wanted to push aside the heavy lapels of his redcoat uniform, unbutton his white shirt and splay her hands over his chest. She wanted to kiss him. Taste him. But she only shrugged.

"You know what my goal is, don't you?" he whispered in her ear. Nora shivered as his breath tickled her, and she inadvertently tightened her grip on his shoulders.

"I want to be with you," he said. "Forever."

Nora realized she was trembling. Caught between desire and common sense, it was hard to know how to proceed. Every time she came near Clay she lost her head, but it was far too soon to talk about forever.

If Nora was ever to think of marrying Clay, she needed time to get to know him—to fall in love with him...

Because whatever this was, this warm, encompassing excitement she felt whenever Clay was near, it couldn't be love. It had to be infatuation, or lust, or...whatever you called it when you were alone too long, and someone finally paid attention to you. Love—true love—took time to grow.

Clay refused to give her time...or rather, he didn't have it to give.

"Nora?" Clay said softly when she didn't answer.

"Yes?"

"I'd like to kiss you."

No. She needed to say no. But she couldn't force herself to say the word, not when her whole body wanted him to. She lifted her chin to look up at him again. He bent down and brushed his mouth over hers, and Nora was lost. She went up on tiptoe and clung to him as he kissed her. Time slowed and the moment went on and on until Nora wasn't sure where they were anymore. She was dizzy, and happy, and… in love, despite what she told herself. When Clay stopped dancing and began to move toward the door, she took his hand and hurried after him, not minding that he bundled her out of the barn and into the deep shadows outside.

Just this once, she told herself. Just this one night she'd relax her rules and enjoy herself. Circling around the barn to the back of the building, he found a place hidden from prying eyes. Clay pressed her up against its wooden walls, hemming her in with his body, and gathered her into a tight embrace. His kisses deepened, grew hungrier, and Nora met him willingly, trailing the tip of her tongue along his lower lip, then nipping at him, wanting something she knew she couldn't have.

When he tilted her head back, traced his lips down her neck to the dip between her breasts, Nora finally regained her senses and stopped him.

"No. We can't," she gasped.

He searched her face. "Can't?" His breathing was uneven. Nora knew he wanted her and knew she was close to giving in to him. She wanted him, too, so badly it was like a physical pain. But she was already playing with fire, and if she made love to him she'd start a blaze that could end up burning everyone at Westfield. She didn't intend to marry Clay—not when his actions were being governed by Fulsom's rules. Not when she didn't really know him.

"Just kissing," she made herself say.

His gaze raked her up and down. "I…"

"Clay. That's all I can do."

She watched him struggle to get himself under control. He had a hard time of it and Nora knew many men would stride away and leave her standing alone in the shadows. She'd danced with him, kissed him, come out here with him…

"That's a tall order," he confessed with a lopsided grin, and Nora's heart throbbed again. Damn it, Clay was such a good man. Why couldn't she give in and let his timetable call the shots?

Because she couldn't, Nora knew. Not and be true to herself. "It is for me, too." She hoped he had the self-control to pull it off. She wasn't sure she did.

"Just kissing," he agreed. "But a whole hell of a lot of it. How's that sound?"

"Heavenly." She bit her lip. She hadn't meant to say that out loud. Clay's expression softened.

"Someday I'm going to make an honest woman of you, Nora Ridgeway."

"Clay—"

"Shh. Just kissing for now." But the look in his eyes told her he thought he'd won a victory. Nora knew she should set him straight. It wasn't fair to lead a grown man on when she knew her heart.

Although her heart didn't quite seem to be getting the message. As Clay made out with her like they were teenagers, pressing her back against the wall of the barn, his fervor leaving her breathless, she knew he was right; she wanted forever.

She simply couldn't have it.

An hour later, when Clay walked her to the manor, Nora ached so badly to be made love to her nerves thrummed with desire.

"I won't get to sleep tonight," Clay said when they paused outside the manor's front door. "I'm going to be thinking of you."

She knew what he meant. "I'll be thinking of you, too," she said honestly. She couldn't even pretend otherwise. No way she could sleep in this state.

"We could help each other," Clay suggested, leaning toward her.

Nora angled away. "No, we can't," she said sadly.

"Why not?" He pressed a kiss to the base of her neck and Nora felt herself slipping, wanting to give in.

"Because if you touch me much longer, I'd have to beg you to take me," she confessed.

"I want to."

"I want you to, too."

"Nora..."

She knew all that Clay wanted to say. This was crazy. It was agony. It wasn't fair.

But it was the way it had to be. In the morning they'd still be at Westfield. Clay would still have to marry within six months. That still wouldn't be long enough for them to really know if they could make a go of it forever.

Would it?

Nora wavered. Her body seemed to think it would all work out just fine.

Clay kissed her again. "I'll see you tomorrow." He took a step back.

Disappointed, Nora almost went after him. "Tomorrow," she echoed. For one long moment she teetered on the precipice, ready to ask him to stay despite all her fears, but she waited a second too long, and Clay, like a gentleman, backed away.

"Be thinking of you." He saluted her and turned away, a redcoat returning to his regiment.

"I'll be thinking of you, too," Nora answered softly and went inside, an honorable maiden who hadn't slipped up before her wedding.

Not that she was a Regency virgin, she thought as she trailed slowly upstairs. So why was she acting like one?

Maybe she was wrong. Maybe she knew all she needed to about Clay in order to marry him.

Maybe everything she wanted was right here at Chance Creek.

CHAPTER THREE

"CLAY? YOU UP? We've got a problem."

Clay woke the morning after the wedding when Jericho's voice pierced the thin fabric of his tent. Reluctantly, he turned over, grabbed the nearest pair of jeans he could find and a few moments later scrambled out of his tent to find Jericho and Walker outside.

Jericho handed him a tablet. "Take a look."

Clay took it from him. "What..." He cut off as he registered the images on-screen. All ten men of Base Camp in uniform. Clay wondered how Fulsom's people had gotten hold of the military photographs. That wasn't the worst of it, though. The photos had been altered, manipulated somehow so that instead of normal men they looked like... superheroes. "What the fuck?" He looked to Jericho for an explanation.

"It's the website for the television show," Walker said.

Clay scrolled up to see the title of the site. *Base Camp*. He scrolled down to take in the rest of the site. There were vital statistics listed for each of them, along with a description of the show, complete with video-game-like icons representing each of the goals they had to reach.

Clay scrolled down a little farther and spotted Edward Montague's self-satisfied face. A developer intent on carving Westfield into a cookie-cutter housing tract, Montague made the perfect villain. Fulsom had pulled him into the game to give the viewing public more reason to watch the show—and to care if Clay and his friends met their goals or not.

If they didn't, Fulsom would give Base Camp and the entire ranch to Montague to be decimated and turned into a suburb of McMansions. Not just their community, but the manor, too. Clay and his friends would lose their home and their chance to demonstrate that a good life could consume far less resources than most Americans did. Nora and her friends would lose their B and B.

Clay wanted to succeed. Needed to. But Fulsom wasn't making it easy.

"We knew this was coming. Fulsom is going to advertise the hell of this show, and he's going to do whatever he can to make it controversial and newsworthy," he said to the others as he read farther down the page, stopping when he got to a comment section.

"That's not the problem. Look at the run dates." Jericho grabbed the tablet back before Clay could read more than a few messages. Probably for the best given what he'd seen so far. Several comments denied climate change altogether. A couple of others were more concerned with his friends' looks than the message of the show. One woman said she'd do Boone.

Riley wasn't going to like that.

When Jericho faced the device toward him again, Clay read the text he was pointing at. "That's a full year." He blinked the last of the sleep from his eyes and read it again. "It has to be a mistake." The show was only supposed to last six months.

Jericho shook his head. "Fulsom doesn't make mistakes. He just plays God. Our commitment to the show just went from six months to a year. Which means Savannah and the rest of them are going to flip their lids."

"And leave," Clay finished for him. Now the truth of the matter finally sank in and he understood why Jericho had come to get him. "We could refuse."

"Really? How do you think that will play out?"

Jericho was right; Fulsom held all the cards. If he wanted the show to last a year, it would last a year.

"We have to warn the others before Fulsom arrives." Clay's gaze swept the horizon. He figured it was just after six in the morning. Fulsom and his film crew were due at seven.

"I'm not sure that will matter. Savannah has always hated the idea of this show."

Clay understood his friend's concern. "So does Nora. What do you think Avery will say?" he asked Walker.

Walker shrugged. "She won't like it because her friends won't."

"Yeah, but she won't be as pissed as Savannah will be." Jericho handed the tablet to Clay and shoved his hands into his back pockets. "I was getting somewhere with her before everything happened with the show. Now every time Fulsom fucks with us, he sets me back."

"You two looked pretty cozy last night. I saw you slow dancing at least twice."

Walker nodded in agreement.

Jericho shrugged. "So were you and Nora. You got a ring on her finger yet?"

"No." But after last night he felt closer. "You know, this might work in our favor," he said. "If we can get them to stay, we'll have twice as long to convince them to marry us."

"If we can get them to stay," Jericho said.

"We'll tell them the truth—we had nothing to do with it. Fulsom's the one who keeps changing the game."

"I guess that's the only thing we can do." Jericho didn't look convinced that it would work, though. "Let's try to head this off before things get out of hand."

When they reached the back door of the manor, lights were on in the kitchen, and he could hear women's voices coming from the interior of the house. He wasn't sure if they normally got up so early, but everyone at Westfield knew Fulsom and his film crews were coming today. He supposed the women wanted time to get into their complicated Regency outfits.

He knocked and a moment later Avery appeared in

the doorway. She was dressed in a green gown with a white apron over it, and her eyebrows rose when she saw them. "What's wrong?"

Jericho took the lead. "We just checked out the website Fulsom put up for the show, and it looks like he intends to change the format."

"Website?"

Avery's sharp question must have carried, because Savannah and Nora appeared beside her a moment later. Nora hadn't put her hair up yet in the old-fashioned twist she wore these days, although she was dressed in a blue gown and a neat white apron. With it down she looked softer, sweeter, and Clay's body responded like she'd flipped a switch on him.

"Fulsom's advertising the show online, and his team has built a slick website to showcase it," Jericho said. "We came to warn you."

"I guess I expected something like that," Savannah said.

"Does it say... Does it mention where we are?" Nora interrupted her, concern drawing her brows together.

"It doesn't give the address, but I don't think we'd be too hard to find if someone wanted to. I'm sorry." Clay realized how unsettling that had to be for her. "Nora, are you all right with this?"

"Of course I'm not all right with it, but it doesn't matter, does it? What Fulsom wants, Fulsom gets." The bitterness in her voice struck Clay deep down. If the show put Nora in danger, he had to—What? Stop it?

Tell Nora to leave?

He didn't like either of those options.

Jericho looked confused. "What am I not getting here?"

"The stalker," Walker said curtly. Clay was surprised Walker remembered; Boone had mentioned it to them weeks ago after Riley told him what had happened to Nora. Clay had gotten a reminder the other morning, but Walker hadn't. He didn't let much slip by him, though.

"Stalker? He's back in Baltimore, right?" Jericho said. "He won't follow you here. Besides, it was just some kid doing crank calls. He's probably moved on to someone else by now."

Clay could have socked him for his callousness. "It's a little more serious than that." Nora's lips thinned, and he couldn't blame her for being angry. It didn't matter who was behind the calls. From what he knew they'd been very disturbing, and after the way she'd reacted the other morning, he knew her stalker was still on her mind.

"Okay, you've warned us. We'd better figure out what we want to do about it," Savannah said, clearly wanting to move on from this sensitive topic.

"What *can* we do about it?" Nora demanded.

"There's more," Walker said quietly.

"More?"

Clay frowned at the note of desperation in Nora's voice. He understood it unnerved her to think her stalker might know where she was, but like Jericho had pointed out, a kid with a grudge wasn't likely to follow her here. Still, he valued gut feelings, and Nora's gut obviously was telling her she was in danger. Was she overreacting? Or was something more at work here?

First things first. Time to break the bad news. Or the good news, depending on how you looked at it. "We're not sure yet, but we think Fulsom has decided to extend the show," Clay said carefully. He wished he could take Nora's hand, or better yet, put his arm around her and assure her it was going to be all right, but he instinctively knew that wasn't the right move.

"Extend it?" Her eyes widened.

"On the site it says the show will run for a year," Jericho said, handing her the tablet. Nora took it, scrolled down and scanned the screen. Clay's heart sank as he took in the tightness of her expression. When she gasped, he leaned in to see what part of the site had upset her so badly.

She must have clicked on a link because she'd gone to a page he hadn't seen before. "The Ladies of Base Camp," the headline proclaimed. Beneath it were images of Riley, Savannah, Avery, Nora and Win Lisle, another member of the community. Their photos were as manipulated and showy as the ones of Clay and the other men on the front page, making them look like some sort of Regency pin-up models.

He felt the tremor running through her and bit back a curse. Fulsom was going to hear about this.

"I never agreed to be on a website," Nora said. "I didn't agree to any of this. Don't we have to sign a contract or something before he can put me on his page?"

"I don't think it works that way, but he did say he'd bring contracts today," Clay said.

"Nora." Walker's quiet voice cut through the conversation.

"What?" She turned to face the big man.

"It'll get worse before it gets better."

She shook her head in disbelief. "Well, aren't you an angel of light and hope? How the hell is that helpful right now?"

"The truth always helps," Walker said doggedly. "You need to be ready for what's coming at you. It's going to be hard, but it'll be worth it in the end."

"You don't know that. He doesn't know that." She turned to the others. "Why are we staying here? This is ridiculous."

"The goal hasn't changed," Walker insisted.

Clay instinctively knew what he meant, but he wasn't sure Nora would. When Riley had confessed to her friends the extent of what Fulsom was demanding of the men—and, by default, of them, too—a month ago, Avery had stormed down the hill to Base Camp and called Boone out on the carpet to read him the riot act. Walker was the only one who could calm her down. He'd done so in this very way: by cutting through the crap and getting to the heart of the matter. Climate change wasn't some future issue. It was here now. To stay. They lived in a world worth fighting for; they'd all agreed on that. It was time to go all in or leave the game.

"Do you know how many people are going to see this?" Nora challenged Walker.

He nodded. "You'll be safe," he assured her. "We're here with you. He won't come."

"Can you guarantee that?"

None of them answered her. They'd all seen too much hatred, violence and war to make those kinds of promises to anyone. But this wasn't the Middle East, or Asia, or Africa. This was Chance Creek.

"Move down to Base Camp," Walker said.

Clay held his breath. Would she agree? *Come on, Nora*, he willed her. He'd love it if she was that close all the time. Fulsom would love it, too. It would make filming the show easier. Not that Clay gave a crap about that right at the moment.

"Never." Nora shoved the tablet back into Jericho's hands. "Fulsom promised. So did you. We get to stay in the manor. We get to keep our Regency life. We'll be extras in your show, but that's it. That's enough. More than enough."

Several emotions warred within Clay. Regret that she was right; they were asking too much of the women. Desire for her to want him as much as he wanted her. Anger at Fulsom for making something that should be so easy into something so damned difficult. If he could woo Nora the right way, they'd be dating by now. Instead she was backing away, ready to flee up the stairs to her room.

"Nora, think about it. Twelve months gives us more

time," he began, but she interrupted him.

"Twelve months of being filmed won't help anything," she retorted. "You tell Fulsom he doesn't get to tell us what to do. We agreed to six months, not twelve. And I want my photo off his site." She left the room in a swish of her skirts, and a moment later her footsteps pounded up the central staircase.

"I think it's time for you to leave," Savannah said to the men.

"I think so, too," Avery added.

With the women closing ranks against them, there wasn't much they could do but head back outside. When they reached the back porch, the kitchen door shut with a resounding thud behind them, and someone turned the lock.

"That went well," Jericho said.

"I CAN'T DO this for a year," Nora told her friends a half-hour later, when she finally calmed down and returned to the parlor, where the other two were waiting until it was time to walk down to Base Camp and hear what Fulsom had to say. As bit players they'd agreed to allow the camera crews access to their lives, but none of them had expected to figure as prominently in the show as Fulsom was showcasing them. She sat next to Avery on the couch, while Savannah kept her seat at the piano, running her hands lightly over the keys. "And I can't believe Fulsom put us on his website."

This was so much worse than she'd imagined when they'd agreed to stay at Westfield while the show was filmed. Even if her stalker didn't come after her, she'd know he was watching the show. She didn't think she could stand that.

When neither of her friends answered, she demanded, "Well? Do you want to be filmed for a year?"

"What's the alternative?" Avery asked. "We tried looking for another place once before and it didn't work. We all know we want to live here. Besides, Walker's here."

Nora wanted to scream. Didn't Avery realize her crush on the large man was doomed to fail? Chatterbox Avery was nothing like dour Walker. He wouldn't stand for her cheerfulness, and she'd grow to hate his taciturn ways. Why didn't love bloom between people who stood a chance at making each other happy?

"Do you really want to leave Clay behind?" Savannah asked.

Nora looked at her sharply. "Are you having second thoughts about Jericho?" A few weeks ago Savannah had been just as adamant as she was that she couldn't be with a man who was rushing into marriage for the sake of a TV show.

"If we can stand being on the show for six months, we can stand it for a year," Avery said without waiting for either of them to answer. "Besides, Fulsom said we can live the way we want and run our B and B. What's the problem?"

"The problem is they're going to intrude in our lives for twelve months. And Walker's going to marry someone in order to keep Base Camp, remember?" *And my stalker will know exactly where to find me*, Nora thought but didn't say out loud. She knew how melodramatic that sounded. What kid was going to track her down half a country away?

"Maybe Walker will marry *me*."

Nora snorted. "Don't count on it." She realized her mistake the moment the words left her mouth. "Avery, I didn't mean it like that—"

"Yes, you did!" Avery glared at her. "I don't understand why none of you think he could fall for someone like me."

"It's just—" Nora looked helplessly at Savannah.

Savannah rescued her. "He's nothing like you. You two are as opposite as night and day."

"That doesn't mean we couldn't work together."

"Fine." Nora threw up her hands. "You want to stay? Stay."

"Not without you two. You both promised!" Avery turned from one to the other. "Come on, we've been through all this before. We can't give up now. I swear I'll do whatever I can to cover for you so you don't have to be on-screen very much. I'll keep all the attention on me. Maybe I'll finally score an acting job, or at least get some interest going in my screenplay."

"That won't work," Nora told her. "Fulsom's already put us front and center on his website. We're stars in his show, like it or not, unless we leave now."

"I don't like what's happening any more than you do," Savannah said softly, "but I made myself a promise I would stay and see this through. I gave up on my music once before, and I don't see how I'll ever get a chance to pursue it seriously if I leave Westfield. I'm going to do whatever it takes to get my shot. Like Avery said—this television show might be my lucky break."

"You're both going to stay?" Nora asked. She didn't know why she was surprised. Walker was right; nothing had changed. None of them wanted to leave the manor, or each other. All three of them had gotten tangled up with the men here. Besides, Riley was here—for good. But a twist in her gut reminded her she had far more at stake than the others did. None of them had a stalker. Was she truly safe here?

Walker and Clay seemed to think so—and they should know, she reasoned.

Clay's last words finally penetrated her brain. *Twelve months gives us more time.* Her heart gave a funny double-thump. He was right. If they had a year to get to know each other, maybe that would be enough. Despite her best intentions, a flurry of images passed through her mind. Dating Clay. Getting to know him. Laughing with him, talking with him, kissing him…making love to him. Flustered, she busied herself straightening the long skirts of her gown.

Avery nodded. "I'm staying."

"I am, too," Savannah said. "Come on, Nora. You can survive this."

"But—" Nora stopped herself. Walker was right. Her stalker would be an idiot if he pursued her here where she was surrounded by Navy SEALs. She had to stop making a mountain out of a molehill. She couldn't let that teenager ruin her life. There was a man here—a good man—who wanted to be her husband. Didn't she owe it to herself to find out if she wanted to be his wife?

"All right. I'll stay—for a year." She checked the time and stood up, ready to face Fulsom. "If it kills me."

CHAPTER FOUR

A T TWO MINUTES before nine o'clock, Clay waited
with the rest of the ranch's inhabitants in the
bunkhouse for Fulsom to make his entrance, his leg
bouncing up and down with his impatience to get
started. Thirteen people in all were arrayed on the
folding metal chairs that Jericho had set up for the
meeting. More if you counted the camera crew that had
arrived ahead of Fulsom and were even now discreetly
filming the proceedings. The participants had grouped
themselves by sex, Clay noted. He, Jericho and Walker
sat closest to the door. The six other men, recruited by
Boone some weeks ago, were arranged nearby. The
women sat on the opposite side of the room, their
Regency-era gowns incongruous next to the casual,
modern clothes of the men. Nora perched on the edge
of a metal folding chair, as upright and proper as any
heroine in a Jane Austen novel, her hands clutched
together in her lap. Savannah and Avery sat close beside
her. Win Lisle, who'd come for Savannah's cousin's
wedding—the first Regency wedding the women had

thrown—and never left, sat in a chair equidistant between the two groups. She was the odd person out in this crew. She hadn't been friends with the women before she arrived, and she wasn't ex-military like the men.

Clay tried to catch Nora's attention, but after one quick glance from under her lashes, she kept her gaze firmly on the floor in front of her chair. At least she was here, and so were the other women. He had half-expected them to pack up and leave.

The door suddenly flung open, and Fulsom strode in on a gust of cool, soft air. He paced to the front of the room as if taking the stage at a speaking engagement and stared out at the assembled group.

"Sex!" he boomed suddenly, and more than one person in the room jumped. Nora's gaze flashed to Clay, color flushed her cheeks and she quickly looked away. Somehow gratified, Clay returned his attention to Fulsom, thinking maybe things would work out after all. Like he'd said to Nora, they could use the longer timeline to their advantage and get to know each other much better before speaking of marriage again. He knew where he stood, but Nora was cautious, and he respected that. Just thinking of ways he could change her mind got him a little hot and uncomfortable. He shifted in his seat and focused on Fulsom.

As usual, every silver hair on the man's head was in place, but he didn't look old. He radiated energy and his face remained unlined. It was easy to see why he'd become such an icon. "There. I said it. It's out in the open now."

Clay had to hand it to Fulsom. He had balls. Not only did he not shy away from controversy, he actively courted it.

"People want sex," Fulsom went on, pacing again. "They want to hear about it, read about and see it on their televisions. So that's what we're going to give them: lots and lots of sex." Clad in black jeans, a black T-shirt and boots so trendy Clay was surprised they were allowed out of Hollywood, he made a stark contrast to the rest of the people gathered. Beside him stood Renata Ludlow, the show's director. She, too, was dressed in black, but far more formally than Fulsom. Her black pencil-skirt, black stiletto heels and stark white dress shirt were tailored in a mannish fashion, and her obviously dyed-black hair was scraped back severely into a tight chignon, but her scarlet lipstick and nails, and the extra button she'd left open to show off her lacy bra, added a hint of femininity.

"I thought we made it clear none of us are baring our private lives on-screen," Jericho called out. Usually it was Boone who stepped in to act as moderator between Fulsom and the inhabitants of Base Camp, but with Boone away on his honeymoon, Jericho must have decided to take his place.

"Or our private parts," Angus McBride called out in his thick Scottish accent, eliciting some laughter from the others. He was one of the recruits who'd joined the group recently, but he'd already become a favorite of everyone at Base Camp. He could always be counted on for a laugh, and the man worked like a draft horse, and was as strong as one, too.

"It'll be a family friendly show, of course," Fulsom said. "But I expect romance, flirtation, public displays of affection, weddings..." He looked around to make sure they were all paying attention. "And babies. In fact, I expect babies any minute now," he said with a nod toward Jericho.

"Don't look at me," Jericho protested. "Boone's the one who should be working on that."

"It'll be your turn soon enough." Fulsom surveyed the others. "It'll be everyone's turn. Last night we launched the companion website to the show. The reaction has already been... gratifying." He let that sink in. "Thousands of visits to the site overnight. Dozens of comments, and you know what people are focusing on? Matchmaking. They're already trying to predict who is going to end up with whom. This show is going to be a hit. It's got sex appeal a mile long, and while our audience is focused on the girl–boy stuff, we'll cram so much information about sustainability down their throats they'll be able to give symposiums on it by the end of the season."

Clay exchanged a look with Jericho. If that was true, then going through with the show—and meeting Fulsom's demands—would be worth it. Pride welled up within him, a feeling he'd missed these past few weeks. It had been easy to lose sight of their initial objectives in the mad dash to get Boone to the altar, and to prep for the show. It was good to know they'd be able to get their message out to such a large audience, despite the trouble it raised with Nora.

"So I've got some good news and some bad news, folks." Fulsom leaned forward. "We initially signed on to run the show for six months. We've extended that to a full year. It makes sense. We'll follow Base Camp from spring to spring, seeing your struggles in every season. That gives us time to focus on each and every couple. The audience wants back stories. They want to watch you men woo your potential mates. They want to be in on the proposals and see each wedding. They want pregnancies—and at least one birth. Twelve months." He let that sink in. "A wedding every forty days."

Clay was glad he and his friends had warned the others about the change in time frame already, so there were no surprises there, but he wasn't pleased with that last bit. "Why do they have to be spread out like that? Why not let them happen when they happen?" he called out. He needed all the time he could get to convince Nora he was the one for her.

"Extending the season is a risky bet. We can't lose momentum."

"But think about it—" Clay said. He needed to win this point. He'd drawn the short straw, after all. If he had to marry in forty days he'd have less time to convince Nora, not more.

Fulsom's expression hardened. "One wedding every forty days," he said, overriding Clay. "Without fail." He scanned the crowd, looking for dissension. "Let me make myself very clear, folks. You miss a wedding, the show's over and Montague moves in with his bulldozers. Got it?"

Clay nodded slowly in the sudden silence. Yeah, he got it. The silver lining he'd clutched so tightly to had just been torn away, revealing bigger storm clouds. He supposed he shouldn't have expected anything less. So much for having more time to woo Nora. For a moment his foot stopped tapping.

Then it started up again. He wasn't going to lose Nora. No way. No how.

Fulsom turned to the women. "Surprisingly, your Regency lifestyle has caught the imagination of people across the country—even around the world. That's a positive thing. But here's a negative." He pointed to each man in turn. "Nine men, since Boone is already married." He turned to the women. "Four women, since Riley's taken, too. Now nine men and four women could make for an interesting and controversial dynamic, but this is a prime time show, so we've got to keep it clean. Time to recruit more females. And they'd better wear bonnets."

Clay began to protest, but thought the better of it. They'd known they had to recruit more women, but for Fulsom to demand the new female recruits join the others in their Regency exploits was unfair.

Fulsom turned to Jericho. "So who's going to marry next?"

"Don't look at me."

"It's me," Clay said resignedly. "I drew the short straw."

A murmur swelled among the women. "Drew the short straw?" he heard Avery echo. Savannah shook her head at him. Nora refused to look in his direction, but two spots of color blossomed high in her cheeks.

Fuck me, Clay thought, closing his eyes briefly while he cursed his choice of words. He'd set himself back further than Fulsom had.

"Drew the short straw, huh?" Fulsom guffawed. "We'd better re-create that for the show, and from now on that's exactly how we'll do it. Every time one of you marries, we'll draw straws to see who is next. The audience will love that."

Clay struggled to keep his cool. Every word that came out of Fulsom's mouth made things worse. Nora had twisted her fingers into the folds of her dress and seemed to be engaged in a struggle to keep her seat. He had no doubt she'd like to slug Fulsom, and then turn on him.

"July tenth, folks! That's our next wedding." Fulsom fixed Clay with a hard look. "Don't be late to the altar, son. I'll have Montague standing by with his bulldozers, got it?"

Clay longed to tell Fulsom where he could shove Montague, but he remembered the promise he'd made to Boone, Jericho and Walker after their failed mission to Yemen. Remembered the suffering he'd seen there and the political civil war that was really about dwindling resources due to climate change. He'd made his vow to help change the world, and he'd keep it, no matter how big an asshole Fulsom was turning out to be.

"Don't worry," he ground out. "I'll be there on time."

So Clay had drawn the short straw, had he? Fury and humiliation battled inside Nora. Had everything Clay had said and done been a lie? Did his kindness and seduction stem from nothing more than a deadline after all? He'd said earlier they'd have a full year to get to know each other. He'd pretended he wanted that, too. But all along he'd known he had to marry next and he'd used every opportunity to push their relationship along.

Damn him, Nora thought, close to tears. She'd let herself believe—after everything she'd been through—that there was one man who was different from the others. That Clay was better—that he truly cared for her.

But that was all a lie, wasn't it? He cared about winning. About the land. About his stupid sustainability baloney.

He'd better not propose to her, Nora thought wildly. He'd better not come near her. Marry in forty days? That was barely over a month. If she refused him—and she would refuse him—who else would he ask?

So much for the slow courtship she'd dreamed about all the way down to Base Camp. Moonlit walks, long discussions, passionate nights of lovemaking...

But that's not how this would go, would it? She'd be lucky to get a few fumbles in the dark, some stolen conversation in between being filmed. A quickie in the barn.

And then she was supposed to stand at the altar with a man little better than a stranger, pledge her life to him and wonder what happened in five years when she found herself with a kid or two—a single mother, Clay long gone...

Alone.

Anger sizzled through her veins and she grabbed hold of that emotion, far more comfortable with it than the pain that came with knowing she'd been fooled again.

She'd let Clay kiss her last night—a lot. She'd almost opened herself to the possibility of...something. And it was all because he'd drawn the short straw?

Fuck that.

Men were users. They lied, they let you down, sometimes they were violent. In every case you were better off without them.

Maybe she'd felt safe and happy in Clay's arms for a little while last night. Maybe he'd awoken a passion she'd thought was gone forever.

But now she felt... cold. Bitterly cold.

To hell with Clay—and to hell with Fulsom.

"As you all know, filming has begun," Fulsom went on, oblivious to her inner turmoil. "Which means you will all remain accessible to the camera crews twenty-four hours a day, seven days a week."

"Except when we go to bed," Jericho called out.

"We've already clarified we won't film your *private activities*." Fulsom finger quoted the words. "But you will accommodate the film crew and Renata here. I want everyone to be clear on that. If I hear otherwise, there'll be hell to pay. Unless Renata has asked you a specific question, or given you specific instructions, you are to go about your business as usual, whether or not you are being filmed. Renata will conduct interviews from time to time. Some of them will figure in the episodes put out each week. All of them will land on our website, along with other social media content like quizzes and polls."

Fulsom's words flowed over her. Nora knew she should listen, but a sound like rushing water had filled her ears. Disappointment warred with pain, and echoes of her stalker's messages began to thread through her racing thoughts. Somehow knowing Clay was lost to her made her stalker more real. More present, even though she'd left him behind. Maybe it was because since she'd met Clay, a little part of her had hoped against hope that the Navy SEAL would turn out to be a real hero—a man she could love, could make a life with.

Now she was on her own again.

Touch you. Make you scream. Cut you. Take my time.

Her stalker's distorted words assailed her mind, coming at her from every direction. Nora tried to concentrate on Fulsom, but she couldn't stop the barrage of hateful, violent speech that racketed around her brain and refused to be controlled. She dug her fingers into her thighs and pinched her skin hard.

I'm here. I'm right here. He can't get me now.

The room swam.

"Nora? Are you all right?" Savannah asked in a low voice.

"Yeah." But she wasn't. The room was spinning, her head pounded and Nora was beginning to find it hard to breathe.

"Okay, that's it for now," Fulsom wound up. "Let's get going. I expect professional behavior from all of you. I don't want to hear any complaints from Renata or the crew. Remember, the whole world is watching you now."

The whole world. Including the student who'd harassed her for months. As hard as she tried, she couldn't get his lurid, violent messages out of her head. Nora stood up with the rest of them and followed Savannah outside, fighting to control her emotions. Fighting for air.

She'd thought she'd escaped her stalker when she'd left Baltimore.

Instead she'd brought him with her.

CHAPTER FIVE

W HEN THE MEETING ended, Clay wanted to pursue Nora and explain everything, but he didn't get the chance. Renata cornered him before he could reach the door.

"Clay Pickett? Time for your interview."

"Already?" He'd thought he'd have a little more time before that kind of thing started. He watched Nora leave with her friends, the rest of them talking together in low tones, while she remained pale and aloof. He'd lowered himself in Nora's estimation in that meeting, and he knew he had plenty of work to do to repair the damage he'd done, but it seemed that would have to wait.

"When you're done, come gather your crew," Jericho told him. "Time to get to work on those houses. I'm about ready to pack up my tent for good."

"Will do." Clay reluctantly followed Renata outside. She led him around the bunkhouse away from the crowd to where a middle-aged blond man in cargo pants and a plaid button-down shirt stood with his camera on his shoulder.

"Clay, this is William Sykes. William, Clay Pickett."

The man reached out to shake his hand. "Morning."

"Now, I say this to everyone I work with," Renata went on, her clipped British accent making everything she said sound formal. "Reality television is intensely personal, but reality television also isn't personal."

"You'll have to explain that." Clay didn't hold with double-speak. He had a feeling the angular woman in front of him was going to rub him all wrong before this show was done. Anyone who made her career in reality television had to have a few screws loose.

"Our job is to bring you to life for our viewers. They don't want to know Clay the man who's acting for the camera. They want to know Clay the man. We will catch you at your most unguarded moments, and we will exploit them for the entertainment of our viewers. In that way, reality television is personal. What I need you to understand, however, is that even if we showcase your vulnerabilities, even if we show all the things you've never wanted anyone to see to a global audience, it isn't personal. We're just doing our jobs. Got it?"

"No." Clay shook his head. "That's a cop out. You got it right the first time. You're exploiting my private, personal moments to make money. You can't expect to get carte blanche approval from me. It ain't going to happen."

"Do we have a problem here?" Renata folded her arms across her chest.

"No. You do your job. I'll do mine. Just don't expect me to respect you in the morning."

Renata rolled her eyes. "Fine. Play it that way, cowboy. Let's get started." She nodded to William.

Cowboy? He supposed he looked like one to a city slicker. He figured he'd earn that designation soon enough, too. This was a ranch, after all, but they wouldn't be herding cattle. Boone thought bison were a better idea. Enough to feed the community and some left over to sell for a profit. Another ranch in town had already made the switch, so they wouldn't have to pioneer the process. Still, bison or cattle, Clay looked forward to spending a lot more time in the saddle than he had for a number of years. He'd slipped back into his country ways the moment he left the service, and it felt good.

He glanced back at the director. Despite her nonchalance, Clay had a feeling he'd gotten under Renata's skin, and that was interesting. The hard-bitten Brit had some vulnerabilities of her own. Good to know, since she'd spend the next twelve months trying to find his.

"Clay Pickett," she said, switching seamlessly into interviewer mode. "In the next year you'll have to work all day to build a sustainable community on this ranch. But from what I just heard, you'll have to work all night as well to get your wife pregnant. Is Nora Ridgeway going to audition for that part?"

Fuck. Clay struggled to recover from the sucker punch she'd delivered so neatly, all too aware of the camera catching every expression that crossed his face. His fingers clenched into fists, but he held back from snatching the movie camera out of William's hands.

"Keep Nora out of this," he ground out.

"Nora's in this up to her eyeballs," Renata countered. "If you don't answer the question, I'll ask her. Of course, I'll probably ask her anyway. This is the way it works, cowboy. I ask questions. You bare your soul. So are you and Nora an item? There were a lot of expressive looks passing between you in the bunkhouse just now."

He wanted to deny everything because he knew Nora would hate for him to talk about her on camera. But Renata was right, this was exactly what he'd agreed to. And lying wouldn't help.

"I'd like us to be," he admitted. "I'm not sure how Nora feels yet." That wasn't exactly true, of course. He had a pretty good idea what she was feeling right now, but he wished he didn't.

"She's awfully handy, at least. Living just a quarter mile away in the manor."

"That's true." It wasn't the reason he was pursuing her, though. He hoped like hell Nora didn't think it was.

Renata leaned closer. "Is she the one?"

Clay grinned suddenly. He could play this game. "I'm going to damn well find out."

ROALD RAISED HIS broad-sword high and sent it crashing down on Finn's head. "That's for the destruction of my village." He struck again. "And that's for the innocent lives you took."

Finn parried the first blow, ducked the second one and swung his ax to meet the third. "No one is innocent in this war—"

"Nora Ridgeway!"

Nora jumped and dropped her pen when Renata strode through the manor's front door and into the parlor, where she'd been snatching a few minutes to work on her novel. She'd made it back to the house, high-tailed it up to her room and sat on her bed, breathing hard, counting from one to ten and back again, over and over like she'd done with Clay several days before, until she'd finally gotten hold of her emotions and her pulse had slowed back to normal.

Nora didn't know what was happening to her. Why had her fear popped up now when she'd kept it under wraps for so long? Was it really because her interest in Clay had distracted her all this time—and now that distraction was gone?

She couldn't let her stalker take control like this. She'd made a new life here and it was a good one despite Fulsom's and Clay's actions. Maybe it was knowing her stalker would be able to watch her on television each week that had turned her into this gibbering mess. She'd hoped if she kept to the manor, she'd be left alone.

Obviously that wasn't meant to be.

She hurriedly shut her notebook to hide her novel. It was an epic historical romance set in the Scottish Highlands. She'd always been a sucker for an accent and a kilt. Still, she found crafting a story harder than she'd expected after all those A's she'd received in her English classes back at Boston College. She was fine for a paragraph or two, and then she'd get stuck.

For hours.

Focusing on the story was far easier than thinking about what had happened this morning, though. Or the way her throat had closed and she'd fought to breathe in the bunkhouse.

A cameraman followed Renata in, and then another man who held a microphone on a boom, and suddenly the airy, sunlit parlor felt small and cramped. Nora stood, shoved her notebook in a desk drawer and shut it tightly. Normally she'd write on her laptop when she was at home, but since all of them were short on cash, and their original plan had been to do nothing except work on their dream goals for six months, they'd made many concessions when they'd arrived at Westfield, including using as little electricity as possible. They charged up their laptops and the single phone they shared during "cell phone hour," as they'd taken to calling it. She'd forgotten to plug in her laptop yesterday and was now paying the price.

"Let's see. Let's have you stand in front of that gorgeous piano. That will look stunning."

Reluctantly, Nora stood and crossed the room as directed, her dress swishing around her ankles as she moved, reminding her how strange she'd look to the audience. Could she make a run for it?

No, Renata would follow and make a big deal over it. She'd end up getting more screen time, not less.

I'm here to write, she reminded herself. *There's nothing remotely interesting about me. Viewers will get bored of me in about two minutes and then everyone will leave me alone.*

She felt pretentious posed by the piano, especially since she didn't play, but Renata seemed happy with the arrangement. When the cameraman was satisfied that the light was acceptable, she began.

"Clay's pretty hot, huh, Nora? All those muscles?"

Nora blinked. She opened her mouth, then closed it again. "I... uh...wouldn't know," she finally gasped.

"Funny, you couldn't keep your eyes off him in our meeting just now."

"I... I'm not—I didn't... That's not true!" Nora was appalled. She hadn't pictured anything like this when she'd agreed to be on the show. It wasn't that she was naive—she knew what reality television was like, but she didn't expect to be attacked for looking at Clay.

"So you're telling me you don't find him the least bit attractive?"

"I didn't say that!" Nora felt her cheeks heat. Damn it, she hadn't meant to say that, either.

"So you do find him attractive."

"I didn't—" Nora broke off in confusion.

"You can't have it both ways," Renata retorted. "So which is it?" The smile she flashed at Nora was down-right evil. Nora promised herself she'd get her revenge.

"I guess... I guess I do find him attractive," she admitted through gritted teeth.

"He needs to marry in the next forty days." Renata eyed her shrewdly. "Will you be the blushing bride?"

"Absolutely not," Nora snapped. "Now, if we're finished here—"

"Oh, no—you don't get to leave yet." Renata

moved to intercept her when Nora headed for the door. "We've only gotten started."

CLAY DIDN'T SEE Nora again until that evening, after Renata had made it clear to everyone who'd listen that she wasn't happy with the lack of interplay between the men and women so far. With Nora, Savannah and Avery up at the manor all day, Riley and Boone off on their honeymoon, and the rest of them working on Base Camp, Win was the only woman in contact with the men, and she'd spent most of the day separating and transplanting seedlings.

"I want everyone to eat dinner together," Renata had finally snapped. "I'll send word to the women and tell them to be here at five-thirty. I want lots of interaction."

"We'll do our best," Jericho had said. Now Kai Green, an ex-Marine from Long Beach, California, who was slated to help Jericho with the solar, hydro and wind power projects, was serving up a version of all-in-one mini quiches he'd baked in oversize muffin tins in an array of solar ovens he'd positioned around the site. Clay had never considered quiche a manly food, but you could hold these in your hand while you milled around or sat on a log near the campfire, and Kai had packed them with enough cheese and tasty bits to fill him up when he'd eaten two or three. With a tossed salad on the side, and a bottle of beer, it did the trick.

When he spotted Nora negotiating the rough ground, a plate in one hand, her long skirts held up with the other, he motioned her over. "Sit here beside me." He patted the log.

"I was going to eat with Savannah and Avery." But she hesitated long enough to give him an opening.

"Come on, Nora—we need to talk." He led her to a log set a little apart from the others and waited until she sighed and sat down. "How are you doing?"

"Fine." Nora's stiff answer let him know that wasn't true.

"Did Renata come after you? She grilled me like an Italian sausage."

"Me, too." Despite his quip, Nora didn't look at him. Instead she concentrated on her quiche as she took a bite of the crust.

"What did she ask you?"

Nora didn't answer at first. She took another bite and chewed it. Finally swallowing, she said, "About you. Whether or not we are an *item*, as she put it." Her tone was so cold, Clay knew he had a lot of damage to repair.

"What did you tell her?"

Nora looked at him sidelong. "The truth. We aren't."

Ouch. Clay guessed he shouldn't have expected any other answer, no matter what had passed between them the night of Boone and Riley's wedding. "I'd like to be. You know that, right?"

Nora shook her head sharply. "I'm not looking for a relationship, and I'm definitely not interested in marrying you."

"Why not?" He set his plate down, his appetite

gone. This was worse than he'd expected. Surely Nora knew he didn't want things to go this way.

"For a lot of reasons."

"Have you seen this?" Jericho approached them, his tablet in his hand again. Clay was beginning to think the thing was surgically attached to his friend. "They've already posted videos on the site. I didn't think they were going to do that for at least a week." He lowered himself onto the log between them, oblivious to the tension in the air, and Clay snatched his plate out of the way just in time before Jericho sat on it. "There are a ton of comments about you two."

Nora leaned in to see, and Clay fought back his impatience, knowing this couldn't be good.

"'Clay and Nora, Perfect Together? Or Perfectly Awful?'" she read aloud. "What is this?"

"It's a poll," Jericho said. "Visitors to the site get to vote on if they think you should be together. It's about fifty-fifty right now."

Clay growled and snatched the tablet out of his hand. "Fuck them."

Nora grabbed it away from Clay. She scanned the site. "Listen to this." Her brows drew together in an angry slant. "'Nora Ridgeway just wants Clay's land,'" she read from the comments.

"What?" Taking the tablet back, Clay looked again and saw that Renata's team had filled the site with new content. There were new photos, excerpts from interviews and *fun facts*.

And then there were the pop quizzes and opinion

questions, such as, "How Sustainable Are You?" There was a ten-question quiz to get an answer. "In a Tent, Or Under the Stars?" That one had elicited a number of dicey responses. "Who's the Hottest Navy SEAL?" Clay scrolled quickly by when he noticed Jericho was winning.

He found the post Nora had referred to and scanned through the comments. Some of them were nice enough, with people pulling for them to be together. Others took sides. "Clay's too good for Nora." "Nora should find a man who owns a real house."

Interspersed among them were nasty comments that set Clay's teeth on edge. "To hell with Nora. What about Savannah? She's hotter." "Clay's just using her." "Good on ya, Clay. The quiet ones are the best in bed."

What kind of people wrote things like that? Who even cared what happened on a television show? For all they knew, the whole thing was staged.

None of that mattered; if it bugged him, he could only imagine how Nora felt. "Jesus."

Nora kept quiet. Jericho, finally taking in the atmosphere between them, took back the tablet and stood up awkwardly. "Sorry. Guess you didn't really need to see that."

"They're just a bunch of idiots," Clay told Nora when he walked away. "Who gives a shit what these people think?"

Nora set her plate down on the log with a thud. "I do. I'm a teacher, for God's sake. Have you thought about that? And now people are talking about my personal business on the Internet. Anyone can look in and make a judgement."

"They're talking about whether or not we should marry. You know my answer."

"That's never going to happen." Nora turned away.

"Why not?" He glanced up, became aware that one of the camera crews had approached them during their conversation and wondered how much of that last bit they'd captured. The boom dangled over Nora's head. The cameraman, standing behind Nora, kept his camera focused on Clay. Clay knew he should warn Nora. Knew, too, if he did he'd be up to his ears in hot water with Renata and Fulsom.

Besides, he wanted to hear Nora's answer. He held still and waited.

"I don't know you well enough to marry you," she said, finally meeting his gaze. "And you have a deadline to marry *someone*, so I'll never know if you really want me, or just a random body to fit the bill." She stood. The crewman yanked the boom higher so she didn't hit her head.

Clay stood, too. "You know I want you. And if you don't know that, I'll gladly prove it any time, day or night—"

"Stop it," she hissed.

Had she noticed the cameras? No, not yet. She was concerned with the people around them. Clay continued. "I can't make it any more clear how I feel about you." He reached for her hand.

She pulled hers back. "Why me?" she said.

"Why do I want to marry you?" He chuckled. "Hell, women talk about romance, but I'm starting to think they don't know anything about it. You all pick and choose when it's the right time to fall in love, you decide how much time has to pass before you know if you've met the right man. You think about how much your potential husband will earn. You consider whether he'll be a good father, and on and on. Men just see a woman and—" he snapped his fingers "—that's that."

For the first time she hesitated. "So you saw me. And now you want to marry me. It's that simple?"

"That about sums it up." He willed her to understand. Sometimes you just knew, and that's how he'd felt the first time he'd seen her. She was the woman he'd been searching for without even knowing he was looking.

"That's… crazy. You know that, right?"

"No, it's not. It's just a fact. It's how I feel."

Nora was quiet for a long time. "I don't buy it." The bleakness in her voice said she wished she could, though.

Clay grabbed onto the possibility that opened. "I know you don't," he said. He reached out and this time succeeded in taking her hand. He wished he could do more, but first he needed to earn her trust—and her love. "That's why I'm going to prove it to you."

WHY WAS SHE letting Clay hold her hand?

Nora wasn't sure. She'd been furious with him—and Fulsom—and herself—all day, but in these last few minutes he'd reminded her of the man she'd fallen for when she'd first arrived at Westfield. In those first moments of knowing Clay she'd felt like he understood her almost better than she did herself, and now she couldn't help wondering how their relationship would have progressed if it wasn't for Fulsom's interference—and her past. Suddenly she wondered if she could even be with a man given the way her fears kept flaring up.

She refused to think that way, though. She wouldn't let a teenager with a sick, twisted imagination affect her so deeply. After all, the touch of Clay's hand didn't frighten her now. Instead, it awakened a trace of the desire she'd felt last night. For one second she remembered a time in which love, lust, want and need were part of her emotional vocabulary—before her mother's death, her stalker's verbal attacks. Nora ached to have that back.

Then Clay's words sank in. Prove it to her? How?

When you're my student, I'll teach you things you'll never forget. Her stalker's distorted voice insinuated itself into her thoughts again, and Nora tugged her hand away.

"Nora—"

"I don't want you to prove anything." Certainly not when she knew what had spurred his pursuit of her. That damned short straw. She spun away from him, needing distance from the onslaught of emotions tangling around her heart, came face to face with one of Fulsom's cameramen and realized he'd been filming the entire conversation.

And Clay had known it all along.

"Nora—"

She didn't wait for his explanation. Anything Clay said now would only twist the dagger his actions had already plunged into her heart. Last night he'd made her feel... something. He'd kissed her. He'd made her want more before common sense came to her rescue.

And it was all for the show.

"Nora!" Clay scrambled after her as she shoved her way past the cameraman.

"Fuck you!" Not very mature, but maybe this scene wouldn't make it into the show if she dropped a few blue words. The young man who held the boom stepped into Nora's path, and she almost ran into him. Clay caught up to her and took her arm.

"Just wait a minute. Let me—"

"What's going on here?" Renata came running, a neat trick on her high heels on this uneven ground. Nora wished she felt nearly as in command of herself as Renata always seemed to be. Even now, not a hair on the woman's head was out of place. In contrast, Nora could feel her updo slipping down. Her bonnet hung from its strings around her neck, and she was breathing hard, her face hot with anger. She wanted to keep running but now she was surrounded.

Renata faced Clay and Nora and put her hands on her hips. "Get. Over. Yourselves." She looked pointedly at each of them. "Got it? We're here. We're filming. You agreed to it. No more screwing around."

Angus, passing by, laughed long and loud. "And here I thought screwing around was the whole point of this show."

The cameraman smiled. Renata rolled her eyes.

Nora had had enough. She pushed past the cameraman and headed for the manor at a dead run.

CHAPTER SIX

"**A**RE YOU READY to be the next matrimonial victim?" Curtis Lloyd asked when Clay approached the building site the next morning, still smarting from his confrontation with Renata and the way the film crew had botched his attempt to change Nora's mind. Despite Renata's continued shouted threats, Nora had refused to turn around. She'd dashed off back up to the manor, and he hadn't seen her since.

"I guess so. Unless you want to beat me to it?"

Curtis chuckled. He was a burly ex-soldier whose thick build belied a man capable of producing the finest finish work Clay had seen—except for that done by Clay's own father. He looked forward to having the man's help to build the ten tiny houses Fulsom had demanded. He'd shown Curtis his plans for the homes weeks ago, and they'd worked together to hammer out details and problem-solve, buy the lumber and hardware they needed, and even prep a few of the more complicated interior pieces, even though they were supposed to wait for filming to start. Even so, they'd have to work hard. Fulsom had extended the deadline, but the houses needed to be complete before the cold weather set in this fall.

"I'd need a woman for that," Curtis said. "So far whenever a likely one steps foot on this ranch, someone grabs her up before I even get a look at her." His words were humorous, but his tone said he wasn't entirely kidding. Clay made a note to tell Boone when he returned from his honeymoon he'd better step up his matchmaking.

"Don't panic. Boone'll find someone for each of you."

"He'd better find me a bunch of them. I want a choice. I figure twenty or so. I'll have to date them all, of course, before I pick one. Right, Harris? What do you say?" he said to the other member of Clay's building team.

"Boone will be lucky if he can find one."

"For me?" Curtis drew himself up. "The ladies love me."

"For me."

Clay jumped in to smooth over the awkward moment. "He'll find someone for both of you." He wondered how easy it would be to find a match for Harris, though. There was nothing wrong with the guy except the quiet, serious man held back so much. Harris Wentworth was a sniper—one of the best Clay had ever known. Unlike the other men, Harris never spoke about old missions or mentioned his time in the service. Still, even a civilian would know he'd served. There was something in his eyes that made it all too clear. Clay had been surprised at how well Harris fit in here. A man like him—a loner—might have had trouble adjusting, but he'd gone along with all the demands they'd placed on him, even when it had come time to learn the complicated Regency dances and attend a ball. In fact, Harris had turned out to be the best dancer among them. "I had lessons as a kid," was all he'd say when questioned. He was a man who kept things close to the vest.

Clay could appreciate that, but most women wouldn't.

"What about Nora and the others? Don't they have some friends they can bring in?" Curtis asked.

Clay knew how Nora would react to that idea. "I'm not sure that's going to happen."

"I still say twenty women apiece ought to do it," Curtis went on.

"I just want one," Harris said quietly. He nodded to the plans rolled up in Clay's hands. "Ready to get to work?"

"No one is innocent in this war, least of all the women." Finn *parried another blow with his rough-hewn ax. Its shaft was made from an ash tree. Cut down three springs ago, aged in a dry place and hardened in a complicated and interesting process, its blade was reminiscent of the Lochaber style, elongated, with a...*

Nora sighed, back at her desk that afternoon. The scene she was writing had lost all momentum. But she wanted her readers to understand the intricate process that was required to make a battle-ax, and to thereby understand how amazing it was that men could make such tools under primitive conditions back in the 1700s. The teacher in her loved those details and wanted to share them with everyone else.

But whenever she tried, the action fell flat.

It didn't help that she kept thinking about Clay. About the way he'd promised to change her mind about marrying him last night.

And the way the cameras had captured the scene, turning it into a farce.

She'd tossed and turned far into the wee hours, trying in vain to clear her mind of Clay's words and kisses, Fulsom's puffed up announcements and her stalker's threats. She'd finally fallen asleep and woken to a dawn in which she felt drained of all emotion except a helpless resignation that this wasn't a world that thought it owed her any happiness. She'd have to be content with the scraps she could gather for herself.

She tore out the page, balled it up and tossed it in the cardboard box Riley had set next to the little trash can for recycling, already half-full of similar sheets of paper. If only she could skip the story and just teach her readers about the way the Scottish highlands had been divided up by clans and then draw a comparison to modern-day Syria and the way family ties were driving the difficulties there, too, then maybe her readers could gain some insight into—

There she went again.

She wasn't a teacher anymore.

Nora stood up again and paced across the room, her

skirts swishing as she moved. Could she ever have been a very good one, seeing the way things had ended? Besides, when she'd studied English at Boston College, she'd planned to write, not teach. Teaching literature was what people did who couldn't write it themselves—or so she'd joked back in school.

It wasn't funny anymore.

What would Jane Austen do in her position? Nora wondered. Jane hadn't had it all that easy, either. For all the happy endings to her stories, she hadn't found one for herself. Was that to be her lot in life?

A spinster?

Nora frowned at the old-fashioned word, and the barrenness it implied. This was the twenty-first century. Being alone didn't mean being barren. She could have a full life. A wonderful career. Heck, she could have a child if she wanted one.

But could she have any of that here, living with the friends who had become her surrogate family? Or would she have to move and start all over again?

If she couldn't teach—there didn't seem to be a job for miles in Chance Creek—and she couldn't write, as evidenced by her recycling bin, then what use was she here? Was she doomed to be a glorified housemaid in Riley, Savannah and Avery's Regency B and B and wedding business? It had been fun to plan and execute the first two Regency weddings they'd taken on—Riley's and one for Savannah's cousin Andrea—but Nora wasn't as enamored of the enterprise as her friends were. She loved Jane Austen's books, and as much as she had resisted at first, she adored putting on her Regency gowns every morning. She especially loved that they represented her vow to dedicate herself whole-heartedly to her writing.

If only she could make some progress.

She sat down at her desk, wrote a line or two, but the sound of horses' hooves clip-clopping up the driveway caught her attention, and Nora looked out the window to see Maud and James Russell pull up in front of the manor.

"I'm off to a doctor's appointment. See you later," Savannah called out as she headed toward the door. Outside she allowed James to help her up in the old-fashioned barouche and took a seat opposite Maud, while James ascended to the higher driver's seat right behind the horses. As James clucked to the horses and they set off, a cameraman came huffing and puffing up the hill, running as fast as he could go. Through the open window, she heard him calling out to James to stop, but James didn't hear him—or he pretended not to—and kept going.

Good for him. There was no reason for all their neighbors to get swept up into their reality television hell.

She figured the Russells would get their fair share of screen time, though. The older couple shared their love of all things Jane Austen, and had been a big help since they arrived. James loved acting as a Regency-style taxi service and brought them to and from town whenever they liked. Maud had saved their bacon by organizing a

Regency ball on extremely short notice for Andrea's bridesmaids to attend the night before her wedding. None of them had expected much more than a few extra men and some recorded music, but Maud had pulled off a miracle—a full-on ball with dozens of guests, candlelight, a quartet of musicians and lovely refreshments.

Nora liked the bluff, old couple as much as any of the others, but she found their almost daily visits too much when she needed to write, and now she would be interrupted by Renata and the cameras every day, too. Maybe the whole experiment was a waste of time, just like she'd said in the beginning.

Maybe she should leave.

Someone knocked at the back door, and Nora gave up. She tossed down her pen and walked briskly to the kitchen in a rustle of fabric. Avery was already opening the door when she entered. Judging by her good spirits, she must have made progress on her screenplay today.

"Hi, Walker," Avery said. "Come on in."

"Is Nora in?" As usual, the big man didn't mince words. Nora was never sure how to take Walker. Boone at least she understood. He spoke his mind and was clear about his needs and expectations, and she wasn't surprised Riley had fallen for him so hard. Nora was still on the fence about the others, though. Walker simply didn't talk enough, but Nora had a feeling he didn't miss much. Jericho was too good-looking with his blond hair and chiseled cheekbones.

"I'll get her." Avery sounded disappointed, and

Nora bit her lip. She wished Walker would give her friend some sign about how he felt about her. Sometimes he seemed interested. Other times he was impossible to read.

Men.

"I'm right here," she said, crossing the kitchen.

"I need to talk to you." Walker stayed where he was.

Nora was surprised by his statement. She'd barely exchanged two words with him so far, but when Walker held the back door open, indicating she should precede him outside, she did so, trying not to notice Avery's wistful expression. She winced when she spotted a camera crew a dozen feet away.

"What's this about?" she asked testily when Walker followed her outside.

"Heard you miss teaching."

Nora nodded. She did miss it. A lot.

"Got a job for you. Kind of like teaching."

Nora's pulse quickened, but she waited for him to go on. Really, Walker's reticence would drive her insane if she let it. "Details," she snapped when he hesitated. If he could be short spoken, so could she.

"It's a more of a writing thing."

Nora's heart fell again. She was already struggling enough with her novel. "What kind of writing?"

"Curriculum. For seventh grade."

"Middle school curriculum? That's not in my wheelhouse at all."

Walker shrugged. "Thought I'd tell you." He turned to leave.

Nora hurried after him. "Wait. What's the subject?"

He turned back. Thought a moment. "Crow."

"Like... the bird?" A single subject curriculum? She supposed that might be interesting—a little.

He shook his head once. "My people."

His people? Suddenly, she understood—he was talking about a Native American history curriculum. "Walker, that's not appropriate. You can't hire a white woman to write Crow curriculum. Who would use it?"

"Wouldn't be working alone. My grandmother's the one in charge, but she's busy. She's the principal of the middle school on the reservation. She'll tell you what to write. You write it. Two hours a day after school."

Walker had a grandmother? She wasn't sure why she'd assumed he'd dropped out of the sky fully grown. He simply seemed so self-contained. She'd never considered him having parents, let alone an extended family.

Especially not a grandmother who was a principal. That was interesting. One thing could lead to another, after all. Maybe if she worked on this project, she could find a way into the Chance Creek school system. She had no doubt all the educators knew one another in this part of the state.

"Why me?" she asked suspiciously.

Walker shrugged. "Why not?"

"Because there must be other people far more qualified for the job. People within the tribe?" As much as the idea grabbed her imagination, she couldn't bear the possibility of being taken to task for overstepping her bounds. She'd seen educators skewered for passing themselves off as experts on cultures they didn't belong to.

Walker winced. "Nation," he corrected.

"I'm sorry?"

"Tribe's the wrong word."

"See? I'm not qualified for the position."

Walker waited a beat. "Thought you might be interested," he said again in a way that told her he understood some of her struggles here. But how could he? It was as much a mystery as the man himself.

Did he think she'd leave the ranch if she didn't get a chance to teach?

That could be the reason, she decided. None of them would get to stay at Base Camp unless all the men married. Maybe Walker was making sure Clay got his shot.

She knew better than to ask him about it, though. Instead, she found herself nodding slowly. "I am interested," she said. "Except..." She trailed off and looked down at her dress. She'd made a vow to her friends to uphold their Jane Austen life for six months—twelve months now. And she was supposed to write every day—not take an outside job. Even if it was only a couple of hours a day. She'd promised to help her friends with the B and B and weddings, in addition to writing. Even if they didn't have any guests booked yet, surely they would soon. How could she possibly juggle all of that?

She couldn't, Nora realized. She should say no.

Walker waited, as if he could read the debate raging inside her mind. "I'm interested," she said again.

She *was* interested.

She'd make it all work somehow.

WHEN BOONE AND Riley returned from their honeymoon, they were both sporting the self-satisfied smiles of a couple who were truly in love and had just spent forty-eight hours alone together. Clay tamped down his jealousy and greeted them with a genuine smile. After a lot of good-natured ribbing and congratulations, Riley headed up toward the manor to visit with the other women. Boone turned to Jericho and Clay, and gestured to them to follow him into the bunkhouse.

"We need more women," he said bluntly as they took seats in the folding chairs strewn around the room. Clay was getting so used to the cameramen following them around he barely noticed William and a couple of other men come in behind them and take up a position in one corner.

"That's right," Jericho said in a tone Clay couldn't quite decipher. Did he want more choices for himself because he and Savannah were on the outs? Or did he want more choices for the other men so no one else would try for her?

"Clay, you're up next. I'm about to place a few ads. Want me to ask for anything in particular?"

"No." Clay bristled at the idea. He wanted Nora and only Nora.

Boone rubbed his face. "Look, I know you think

Nora is the one, but from what I've heard, she doesn't seem to be on the same page, and you've got a deadline."

"I know—"

"All I'm saying is let me find a backup. Just in case."

Jericho looked away. Clay couldn't blame him for his discomfort; this had to be the strangest predicament he'd ever found himself in.

"I want a month."

"A month?"

"To try with Nora. Go ahead and find a backup, but I don't want to see her or hear about her for a month."

"That leaves you ten days to marry if you fail." Boone leaned forward. "We can't—"

"If I can't convince Nora to change her mind by June thirtieth, I'll marry whoever I find at the altar on July tenth." To allow Boone to bring in another woman now would be tantamount to admitting defeat—to himself and to Nora. He felt sure Nora would take one look at her and harden her heart against him for good. He wasn't ready to take that chance.

Boone nodded finally. "Okay, have it your way. I'll try to have a woman waiting in the wings, ready to go, but I won't bring her to Base Camp until July. Deal?"

"Deal." Clay didn't let himself think what it would be like to marry a perfect stranger if Nora didn't change her mind. It wouldn't matter. He was a goner where Nora was concerned. If he couldn't have her, he didn't really care who showed up at the altar.

"Describe your ideal woman," Boone said.

Clay described Nora. "Smart, dedicated, knows what she wants." He knew the cameras were catching this so he made short work of it.

Boone leaned forward. "I need more than that. You're going to have to marry her if Nora doesn't pan out. Give me enough so I don't completely screw this up."

"If it's not Nora, it'll be screwed up no matter what."

"I'm on your side here." Boone didn't give an inch.

"Right." Clay surged up out of his chair. He couldn't sit still while they were discussing this.

"It wasn't any easier for me," Boone tossed at him as Clay paced across the room. "I had my work cut out for me with Riley, or have you forgotten that already?"

"Not like I've got with—" Clay cut off his sentence, glancing at the cameras. He couldn't go on with them filming—sooner or later Nora would watch this conversation. "Forget it."

Ed Wilson, the closest cameraman, made a chopping motion, turned off his camera and let it point toward the ground. He was a fiery redhead with a build that made him look like one of the military men in Base Camp, and Clay had already figured he'd be a hard one to dodge. "Clay, we've had this discussion before. Whatever happens during the next year happens on camera. You might as well speak your mind. We're not going away."

Clay stopped in his tracks. "This isn't any of your business."

"I've got a contract back in my tent that says you're wrong."

"Yeah. Whatever. Fine." Clay was done with this discussion.

Ed turned his camera back on. After an awkward silence, Boone said, "I guess I'll write that ad."

"I'll get back to building houses." Clay exited the bunkhouse and didn't look back to see if a camera was following him. Of course it was. And would be for the next twelve months, whether or not Nora married him.

He knew he needed to get over his urge to conduct his wooing of Nora in private. That wasn't going to happen, and if he kept curtailing his actions around the cameras, he was going to blow everything. He wouldn't win Nora by holding back, or trying to make a secret of his feelings for her, either. That would only come across as hesitation to her.

Like his feelings were insincere.

They weren't. She needed to know that. Everyone did.

Time to stop being so squeamish about being filmed.

He changed direction. Instead of heading to the building site where Curtis and Harris were hard at work on the first of his tiny houses, he headed up the dirt road that led to the manor, making sure the crew followed him. He'd show everyone exactly how he felt about Nora.

The three-story house with its stone facade stood as proud as ever on a rise of ground. His long strides ate up the distance and in only a few minutes he approached the backyard—in time to see Walker exit the manor's back door, tip his hat to Nora, tip it again to Riley, who was just heading up the back porch steps, and turn his steps toward Base Camp.

Jealous fury surged within Clay, an emotion he wasn't on good terms with. A couple of days ago he'd felt confident about his ability to woo Nora, but after all his mistakes, their run-ins with the film crew and the knowledge he only had forty days to get her to the altar, his confidence had drained away. Walker had shown no interest in Nora so far. But then when did Walker betray his emotions about anything? Had Clay missed some obvious signs of the man's intentions toward her?

Clay strode toward him. "What're you doing here?"

Walker met him halfway. "Came to see Nora."

"Why?"

Walker shrugged and kept going, right past Clay, who stopped and whirled around.

"Why?" Clay repeated.

"Wanted to," Walker called back over his shoulder.

Was Walker yanking his chain? Clay wasn't in any mood for that. "Stay away from her."

Walker stopped. Turned slowly around again.

Clay didn't care if the man had been his superior officer. This wasn't the Navy, nor was it the reserves. This was just Westfield. They were on equal terms here. "You heard me. Stay away from her."

Walker gazed at him a long moment, his dark eyes betraying nothing. "No can do."

He walked away, leaving Clay to follow him a few paces before reason stopped him in his tracks. What was he going to do, fight Walker—on camera? Walker didn't want Nora. And Nora sure as hell didn't want Walker.

At least, he didn't think so.

Doubling back, he had to force himself to walk, not run, to the manor's back door. By the time he reached it, Nora and Riley had withdrawn inside. Hot, tired and frustrated, Clay didn't bother to knock. He went right in and found the women gathered around the kitchen table congratulating Riley and talking animatedly.

"Nora? Got a minute?"

He thought she might say no, but she nodded. "Excuse me. I'll be right back," she said to her friends.

With a baleful glance at the cameramen following him, Nora led Clay into the parlor. The cameramen trooped around to get the best angles, making so much noise that there was nothing for it but to wait for them to gain their positions before he began to speak. Nora sat down at the desk and fiddled with a jade paperweight, one of the many doodads with which the manor was decorated. Clay paced until he could speak again.

"Would you...?" He searched for a way to finish the sentence. *Marry me?* No, he couldn't say that. "...like to go to dinner with me?" he finished instead.

Nora made a face. "I don't think so."

"Why not?" His frustration rushed back with a vengeance.

Nora bit her lip. "Clay, we...we're just not..."

Clay rubbed the back of his neck. He'd never been a man of words. He preferred action, but there wasn't any action to take here. He wished someone would hand him some orders and a target. A concrete job. "Nora, you gotta give me a chance here." He wasn't one for begging, but what were his options?

"We're not going to be together," she said. But she didn't look at him, Clay noticed. Instead, she plucked at her gown. "Besides, I'd be pretty conspicuous at a restaurant, don't you think?"

Clay stilled. Maybe that little joke was just a nervous gesture on Nora's part—a way to lighten the tense mood.

Or maybe it had been a tell. Did she want to go on a date, despite everything?

Maybe she did.

He thought fast. "A picnic, then. Down by Pittance Creek. Just two friends eating a sandwich and talking."

"Friends?" She looked up.

"Friends," he repeated. "You can handle that, can't you?"

"I guess so." She didn't sound too sure, though. When Walker's face popped into his mind, Clay could only shake his head. Nora didn't like Walker. That was...stupid. This was about Fulsom and his timeline.

Still, the thought galled him. "Tomorrow night," he said quickly. "I'll come and get you at six."

"O-okay." Nora glanced at the camera again and bit her lip. Clay sensed she was about to change her mind.

"How is your writing going?" Time to change the

subject.

At first he thought she would refuse to talk about it. In fact, he was pretty sure she was about to make up an excuse to cancel their date.

"Getting a lot of words on the page?" he prompted her, unwilling to give her a chance to do so.

"Not that many," she finally admitted. "There've been a lot of distractions lately."

So much for chitchat. "I won't keep you from it then." He began to back away, but something stopped him. A desire not to leave things in such a lackluster way. Nora could call off their picnic any time between now and tomorrow night. He needed to remind her of the sparks they'd shared the other night—keep her thinking of what they could have together. Instead of leaving, he took a step forward and moved to drop a kiss on her lips.

But Nora pulled back abruptly and shook her head.

Shit. Clay froze, painfully aware the cameras were filming everything, including his advance and Nora's retreat. He hesitated like a deer caught in the headlights before the urge to do something—anything—to repair the situation had him reaching out and giving her shoulder an awkward pat. "Good luck with the writing," he said, cursing himself for not coming up with anything better. He knew damn well Renata would use this footage. He could imagine her running it over and over again in a show—him leaning in for the kiss, Nora backing away, his awkward shoulder pat. He'd look like a prime idiot.

His pride stinging, Clay couldn't help himself. He caught Nora's chin in his hand, tilted her head up and kissed her for real. Her mouth was so sweet under his. He wanted the moment to go on forever—

The sharp pain that exploded in his temple made him drop his hand and stumble against the desk. "What the fuck?"

Nora, the jade paperweight in one hand, half-stood from her chair, then collapsed back into it, her other hand flying to cover her mouth. "Oh, my God. Clay— I'm so sorry! I didn't mean—"

Clay touched a hand to his temple and felt a trickle of blood. She'd bashed him with a rock—and the damn cameras had recorded everything.

Avery rushed in from the kitchen, followed closely by Riley. "What happened? Clay—why are you bleeding?"

Numb with shock and self-recriminations, Clay couldn't find the words to answer her. He strode through the house and out the back door. It served him right for the way he'd acted. Nora had let him know in no uncertain terms she didn't want his kisses, and he'd gone and stolen another one anyway.

Still, to know that scene would be replayed on televisions all across the nation made his blood boil. He wasn't sure he could stand the humiliation.

But what choice did he have?

Clay needed some time alone to settle down, but he hadn't gotten fifty feet from the manor when he met up with Angus.

"There you are. You're needed at Base Camp."

"What is it?" Clay looked back, spotted the camera crew following close behind him and strode on.

"Your father," Angus answered in his thick Scottish burr, falling in with him. "He's come calling. And he's got a suitcase."

"NORA, WHAT HAPPENED?" Avery demanded again.

"Did Clay do something?" Riley asked.

Nora covered her face with her hands. Some of the crew had trailed after Clay when he left, but not all of them. She was still being filmed.

She couldn't believe she'd done that. She could have hurt Clay. Could have killed him, even. She hadn't even registered when she'd gripped the paperweight and hit him with it. Instinct had kicked in when he grabbed her chin.

She'd fought against the attack.

Nora dropped her hands into her lap. Clay hadn't meant to attack her. He'd meant to kiss her. He liked her.

Not everyone was a sick, twisted criminal like the kid who'd stalked her.

"I didn't mean to," she said helplessly. "He surprised me."

"How?" Avery dropped to her knees by Nora's side. "Did he hit you?"

"No! He... kissed me," Nora admitted.

Riley made a noise that sounded suspiciously like a laugh. "And you clobbered him with a paperweight?"

She gestured to the piece of jade Nora had dropped back onto the desk.

"I don't know why. It was a reaction—"

"Clay probably got the message," Avery said seriously. "I don't think you'll have to worry about him again."

Nora met Riley's gaze and pleaded with her for understanding.

"Is that the message you meant to send?" Riley asked gently.

"I don't know." Nora fought against the tears that threatened to fall. She refused to cry when the cameras were on her. Or ever, for that matter.

Why was she suddenly so jumpy when she'd left her stalker a thousand miles away? She was safe here. Everyone had told her that. Were her instincts so warped now that she'd mistake friendliness and attraction for a brutal attack from here on in?

Shame burned through her again at the thought of what she'd done to Clay. In a few minutes, everyone in camp would know about it. Soon enough, the entire viewing audience would, too. She could imagine the comments she'd receive then.

Was her face bright red? Was it clear she was fighting off tears? She wasn't sure how to get out of the parlor and away from the cameras, but Riley came to her rescue. She nudged Avery and said, "It's probably time for a snack. Should we bake some cookies, Avery?"

"Cookies? But..." Avery trailed off, got the message and started again. "Yes, that sounds terrific. Let's make double chocolate chip." She suddenly sounded as breezy as June Cleaver.

"Come on, Nora. Let's go wash up." Riley took Nora's hand, squeezed it meaningfully and pulled her to her feet.

Bless Riley and Avery, Nora thought as they all retreated to the kitchen.

"Do you remember the time you challenged Dean Boslow to beer pong back at school?" Avery said to Riley in that same chipper voice she'd used in the parlor.

"How could I forget?" Riley said. Nora saw the cameraman focus on her and hoped her friends could come up with enough college stories to keep his attention while she got herself together.

A half-hour later, when their stories had degenerated into general, stilted conversation, the camera crew finally packed things in.

"See you down at Base Camp for dinner," one of the men said as they left.

"See you," Avery chirped and shut the door behind them. "Fuckers."

CHAPTER SEVEN

"GET THOSE CAMERAS out of my face before I smash them to hell," Dell Pickett said as Clay tried to urge him away from the bunkhouse. A tall man, broader in the shoulder and thicker in the chest than Clay, Dell's short, dark hair stood on end as if he'd run his hand through it in exasperation more than once today. He had the swarthy coloring of someone who'd worked outdoors all his life, and he was dressed in a battered old pair of dungarees and a Chance Creek High wrestling team shirt—his go-to outfit when life was getting him down.

Clay had managed to duck into the bathroom and clean the blood from his wound. It was a shallow cut but he was getting a bump on the side of his head. He hoped like hell it didn't show up on camera.

"Dad, you're on the set of a reality TV show. That means you're going to be filmed if you stay here. The show runs for the next twelve months. I told you that." He was worried about his father's sudden appearance—and that ratty old T-shirt. The man was thirty pounds heavier than he'd been in high school. The shirt had stretched with him over the years, but it was in rough shape, and Clay's mother never let Dell wear it out in public. Something was wrong.

"I'm not going to be on any TV show. You all can talk to my lawyer if you don't like that." Dell spoke with an authority that snapped like a whipsaw. Clay had always joked with his friends that the officers the Navy had appointed to train him should have gone to Dell for lessons. His friends had agreed.

"You are if you're around me between now and next June." He knew from past experience he had to meet his father's aggression head on. Once Dell made up his mind about the way something should be, there was no changing it. Clay had to head him off at the pass. "Come on, let's take a walk." He led the way toward the rutted track that led to Pittance Creek. Hopefully, the cameras would fall back and he could find out why his father was here. Dell had dropped his suitcase in front of the bunkhouse, as if he planned to move right in. He'd been disgusted to see there were no bunks in there.

"Those men are still following us," Dell said a minute later.

"And they'll keep following us, so say what you have to say. What gives, Dad? What's with the suitcase?"

If Dell's shoulders slumped a fraction of an inch, Clay figured he was the only one who'd notice. A stranger would have thought Dell was the one in charge, the way he was marching through Base Camp, but that little sag told Clay a lot.

"It's your mother. She's lost her mind."

"I doubt that." Clay's mother was the most rational woman he knew. As office manager of a local walk-in clinic, organization was her strong suit. Unfortunately Dell saw any opposition to his opinions as akin to lunacy, so this wasn't the first time Clay had heard him dismiss his mother that way.

"She told me to get out, so I got out."

"What happened before that?" He couldn't imagine Lizette kicking anyone out without a good reason.

"Well..." Dell muttered something. Clay caught the words "job" and "disagreement" and "parting of the ways." Still, it took him a minute to put it all together.

"You lost your job?"

"Didn't I just say that?" Dell growled.

Shit. That was a new one. No wonder his dad was so close to blowing his stack. Clay knew he'd have to do some damage control, fast. "When?"

More grumbling. "April," Dell finally said.

"You've been out of work for two months?" He didn't blame his mother for throwing in the towel. Clay shuddered as he remembered childhood vacations, the only time Dell didn't work ten or more hours at a shot. The man could barely stand to relax for a day, let alone the week-long camping trips his mother had organized with her two sisters and their families in the mountains. While Lizette lounged with the other women and the kids had raced around and played pick-up games of football, baseball, badminton and more, or splashed in whatever creek or lake they camped next to, Dell had tried to expunge his extra energy collecting firewood, fishing or climbing every peak in a fifty-mile radius. Soon he would run out of excursions to make and patience with fishing and kids, and become so irritating that Lizette would threaten to send him home. Instead, she'd make up reasons for him to travel to Bozeman and pick things up at the shops there. Dell would happily jump in his truck and be gone for hours hunting down the obscure items on her list, thrilled to be doing anything other than sitting still. He'd visit three stores to find the lowest price for his purchases, although he'd only save pennies. Without a challenge, the man was lost. Clay had come by his own excess energy honestly.

"I've looked for work."

Clay could guess what the problem was. Dell was a whiz at carpentry. He also could be an annoying son-of-a-bitch and he'd had run-ins with other contractors in the past. His previous employer had kept him on a long time, so if he'd finally kicked him to the curb, Dell must have pushed him past his limit. Now Dell wouldn't have a good reference when he applied for other jobs.

"Maybe you need to broaden your search."

"Broaden it? Where? To Wyoming?"

"What about Abe or Chris? Can't they help find you work?"

"No."

"Rachel? Naomi?"

He exhausted his list of siblings, and when Dell shook his head after Clay said each name, Clay began to understand how dire the situation was. When Dell settled into a simmering silence, he realized he might be his father's last stop.

"Mom really threw you out?" he ventured.

"Yes, she did." Beneath the bluster, Clay heard his father's pain. Gruff and hardheaded as he was, Dell was a family man. Without Lizette he had no reason for being. He wasn't one for flowery speeches or declarations of love, but Clay had never doubted his father loved his mother. He showed it by all he did to support the family. And if he couldn't support his family, Dell would be questioning his place in the world. It was all he knew.

"How long do you think you'll stay?"

Dell shrugged again.

"All we've got are tents, but I'm sure there are extra ones."

"I'm obliged to you," Dell said stiffly. "I'll help out to pay my way. Looks like you've got a project going."

Clay's heart sank. "Yeah," he said slowly. "I guess I do."

CHAPTER EIGHT

CLAY SHIFTED UNCOMFORTABLY in his tent later that night, all too aware of Dell a few feet away in a separate one. When he'd left his father to get set up earlier in the day, he'd expected him to choose a site some yards away, since everyone else had given each other a little room. But his father had lined up his tent right next to Clay's and barely left any ground between them. It was embarrassing. This wasn't a Cub Scout camp out, and he wasn't some sniveling six year old who needed to be close to his daddy.

Apparently his dad needed to be close to him.

After Dell had placed his suitcase in his tent, he'd roamed Base Camp, poking his nose into the various projects just getting underway and offering his unsolicited opinion in that gruff, no-nonsense tone he had until Clay had been goaded to use his mother's old distraction technique when he noticed a cameraman trailing Dell intently. It would be too easy for Renata's minions to make his father a laughingstock on the show in his present condition. Clay had quickly composed a list, included an item or two he didn't think it possible to find in Chance Creek, and passed it to his father. Dell had brightened, just like in the old days, and made a beeline for his truck.

All too conscious of the fuel he was wasting in exchange for some peace and quiet, Clay had gotten some work done before he returned, but not as much as he'd hoped. Meanwhile, Nora was on his mind. It didn't take a genius to put two and two together and get four. Nora's hesitance—and the way she'd clouted him with that paperweight—could only mean one of two things. Either she really, truly disliked him, or she'd been spooked badly by the man who'd stalked her, and she'd overreacted when Clay had surprised her. Clay was beginning to understand that in his haste to get Nora to the altar, he'd vastly underestimated how much her stalker had spooked her, and his urge to steal a kiss had only made things worse. His only consolation was that she'd welcomed his kisses at the wedding, even though he'd frightened her badly only a few mornings before. His advances weren't the real problem; the television show was. Clay could understand that. Before, she'd felt anonymous here in Chance Creek. Now her location would be broadcast to the world. No wonder she was anxious. If he wanted any chance with her, he needed to soothe those fears.

In Clay's mind, spending more time with Nora was the obvious solution. He was a Navy SEAL, after all. He could be her bodyguard. Unfortunately he could predict her reaction to that. She'd say he was only motivated by

Fulsom's deadlines, and his unwanted attentions would end up making her feel less safe, not more. All day long his problems twisted and turned in his brain, and by the time he went to bed, they'd created so many knots he couldn't unravel them.

He must have drifted off to sleep at some point, though, because when Clay woke up again he found sunlight shining on his tent. He'd overslept. A series of shudders in the canvas around him alerted him that Dell was awake and moving about in his tent. Clay figured he'd better get up, too. His one shot was his date with Nora tonight. It had to go off smoothly.

Clay sat up, groaned at his throbbing temple, touched the sore spot and winced. First he needed to apologize, then he needed to make sure they were still on track for tonight. He'd do that now, before the filming started.

When he met up with Dell and the other men at the morning campfire, however, he got a taste of things to come. For one thing, the cameras were everywhere. It was later than he'd judged it to be—no time to go and talk to Nora now. For another, Dell was already riling up the other men in that inimitable way he had.

"Whoever made this coffee needs to learn how to do it right," Dell was saying to Jericho when he reached them. His father went on to explain a complicated process that had Jericho giving him the side-eye. Clay hastened to step in.

"Dad. What are your plans today? Do you have any interviews lined up?"

With an uneasy glance toward Jericho, Dell edged away from the fire. "I already told you, I contacted the employers around here. No one's hiring."

"You'll have to find work somewhere. Are you sure you can't convince Mr. Silverton to take you back?"

"I wouldn't go back," Dell snarled. "I don't need his money."

Clay pulled him farther aside as the camera crew closed in again, hoping to conduct this conversation in private, but Ed broke off from the others and followed them. "Look," Clay said in a low voice. "You need *someone's* money."

"Looks like there's plenty of work here. Half this crew are loafers—you can tell by the way they—"

"Dad, these are hand-picked men. All ex-military. Show some respect." His tone had grown sharper than he'd meant it to. Dell puffed up like a rooster, and Clay knew he had to head him off. "This isn't a paid gig," he continued. "We're getting room and board, such as it is. Our materials and food are covered. Once we've got our community up and running, we'll have to figure out how to make it profitable. A big part of that will be ranching. You've never liked that."

"Ranching. Fat lot of good that'll do you."

Clay knew his father hated ranching for two reasons. First, because his old man had wanted him to take up the family business, something Dell refused to do. Second, because he was only two years into the architecture degree he'd wanted so badly when his parents lost their ranch in a combination of bad practices and worse luck. Dell had to quit school and go to work to help them out as they sold off the property and struggled to cover their debts. He'd gone straight into construction, and never made it back to finish his degree. Despite his temper, he'd done well for himself over the years—until recently. As cussed as he was, he was a good worker. Clay doubted he had enough saved for the future to retire now, though.

"You're telling me you're not getting any money for this?" Dell demanded.

"Not yet." Clay was all too aware of Ed filming their conversation. "Anyway, I can put you to work today just for something to do, but it won't be paid. You need to look for a job."

"I'll check the listings." Dell stalked off, but all too soon he was back at Clay's side on the building site.

"Nothing new," he said tersely, which meant Clay spent his day finding tasks for him to do around Base Camp instead of finding a way to patch things up with Nora. When he noticed Walker walk past and head up toward the manor, an ugly streak of jealousy surged through him. Was he going to see Avery?

Or Nora?

"JOB'S YOURS," WALKER said when Nora opened the front door to the manor and found him on the steps. Dressed in her work gown, a large white apron covering most of it, she had been cleaning the first-floor bathroom when he'd arrived. Savannah was upstairs making up the bedrooms. Avery and Riley had gone down to

Base Camp to consult with Boone about plans to make the manor more energy efficient.

"What does that mean?" She stood back to let him come in, but though he stepped into the doorway, he didn't come in any farther. Behind him she could see a camera crew waiting to come inside and film the proceedings. She was sure he knew they were there, but he didn't acknowledge them.

"My grandmother will come by tomorrow after school."

"Doesn't she want to interview me before hiring me for the job?"

Behind Walker, a cameraman Nora thought was named Craig Demaris cleared his throat.

Walker shook his head, keeping his position.

"What about references—does she want a list of them to call?"

He shook his head again.

Nora eyed him. This wasn't the way things were done in Baltimore. "She doesn't even know if I am who I say I am!"

Craig cleared his throat again. "Walker? You'll have to move, buddy."

Walker ignored him. "Got some ID?" He leaned against the doorjamb and waited as if he expected her to fetch it.

"Yes. Upstairs." That was more like it. With a copy of her ID, at least his grandmother could verify a few things. Nora liked everything to be done by the book. This loosey-goosey way of hiring made her nervous. She climbed the two flights to her room to fetch her purse. Downstairs again, slightly out of breath, she pulled out her driver's license. Walker looked it over. Handed it back.

"Good."

Nora blinked. He couldn't be serious. Wasn't he going to photocopy it or something—?

Wait. Had the corner of his mouth hitched up a fraction of an inch, just for a second? Was Walker... teasing her?

No, she decided. Not him. Although...

No.

"That can't be it," she exclaimed, disconcerted by this whole situation. "This isn't any way to hire a person."

"Walker!" Craig said. "Let us in, man."

"This is Chance Creek." Walker seemed to think that explanation enough. "Three o'clock. Be ready."

Three o'clock was right in the middle of her writing time. There wasn't anything for it, of course. She wanted the job. She'd have to write in the evenings. If Walker's grandmother left by five, she'd be on time for dinner down at Base Camp, anyway. She knew Renata would have things to say if she was late.

Nora looked down at her dress. "She's going to think I'm pretty strange."

"For fuck's sake, Walker—" Craig said.

"It'll be fine." Walker turned to go.

"I'll be ready," she called out as he walked slowly down the stairs. He didn't bother to reply. Craig and the others trailed after him as he went, the cameraman berating Walker. Walker kept going, as stoic as ever.

Nora shut the door, re-examining her feelings about taking this on. Here she'd finally gotten the opportunity to really give writing a go, and she was allowing a new responsibility to take a chunk out of her day. Was she sabotaging herself?

More like distracting herself, she decided. It was a project she could sink her teeth into. Maybe then she'd forget the anxiety twisting her innards into knots.

Besides, it was only temporary. She'd write up the curriculum under Walker's grandmother's tutelage, then return to her Jane Austen life.

Savannah cleared her throat behind Nora, and Nora spun around, startled. "Savannah! You scared me."

"Sorry. I just finished the bedrooms." She waved behind her to indicate the stairs. "Did I just hear you accept a job, Nora Ridgeway?"

Nora nodded, guilt flooding her cheeks with heat. She'd hoped to have time to craft an explanation that would make up for her breaking her vow. "It's education-related—" She squeaked when Savannah hugged her. "What's that for?"

"I know how much you miss teaching, so if you've found something that makes you happy, then I'm glad. Above everything else, we want you to stay here. Write if that makes you happy. Teach, whatever. Just... stay."

For the first time in twenty-four hours, Nora smiled. She hugged Savannah back impulsively.

"Are you busy right now?" Savannah asked.

"Not really. I need to finish up the bathrooms, but—"

"I'm going stir crazy. I'd... like a new dress." She blushed a little when Nora raised an eyebrow. "I know, I know, we're supposed to be economizing, but I'm feeling frivolous. Is that really so bad?"

Nora shook her head, taking in the circles under Savannah's eyes. Wrapped up in her own cares, had she missed something? Savannah didn't look like she was sleeping well. "Of course not." She wondered if this was about Jericho.

"Should I call James Russell or a taxi?" Savannah was keeper of the cell phone today and she pulled it out of her pocket.

"James." Nora could use a carriage ride right about now. The slower pace suited her mood.

As usual, James was all too pleased to have an excuse to get out his horses, and in less than half an hour he was climbing down from his high seat to greet them and help them into the carriage. Nora swore the man would drive all over Montana in his barouche if he could.

"Cameras. Twelve o'clock," Savannah said suddenly. Nora sighed when she turned and saw the crew hastening up the hill to catch up with them.

"Wherever you're going, we're coming, too," William said, puffing with the exertion.

"Not in my barouche." James straightened to his full height, and almost managed to look intimidating in his old-fashioned waistcoat, but Savannah put a hand on his arm.

"It's all right."

"Are you sure, my dear? I think the way these people are hounding you is deplorable."

"It's fine."

Nora didn't agree, but there wasn't anything for it. William, Byron and a young female crew member she didn't know climbed carefully into the barouche, trying to keep their equipment steady. Nora and Savannah got in after them. Nora knew they were filming the ride, but she and Savannah both made a big deal of looking at the scenery rather than talking. She suspected this particular footage wouldn't make it into the show.

James took them to the Reed place, a large spread east of Chance Creek, where Alice Reed, an expert seamstress, lived. Nora relaxed a little along the way, despite the camera crew. She was blowing things out of proportion over this job. It was temporary. It was only two hours a day. She'd still have plenty of time to write.

"I'll be back in an hour to pick you up," James said when he deposited all of them in front of Two Willows, the big, old white farmhouse where the Reed sisters lived.

"Thank you," Nora said, and she and Savannah waved as he clucked to the horses and drove off.

"It's such a civilized manner of transportation," Savannah said. "Don't you agree?"

Nora shrugged. "As long as someone else is driving. Those horses scare me."

"Me, too, although I think we're going to have to

get over that."

Alice was waiting for them on the porch. "Come on in. I expected you a half-hour ago."

"I was so desperate to get out of the house, I didn't even call to warn you we were coming," Savannah said with a laugh. "I figured we'd visit with one of your sisters if you were out. I'm sorry about our entourage." She waved a hand at the crew following close behind them.

"Did James call to let you know?" Nora asked Alice.

Alice shook her head. "Just had a hunch you'd be by." She led the way inside as Nora exchanged a look with Savannah. Savannah shrugged, and Nora decided to let it go. Alice was a dreamy young woman Nora thought belonged in a fairy-tale illustration. Her long hair was always half braided, half coming undone, and no matter what she wore she couldn't hide her beautiful figure and regal bearing. She was like a princess caught in a spell. Nora wondered if a prince would ever come along and spring her from her enchantment.

Nora hadn't been to Two Willows before. Previously, Alice had come to them when they needed dresses. It was an old house with a generous front porch and large rooms. Like their home, the kitchen was at the back. Alice led the way and sat them at a large wooden table Nora thought must have been there for a century at least. The crew took their time taking shots of the house and Alice.

"What can I do for you?" she asked when she'd poured them both large glasses of ice water, and added a slice of lemon and a mint leaf to each.

"I'd like a new dress," Savannah said, a little sheepishly. "Something... that will solve all my problems. Can you make me a dress like that?" She smiled at Alice as if to say she knew that wasn't possible.

Alice looked her over with a critical eye and nodded. "I believe I can. Let me take some measurements and we'll look at fabric. Come out to my workshop."

They brought their glasses and followed Alice out the back door across a lawn toward a carriage house set to one side and behind Two Willows, trailed by the crew. It was a white two-story building with four bays and a row of windows set on top of them that hinted at apartments over the garages.

Alice let them in a door to one side, up a flight of thick wooden stairs and into a room that took Nora's breath away. Large windows on all sides let sunlight stream into the huge space. Racks and racks of clothing were placed around the room. Several large worktables filled the interior space, with sewing machines of all kinds positioned on them. One corner of the room had been made into a fitting area, with draperies to give privacy to a small cubicle, and several large mirrors were set up in an open space so that you could see all sides of yourself at once. In another corner there was a small kitchen, and Nora spotted a bathroom through an open door. It seemed Alice never had to leave her workshop if she didn't want to.

"Holy moly," Savannah breathed, her eyes alight. Even the crew members stopped to take it all in before furiously getting to work to record it all.

Alice laughed. "Do you like it?"

"I love it. This is a workshop fit for a queen," Nora said. Just like she'd thought: Alice was living in a fairy tale. Doomed to sew forever until her prince came by.

She shook off her fantasy as Alice beamed. "That's what I feel like when I'm here. Come on. Let me measure you." She took Savannah to the fitting area while Nora drifted around the room and pulled outfits off racks. She spotted a redcoat uniform like the ones the men had worn at the ball and weddings, a southern Civil War–era hoop skirt, a flapper dress, a white gauzy gown that looked like something Cleopatra might wear...

"This is amazing," Nora called over to the others. "Alice, you could furnish a Hollywood movie studio."

"Sometimes I do," Alice said simply, pulling out a measuring tape. "But mostly I just enjoy making them."

Alice was a true artist, Nora thought. She didn't need any monetary gain to commit to her craft. She didn't need a vacation from her day job or her friends around. You couldn't keep her from it.

Why didn't she feel that way about writing?

She tuned out Savannah and Alice's conversation, and the attempts of the film crew to record everything. There was no doubt writing called to her. But every story she started seemed... wrong. She must be messing up somehow.

"Alice, how do you know what costume to make next? If someone hasn't asked for something specific?"

she called over from the rack she was looking through. She loved the feel of all the different fabrics.

"I run my hands over the fabric until I feel the heat of a possibility," Alice said. "Or I go for a long walk until it springs into my mind. Or I take a bath. I always think of costumes in the bath."

"That's the way I pick music to play," Savannah said. "It's like it comes out of my fingers without me thinking or making a choice at all. Sometimes when I run my hands over my music books, I know what to pick out without even looking at it. The pages open and there's the song to play."

Nora let her hands fall to her sides. "Writing never feels like that to me." Only teaching did. She came up with curriculum ideas all the time.

"Don't give up yet," Savannah said as Alice finished with her measurements and stepped back. "It'll come. You're just starting."

"You'll know when it's right," Alice added. "Listen to your body. It never lies."

CHAPTER NINE

CLAY HAD BEEN waiting by the front door of the manor for nearly twenty minutes when James's barouche finally pulled up around noon, and he spotted Nora and Savannah inside. It had been strange to find the manor, usually full of female laughter and chatter, empty of life, and for one awful moment he'd thought the women had decamped before he remembered Avery and Riley were down at Base Camp talking to Boone. The door was unlocked and he could have waited inside, but that didn't seem right. When he spotted the crew in the barouche with them, his irritation flared, but he covered it up with a comment or two to James as they all climbed out.

"Can we talk?" he asked Nora as they watched James drive away.

"I guess we'd better. Would you like a glass of lemonade?"

He'd prefer something far stronger, but said, "Sure."

Savannah led the way inside. She went into the parlor and began to play the piano. Nora led the way into the kitchen. Clay followed her, and the crew followed him. So much for his hope they'd go record Savannah's performance. He watched Nora pour two drinks, smiled at the hopeful look on Byron's face that soon faded when she didn't pour any more, and held the back door open for her.

Outside on the porch, he took a seat across from her on the wicker furniture. The crew arranged themselves around the perimeter of the deck. Clay did his best to ignore them.

"How's your head?" Nora asked, handing him a drink.

"Sore."

"I really am sorry about that." She finally settled in her seat and took a cautious sip of her drink.

"Want to tell me about it?"

"Not really." She placed the drink down on the table. "Let's just say I like to choose when and where I'm kissed."

"I guess I was trying to be romantic. Like when I surprised you at the creek."

She raised an eyebrow, and Clay coughed to cover his embarrassment. He leaned back and balanced his drink on his knee, keeping hold of it so it didn't crash to the porch floor. "It is romantic sometimes when the man takes charge, right? Makes you feel all feminine?" Hell, he was digging himself a nice big hole, wasn't he? He'd meant to apologize, and now Nora was staring at him like he'd lost his mind. "I mean, sometimes girls like that." Fuck, that was smooth.

"Girls?" If her eyebrows went any higher they'd disappear under her hair.

"Girls. Women. You know—"

"Dude, shut the fuck up," William said. "You're just making it worse."

"Stay out of it," Clay snapped back at him. William shrugged and went back to filming.

Nora didn't blink. "I'm not one of those *women*."

"Oh. Okay." Clay fiddled with his drink. Lost his grip on it. It clattered to the porch floor but didn't break.

Nora winced. "You know what? I don't think—"

Clay couldn't take it anymore. "Look, Nora. You know I like you." He ignored the mess he'd made and the glass lying on its side on the porch floor. "You know I'd never in a million years hurt you. I wasn't raised like that, I wasn't raised to push a woman around and I don't need to prove my manhood by forcing myself on one. I wanted to kiss you, you didn't want to kiss me and I got embarrassed."

She scanned his face as if checking to see if he was telling the truth. Clay sat and took it. "Okay," she said finally. "That I believe. And I'm sorry. I wanted to kiss you, too. I just… couldn't."

Surprised at her candor, Clay picked up his now-empty glass and put it on the wicker table. "Sorry about your deck. I'd better pour some water on that before the wasps come."

"In a minute." Nora leaned forward. "The problem with this scenario is that I don't fall in love fast under the best of circumstances. I need time to fall for some-one. Lots of time. We don't have that, and that's not going to change."

Clay shrugged helplessly. "The problem with this scenario is that I want you and no one else."

A silence stretched out between them that neither rushed to end. Finally Clay said, "I'd still like to take you on that picnic. I'll keep my hands to myself. And my mouth."

Nora smiled, then quickly frowned, but in the end she nodded. "Okay."

OKAY? HAD SHE really just said okay? Nora wanted to bury her head in her hands, but Clay's truthfulness had impressed her and she'd wanted to reward it.

And, if she was honest, she wanted to spend time with him. A picnic sounded like a lovely retreat from the stress of the past few days. It would be a way to start over, maybe. A return to normalcy, if that was possible under the circumstances.

"I'll pick you up at six," Clay said. He grinned. "I guess that means I should get back to work now."

"How are the houses going?"

"We're working as fast as we can, now that we've gotten started. I don't want Boone and Riley to have to wait long to move into theirs, and Harris is framing up the second one while Curtis and I work on the first."

"It's so strange not to have Riley at the manor any-more." That sounded too wistful. "I'm happy for her," she said for the benefit of the cameras.

"She'll still work with you on the B and B stuff."

"That's not quite the same. I wish we'd had more time here alone before you guys came." She bit her lip again. "Sorry. That wasn't very nice."

"It was truthful. That's better than nice sometimes. We kind of wrecked it for you, didn't we?" He set his hands on his knees as if about to launch to his feet. Nora hid a smile. Clay was always a ball of barely restrained energy. She had a feeling he'd be amazing in the sack.

Where had that thought come from? Nora refrained from rolling her eyes, but she was relieved that she could joke—internally—after how tense things had been these past few days.

"In a way. But in a way it's more interesting," she made herself say. She meant it, too. "Men do awful things sometimes, but they're also kind of wonderful now and then."

"I'm sorry for scaring you. Both times."

She looked down, embarrassed by the word he'd chosen. Scared. He was right, though; he had scared her, and she didn't want to be scared by passion.

"You just surprised me. Both times," she echoed.

"I know that it must be hard given your past—"

Nora didn't want to talk about her stalker on camera. "Clay," she interrupted. "What should I wear tonight?"

He blinked. "Uh…"

"Should I dress up?" She leaned toward him as if his answer was the most important thing in the world.

"It's… a picnic. Don't wear anything that can't get dirty," he said slowly.

"Okay." She stood up. "I'd better get back to work."

"All right." He stood, too, although she could tell her sudden dismissal confused him. She picked up both glasses, and when she straightened, he moved closer to her, as if to come for another kiss. But he must have remembered what happened last time, and stopped just as he began to bend toward her. "Until tonight, then," he said and backed away again, leaving Nora a little disappointed.

"Yes. Until tonight."

They stood there awkwardly until both moved at once.

"Sorry," she said, nearly bumping into him.

"No, I… See you later." He dodged around her and made it to the porch steps. With a salute he headed in the direction of Base Camp.

Nora turned to find the camera crew watching her, all of them wearing nearly identical expressions of pity and disgust.

"You two are so completely lame," William said.

CHAPTER TEN

"**O**H, MY GOSH, we got an inquiry," Avery said when they'd eaten lunch and settled down to work. "Sorry," she added sheepishly. "I was looking up something for my screenplay and couldn't help checking e-mail." She was seated on the divan in the parlor, holding the cell phone they shared. Savannah was back at her piano. Nora was trying to write at her desk, even though the music distracted her. Riley had stayed at Base Camp with Boone even after their meeting was done, and Nora wondered if this was indicative of the way things would go from now on. So much for their vow not to get distracted from their work. Riley had mentioned sketching down at Base Camp, but with Boone there, Nora wasn't sure how much she'd actually get done.

"Who from?" Savannah asked. She stood up and came to sit by Avery, piano forgotten.

"A woman named Hortense. She wants to bring three friends for a weekend. At the end of July—long past the next wedding." Avery snuck a look at Nora.

Nora busied herself by taking a sip from her glass of water and setting it carefully back on the desk. She tried to find her place in her manuscript, but found herself re-reading words she'd already perused a half-dozen times.

"The end of July?" Savannah sounded discouraged. "That's not for weeks—and it's not a very long stay. I think we should require a minimum number of nights, otherwise it won't be worth it for us to do all the preparation work."

"We're just starting, though," Avery said. "I think we should take every customer we can and treat them like queens. Once we have a following, we can set stricter rules."

"Did she ask for any specific activities?" Nora made herself enter the conversation.

"Carriage rides, walks, and she's written she'd like painting and horseback riding lessons."

"How old is Hortense?" Savannah smiled at the old-fashioned name. "I'm assuming in her sixties or seventies?"

"She doesn't say. Let me do a search." A minute later Avery straightened. "She looks about twenty."

"You're kidding. That can't be right." Nora stood, pushed her chair back and came to look over her shoulder. "Huh."

"How many Hortense Minns can there be?" Avery asked. "This has to be her."

She had a point.

"What about her friends?" Savannah asked.

Avery did a few more searches. "From what I can tell, they're young, too. What do you say?"

"I say we go for it. Let's come up with a plan of activities first, though, and submit it to them for approval up front. Then we won't have any surprises like last time," Savannah said.

"Good idea." Nora didn't want to be responsible for throwing another last-minute ball. The Russells had saved their bacon that day, but they didn't want to depend on the older couple to keep bailing them out.

"I'll do a canned response for now and tell her we'll send her a proposal within a day or so," Avery said. "But right now I want some tea. Anyone else?"

In the kitchen, Avery heated the kettle on the stove while they discussed possibilities for the weekend. Nora pulled out some muffins and she and Savannah sat down at the table.

"We can pretty much do what we did for Andrea, without the wedding shower parts," Avery said from her position near the stove. "Take them on a carriage ride around the ranch and into town, feed them Regency-style meals, teach them some dances. It should go just fine."

"Friday night we'll do dinner and a basic orientation to the ranch and Regency life. It'll be light out late, so we could definitely do a carriage ride," Savannah said.

"I wonder if—" Nora started. A crash from the parlor cut through her words.

"What was that?" Avery rushed toward the door. Savannah and Nora pushed back from the table and hurried after her. When they reached the parlor, they found a glass shattered on the polished wooden floor.

"That was mine from earlier," Nora said, hurrying to her desk. "But it wasn't anywhere near the edge. How did it fall if no one was in here?" She checked her laptop, worried water might have damaged it, but it was perfectly dry. In fact, there was no water on the desk at all. It was as if she'd set the glass right on the edge and it had slipped off.

But she hadn't. She'd placed it behind her laptop for that very reason. She scanned the room for evidence that would explain the mystery, but nothing else was askew.

"At least it wasn't very full," Avery said, crouching down. As Avery started to gingerly gather up the biggest shards of glass, Nora examined the desk again, a funny feeling coming over her. "I don't get it. Why would it fall over like that?"

"It must have tipped." Savannah bent to join Avery, lifting her skirts out of the way.

Nora knew she should join them, but she couldn't get over the feeling that something was wrong. "How come there's no water on the desk, then?" Had one of the crew members come back? Had they tried to read her manuscript? She wouldn't put it past Renata, but her laptop screen was dark. If someone had touched it, it would have lit up again.

"I don't know what happened. Can you grab the broom, Nora?" Avery said.

"Of course." But she didn't move. Her methodical

mind wouldn't stop ticking over the problem. How on earth could that glass have moved a foot and a half by itself before it fell?

It couldn't, Nora realized.

Which meant someone had moved it.

And that someone might still be in the house.

"Nora—"

She glanced from the open window to the nearby front door. The window had a screen on it; no one could get in there. Was the front door locked? Probably not.

"Shh," she hissed and held up a hand for silence.

"What?" Avery stilled, too, and listened. Savannah did the same.

"I think someone's here," Nora whispered. If Renata thought it was all right to sneak in and film them unawares she was wrong and Nora meant to make that very clear.

If it was Renata…

The other two exchanged a look. Avery set aside the shards and rose to her feet. She crossed lightly to the great room, which they rarely used, peered in, then shook her head at Nora to say no one was there. Savannah and Nora followed her to the kitchen, but that was empty, too. Avery held up her hand, and they all stood still, straining to hear anything.

Nora cocked her head. Was that the scuff of a footstep? She rushed back to the front hall but again it was empty. So was the parlor. She turned to the others and shrugged.

They all jumped when they heard a creak from the direction of the kitchen. It sounded like the back door swinging open.

"Hello?" Nora called out, striding down the central hall toward the kitchen again. "Who's there?" Avery and Savannah were hot on her heels, but when she peeked inside the room, no one was there and the door was firmly shut.

Avery pushed past her to open it and step outside.

"Do you see anyone?" Nora whispered when she and Savannah joined her on the back porch.

"No."

All of them clattered down the steps and split up, Avery turning left, Nora turning right and Savannah heading for the edge of the backyard. Moments later they met up again at the back porch.

"I couldn't see anyone," Avery said.

"Maybe it was the wind we heard," Savannah said. "The windows are open all over the house."

"What about that glass? The wind couldn't have moved it." Avery led the way back inside. Nora shut the kitchen door and locked it carefully, before catching up with the other two in the parlor, where they stared at the shards still lying on the ground.

"Avery's right; I don't see how it could have fallen by itself," Nora said. She remembered the front door and crossed to lock it, too.

"There's no one around. We checked," Savannah said reasonably.

"Outside." Nora looked toward the stairs and lowered her voice again. "What if someone's hiding upstairs?"

Avery shook her head. "That's crazy. Who would do that?"

"Maybe one of the cameramen. Maybe they're trying to dig up dirt," Savannah said suddenly. She hurried toward the staircase. "Who else would be sneaking around in here?"

Nora decided not to bring up her stalker. Savannah's suggestion was far more reasonable. She and Avery hurried after her. In unspoken agreement, they stuck together, climbing all the way to the top of the main staircase and going through the bedrooms one by one. Riley's was neat as a pin. Before her wedding, she'd packed the belongings she'd take down to Base Camp, now that she'd be living there with Boone. The rest of her things were stored carefully away here. Savannah's was less tidy. She had a habit of tossing possessions aside when she was done with them and not returning to put them away. Nora's was neat enough, but Avery's looked like a tornado had gone through it. All of them were empty.

"I really meant to clean up last night," Avery said, her cheeks a little pink. "Then I had a really good idea for my screenplay."

"I'm more worried about the intruder than your standards of cleanliness," Nora said, then felt bad about snapping at her friend. "Sorry."

"That's all right."

They descended to the second floor and checked all

the guest bedrooms and baths. There was no one here, either. Back on the first floor in the kitchen, Nora shrugged. "I guess we were alone the whole time." That didn't settle her nerves any, but she wanted to put a good face on things. She didn't want the others to know how uneasy she felt. After striking Clay with the paperweight, she figured they already suspected she was a bit unhinged.

"There are so many people at Westfield," Avery said reasonably. "I don't think anyone from off the ranch could come and go without us seeing a car, at least."

"It better not have been one of Renata's goons," Savannah said. She looked as distracted as Nora felt. Nora wasn't convinced by any of their explanations. The anxious feeling settled in her gut, as if there to stay.

When a sudden rasping sounded at the back door, and it swung open a moment later, Nora shrieked. So did Avery. Riley, framed in the door, shrieked, too. "It's just me!" She held up her key. "What's wrong with all of you? You look like you've seen a ghost. And since when do we lock the doors? Did something happen?"

Nora cut the others off before they spoke up. "We thought someone from the camera crews might be snooping around in the house." She didn't want Renata to find out about her stalker, which meant she wasn't going to plant the idea in Riley's head. If Riley mentioned to Boone that Nora was afraid her stalker had followed her, he'd rally the troops and set an armed guard at the manor. Renata would run with that for all she was worth. She'd send investigative teams back to

Baltimore to find out all the sordid details, and feature them on the show—blown all out of proportion, of course. Then Nora would be known forever as the victim of a twisted sexual offender—not the kind of woman you hired to teach school.

Nora swallowed hard at the thought of losing her career forever. "Is that tea ready yet?"

CHAPTER ELEVEN

W HEN DELL INVITED himself along to the grocery
store that afternoon, Clay tamped down on his
exasperation. He didn't mind the company, but he did
mind the way his father had interfered with every
project happening at Base Camp. It had been bad
enough when he'd tried to take over building the raised
beds Boone wanted in the community garden, ordering
around the other men like he was in charge. It was
worse when he'd tried to help Jericho figure out a
schematic for the first of their wind turbines and had
almost gotten into a tug of war when Jericho refused to
hand over the plans.

Now he was full of suggestions for the picnic dinner
Clay needed to prepare.

"Meat. It's all about the meat. I'd suggest a roast
beef sandwich for Nora."

"I'm going to get a variety."

"But nothing compares to roast beef at a picnic. I'm
telling you, son. You can't go wrong with that."

"I'll definitely get roast beef. And turkey, and—"

"Beets are good. Pickled beets. Gotta have them on a roast beef sandwich."

"I'm not too sure about that, Pops." For one thing, Dell was the only person he'd ever met who ate beets on a sandwich. For another, beets were one of those things people either liked or hated. And if they slid out of Nora's sandwich onto her gown, he could probably kiss his chances with her good-bye. When you only had a few dresses, you had to take good care of them.

Clay shook his head. Hell, that was a manly thought. He must be hanging around the women too much.

All this wedding and marriage business was enough to make your balls shrivel up. And he was all for matrimony—as long as it wasn't complicated by all these extra problems. Why couldn't he have met Nora, dated her, moved in when the time was right and married her if and when it made sense? Fulsom was screwing everything up.

"Everyone loves pickled beets," Dell continued.

"I like pickled beets," Ed, lugging his camera along, said.

"Two people aren't everyone."

His father settled into an irritated silence.

Once at the store, however, Dell started in again, questioning every item Clay put in his cart, offering alternatives and opinions Clay didn't want. Ed documented everything, and by the time they were heading home again, Clay was close to losing his cool—and he had several items in the bags in back he didn't even like to eat.

"I'll see you later," he said to Dell when they pulled up near the bunkhouse.

"What time are we leaving?" Dell undid his seat belt.

"For what?"

"For the picnic." Dell's exasperation was clear.

Clay opened his mouth. Shut it again. No. His father could not be this dense. "Dad, it's just—"

Something in his father's face made him stop. For the first time Dell was showing his age. Clay couldn't say if it was the wariness in his eyes, or the depth of the grooves bracketing his mouth. His father was braced for a blow, and Clay was about to give it to him.

"It's... six. I need to change. Can you be ready by then?" he said instead, cursing himself the minute the words left his mouth.

His father relaxed a fraction. That made it worth it. Almost.

"Sure thing. I'd better go shave." Dell strode off toward his tent. Clay got out and slowly brought the bags of groceries and the hamper they'd picked up at the Five and Dime store into the bunkhouse kitchen. He started unloading the bags, lost in thought.

This was bad. Real bad.

He was taking his father along on a date.

Something had to give.

IT'S ONLY A picnic, Nora reminded herself as she made her way up to her bedroom to get ready late that afternoon, Savannah and Avery close at her heels. She was grateful they'd offered to assist her. It wasn't that she had a lot of dresses to choose from, but she needed help to change and do her hair. Plus, if she was honest, she was a little spooked to be alone anywhere in the house right now. Riley had returned to Base Camp. Soon her friends would head down there, too, for dinner. Nora was glad she'd be with Clay rather than here on her own.

She'd convinced herself her friends were right, and the glass had fallen over on its own. Maybe she'd taken another sip at the last minute and hadn't put it down as carefully as she thought. She could have set it near to the edge—half on, half off the stack of notes she'd left there earlier.

It was the rational explanation.

Still, she couldn't shake the feeling it wasn't the right one.

Avery helped her change into her other gown, and Savannah got to work on her hair. She brushed it out, gathered it together high on her head, then braided and pinned it into a complicated bun.

"You look beautiful. You'll knock his socks off," she said, turning Nora toward the mirror.

Nora touched her hair. "But is that what I should be doing?"

"You like him, don't you?" Avery asked, hanging her work dress back in the closet.

"I shouldn't."

"But you do."

Nora nodded. "I can't help it."

"Would marrying him be so bad?" Savannah asked

softly.

"Would you marry Jericho?" Nora countered.

Savannah was thoughtful. "Maybe I would. If—" She broke off and smiled sadly. "Who's to say he'd want to marry me?"

Surprised, Nora glanced at Avery, who was looking at Savannah in as much confusion as Nora felt. "Why wouldn't he want to marry you? He's always been interested," Avery said.

"People change their minds."

"Savannah—"

A loud knocking at the front door interrupted them.

"That must be Clay." Savannah urged Nora toward the door. "Hurry up."

"We'll finish this conversation later," Nora told her, but she hurried down the two flights of stairs, and when she opened the front door she forgot all about Savannah and what she'd said about Jericho.

Clay had obviously showered recently, his short, dark hair still damp. He wore jeans, a black T-shirt and a nicer pair of boots than he normally wore working around Base Camp. His broad shoulders strained the fabric of his shirt, and there was something so appealing about a man all cleaned up for a date she had to hold back from leaning in, wrapping her arms around his neck and going up on tiptoe for a kiss. He wore his cowboy hat tonight. She loved him in that hat; another thing that had surprised her. She was a city girl, after all.

How ironic to know she'd like to ambush him in the same way he'd startled her the other day. She had a feeling Clay wouldn't conk her with a paperweight, either.

If he did, she'd be in a lot of trouble, judging by those biceps.

Nora smiled at the frivolous thought. Since when had she stopped being an intellectual and started lusting after six-pack abs and big muscles?

Since she'd started living with a bunch of Navy SEALs, she supposed.

She knew Clay would never hurt her, no matter how strong he was. If only she hadn't hit him, he might try to kiss her tonight. She figured he'd need a lot of encouragement before he did that again.

Could she offer him that kind of encouragement? The edgy panic she'd felt earlier had taken second place to the warm glow Clay's presence always stimulated within her. Still, she couldn't help but worry the desire that twined within her now would disappear if Clay touched her. What if he kissed her and she overreacted again?

Best to keep things civil and platonic, she decided. For a number of reasons.

He smiled back and Nora's intentions melted away. "Evening. Hope you're hungry. I've got a lot of food."

"I could eat something." She drew on her gloves, put on her bonnet and tied the strings into a loose bow under her chin, grateful for a moment to pull herself together. She noticed Clay looking at her fondly when she was done.

"What?"

"You're really something, you know that?" He reached for her hand, and she stepped onto the front stoop with him, shutting the door behind her. She heard the bolt slide home and knew either Avery or Savannah had locked it behind her. She hoped they remembered to lock the other door, as well.

"No," she said truthfully. She'd never felt like much of anything. Certainly not in this last year. She hadn't accomplished much in her life. Her father had left her without a second look. She hadn't been able to prevent her mother's death. She'd run away from the only job that had ever mattered to her.

"You are. It's your eyes. And that smile you don't flash around much. And your graceful hands. And the way you put it all together."

She was sure she was blushing. She wasn't used to praise like this. People either liked her or disliked her. They tolerated her plain speaking or hated it. They approved of her work ethic or thought she was a prude. No one thought anything of her eyes. Or hands, for heaven's sake. The flutters in her stomach were getting the best of her, especially when she caught his eye and saw the desire there.

Nora looked away again, finding it hard to meet his gaze when he talked like that, but she couldn't look at the cameras, either. She looked behind him—and noticed an older man waiting a half-dozen paces away.

"Who's that?"

Clay sagged a little. "That's my dad. I hope you don't mind, he's coming on the picnic with us."

CLAY KNEW WITHOUT a shadow of a doubt that any headway he had made in those first few moments after Nora had opened the door were long gone. As the three of them trailed back down the dirt track past Base Camp toward Pittance Creek, he felt like he could have been on a picnic with the Pope, for all the flirting that was going on. Instead of smiling at him the way she had back at the house, Nora was walking beside his father, asking polite questions and making chitchat about the weather. He was stuck behind them with the cameramen.

He lugged along the heavy basket and cooler his father had insisted on packing as if Armageddon was coming. He put in a word or two when he could hear enough of the conversation to comment on it, but by the time they reached the creek, he thought he knew exactly how this evening would play out.

The cameramen fanned out and took up fixed positions. Clay set down the picnic basket and spread out the blanket he'd brought. He wasn't sure what irritated him more—the cameramen's presence on his date or his father's.

"Is the fishing good here?" Dell asked, surveying the running water while Clay and Nora began to unpack the food.

"Haven't had a chance to try it yet, but it was good when we were kids."

"I remember the way you always came running over here back then. I figured you liked that pretty little girl who used to spend her summers here. What was her name? Riley?"

Hell. That wasn't going to help his case with Nora. "It was the money I liked, Pops, not Riley. Riley just married Boone Rudman, remember?"

"I remember Boone. That boy always did end up on top when you two scrapped."

"We never scrapped over Riley." Clay would be ready to scrap with Dell in a minute, though.

"Oh, you say that now." Dell turned, caught sight of Nora and seemed to remember her presence. "I mean, well, that's all in the past now, of course."

Clay touched Nora's hand when Dell turned back to the water. "He's got it all wrong."

She nodded, but he wasn't sure if she believed him. Or maybe she didn't care. She seemed preoccupied tonight, like something other than their date was first and foremost in her mind. Maybe she'd decided there was someone else at Base Camp she liked more.

"Walker's been to see you a couple of times." He couldn't seem to help himself. Mentioning it was a chump move, but he had to know the truth of the matter.

"He found me a job."

Dell caught that and came back. "What's that you say about a job?"

"Walker found me a curriculum writing job. I start tomorrow."

His father lost interest again and went back to studying the creek. "I thought you were supposed to be writing a novel." Clay was confused. That's why she'd come to Chance Creek, after all. That's why he'd been making it a point to leave her alone during the afternoons.

She nodded. "It's only temporary, but maybe it will help me get my foot in the door of the local school administration. I miss teaching."

"And Walker found the job for you?"

"I'll be helping his grandmother. I was as surprised as you are. I don't know why they'd want me to help. Surely someone on the reservation is far more qualified."

Clay thought he knew why Walker would get Nora a job: because he wanted her to stay. He had some newfound fascination with her.

Clay didn't like that one bit.

Dell chose that moment to return, drop to his knees on the blanket and open up the picnic basket. "I'm hungry. Which one is the pastrami?"

"I thought you said you wanted roast beef." Clay pointed to a sandwich that was clearly marked. Maybe he was making too much of this. Maybe the job was innocent and Walker was just looking out for his grandmother.

"I said everyone likes roast beef. I didn't say I wanted it."

"For God's sake." Clay turned to Nora. He needed to connect with her the way Walker had. What could he do for her, to let her know she was on his mind and he was worried about her welfare?

"Riding lessons," he said out loud. "We've got a half dozen horses down at Base Camp now and you said you don't ride. It's time to learn, don't you think? I could teach you." She blinked and he realized he'd turned the conversation awfully suddenly.

"You're right, I don't know how to ride," Nora admitted. She sat down gracefully on the blanket. "I'm not sure I want to learn, though. I don't really like horses."

Dell finally found the sandwich he was looking for and pushed the basket nearer to her. "I recommend the roast beef."

"Do you have turkey?"

Clay crouched down and helped her find it, relishing the chance to be close to Nora. He wished they were alone. "You'd like them if you got to know them. Horses are intelligent, just like you."

She smiled a little lopsidedly. "I'm not sure I can ride in something like this." She indicated her dress.

Another excuse. Clay wondered if it was because she really was afraid of horses, or if she just didn't want to spend time with him.

She'd agreed to this date, he reminded himself.

"You'd have to ride sidesaddle, I guess. I don't know where you find one of those. It's more difficult than regular riding, too. Can't you wear pants for part of the day?"

"That would be breaking my vow." She didn't sound too enthusiastic.

"Let's think about it," he said.

"Sure." She took a bite of her sandwich. Disappointed, Clay found one for himself and took a bite.

Pickled beets.

Figured.

THE PICNIC WASN'T turning out at all like she expected. Nora couldn't understand why Clay had brought along his father. He didn't seem to want him there, which made everything uncomfortable. If he'd been happy about Dell's presence, she could have settled in for a nice meal and gotten to know more about his family. Between Dell's comments and Clay's barely civil answers, however, she felt like she'd stumbled into a battle. And that didn't even include the annoyance of being surrounded by cameras.

She had found Dell to be a thoughtful man on the walk down to the creek when she'd done her best to keep the conversation flowing. It was only when they'd stopped moving and the two men had begun to interact that things fell apart.

"Dell, have you lived your whole life in Montana?" she asked when the current silence lasted too long.

"Sure have. Right here in Chance Creek."

"What made your parents settle here?"

"My great-great-grandparents, you mean? Probably came looking for a new start. My great-great-grandfather hailed from Rhode Island, but he was a hunter and a fisherman and liked the outdoors. Montana's got room to roam, if you know what I mean."

"That's for sure. You're in construction?"

"I was." Dell frowned. "Been laid off."

Clay made a noise she couldn't decipher. Suddenly the pieces of the puzzle fell into place. If Dell had been laid off—or maybe fired, judging by Clay's bad attitude—was that why he'd come to stay with Clay?

Was there trouble at home, too?

If so, time to move on to a new topic. "Do you know how to ride?"

"He taught me everything I know," Clay said, and for the first time she heard pride in his voice. Encouraged, Nora went on.

"Who taught you?" she asked Dell.

"My daddy, of course. All the Picketts ride. We know our horses, too. Clay here could teach you everything you need to know when you're ready to learn."

"As soon as I find a sidesaddle," Clay reminded him.

"Hmm. Ought to be one somewhere." Dell looked thoughtful.

At least the tension between the two men had diffused. Nora finished her sandwich, enjoyed some potato salad and a slice of cherry pie, then helped Clay pack up the extra food.

"Take your girl for a stroll," Dell said, settling back on the blanket. "I need some shut-eye."

Nora's spirits soared. Judging by the alacrity with which Clay got to his feet and pulled her to hers, he was enthusiastic about this turn of events, too. Her happiness lasted until she realized two of the cameramen meant to come with them. They weren't going to be alone.

Not that they should be.

Clay crooked his arm, and she took it without thinking. They both seemed to realize simultaneously what they'd done. "Is this okay?" he asked softly.

She nodded. Why not? Touching him wasn't hurting anyone, and she didn't feel anxious. Maybe the paperweight incident was a one-off. Without another word, Clay began to amble along the bank of the creek. Full of food and mellow as the evening settled in, Nora took a moment to enjoy herself. She didn't mean to lean against him as she walked, but his shoulder was right there, and with her arm linked through his it was difficult to keep her distance. Besides, it was kind of nice to feel the heft of his muscles under her hands. For the moment she felt... safe.

"It's a beautiful setting," she said when they made their way around a bend in the creek, but what she was feeling went far beyond the loveliness of their surroundings. Clay's willingness to slow things down and just walk with her, rather than try to convince her to move their relationship along, meant a lot to her. As she relaxed, she realized how wound up she'd gotten in the past few days. Here she was with a Navy SEAL. Her stalker was just a teenager. Even if he had made his way out here to Montana, which was highly doubtful, he'd never attack her in Clay's presence. And the broken glass... well, that was just a broken glass, wasn't it? No one had been anywhere near the manor when they'd checked. She had to stop letting her imagination run away with her.

Some of the tension that had tightened her shoulders slipped away. She let her guard down and, with stolen glances, took in Clay's handsome features.

Rounding another bend in the creek, they moved out of Dell's sight. Not that he was looking. The last she'd seen of him, Dell had stretched out full length on the blanket with his eyes shut.

She glanced over her shoulder, saw the cameras had lagged behind a little, and stopped. "Clay—"

"What?" Clay stopped, too. Waited for her to finish her sentence. "Nora, what is it?"

She found she didn't want to talk. Instead, she wanted to let him know how she felt. She went up on tiptoe and kissed him before she could change her mind. She had a fleeting sensation of Clay's hard muscles, his mouth soft on hers, the heat of his hands through the thin material of her dress when he shifted to take her into his arms.

She pulled back just as suddenly as she'd lurched forward.

"What was that for?" Clay didn't pursue her.

"I... I don't know." How could she explain the turmoil inside her? She was too full of hopes and fears and confusion.

When it was clear she wouldn't go on, he simply took her hand. "How about we keep walking?"

She went along with him, but now Nora's thoughts were in turmoil. What had she done? She'd told him just this afternoon she wouldn't do anything rashly, and now she was the one kissing him...

"Don't overthink it," Clay said gently. He gave her hand a squeeze.

Once again he'd made the perfect response. She relaxed again, appreciating the easy camaraderie she felt with Clay, the sense that she'd known him longer than she had.

But she couldn't lead him on. She knew where this was going, after all.

"Clay, I can't marry you."

His stride hitched, but only for a second and then he kept going, although his pace sped up. Nora hurried to keep alongside him.

"You're turning me down before I even ask you," Clay pointed out.

Embarrassment made her reply tart. "You have to marry someone in less than forty days."

"I didn't ask for that deadline, you know."

"You didn't have to accept it."

"Yes, I did."

His response irked Nora. Wasn't it hubris to think one person could make a real difference in the world? "Do you really think you can change anything with a television show?" The bank of the creek was narrow here between the woods on one side and the water on the other. In order to stay side-by-side, they had to walk close together. Clay seemed too big, suddenly. He was all muscles and shoulders and overconfidence.

"Actually, I think you can change a lot with a television show. I hope people become familiar with a lot of terms they don't know. I hope they see us using equipment that isn't in their homes today, and they become less afraid of it. I'd like the idea of paring back a little and choosing possessions more consciously to become part of the American mind-set."

"And you're willing to marry to make that happen."

"Yes."

His utter certainty made Nora curious despite herself. What had happened to Clay that made him so determined to pursue this course?

"Let's keep moving," he said before she could question him, with a backward glance toward the camera crew that was closely following them again. He led her onward. "So this job. What's it all about?"

Nora decided to accept the change in topic. She couldn't blame him for not wanting to bare his soul in front of the cameras, after all. "I hardly know. Some kind of curriculum about Walker's clan for seventh graders."

"If it's for middle schoolers, it should be a walk in the park."

"Nothing about teaching is a walk in the park," Nora said tartly. "Especially not concerning a subject so sensitive. For years, Native Americans were all classed as bad guys—and as too primitive to build societies whose cultures were worth preserving. So much damage has come from that legacy—it'll take hard work to turn it around. It's a big honor for someone like me to be asked to be a small part of it." When he raised an eyebrow, she clarified. "Someone white. I've got to go in there knowing it's Walker's grandmother who needs to take the lead. I can help with organization and ideas, but Crow culture isn't mine to define." She realized she was lecturing him. "I know it seems like a simple thing to draw up a unit on Crow history, but what we teach our children about the past tends to define their futures, you know?"

"That makes sense. I didn't mean to downplay what you do."

"Most people couldn't care less about any of it."

"I'm not most people."

They walked in silence for a minute and Nora tried to recapture her equilibrium. Nothing was going right today, and she wanted to enjoy this time with Clay. Who knew how much longer she'd have with him?

Despite the delicious smell of the pine trees, the sound of the running water in the creek beside them and the last rays of sunlight streaming through the branches overhead, all the light went out of the day when Nora thought about a future without Clay. It frustrated her to know that even though she hadn't been looking for a man when she'd come here, she'd left her heart open to an entanglement. He would be hard to get over, and she was sick of feeling battered and bruised, even if only mentally.

"You're right, you know. I have to marry in a short period of time, and that's not ideal," Clay said suddenly. "Here's the thing. I like you. I'm attracted to you. I'd be a fool not to try to see if you're the one for me." When Nora tried to let go of his hand again, he stopped and grasped her other hand, too, so that she had to face him. "So we've got until July to figure this out and plan our wedding."

"Clay—"

"What would it take for that to be okay for you?"

"There isn't—"

"There has to be a way. Tell me."

As fierce as his determination was, it didn't intimidate Nora. His desire was clean and straightforward—nothing like her stalker's twisted need to hurt. Was there a way to bridge the gulf between them? Suddenly Nora wanted to try.

"I'd have to know you," she said in a rush. "That's not possible, though."

Clay chuckled. "Oh, yes, it is. Try going on a mission with a guy into enemy territory, living with him 24/7 while knowing you're a split-second away from death. You figure out who they are real quick." He cocked his head. "Maybe that's what we need. A shared mission."

"There's no enemy territory in Chance Creek." And she'd rather not face someone who was trying to kill her. Just thinking of the situations Clay must have experienced made her shiver.

"There are other kinds of missions."

"And what—you're going to make one up?"

"Nah. Not me. Boone's the chief around here." Clay grinned and her heart did a little flip. That smile undid her in so many ways. "He's good at finding missions, too. You'd better hold on to your socks, baby girl. Shit's about to get real."

Nora rolled her eyes and turned around. "Settle down there, sailor. You'd better take me back."

CHAPTER TWELVE

H E HADN'T MADE much progress he could document, but Clay felt like he'd taken a giant step forward with Nora during his walk. He'd broached the topic of marriage—the elephant in the room. Now she knew he considered her a candidate, and she knew he meant to pursue her. And he'd come up with a brilliant idea. They needed a common goal—a challenge they could share. He was sure Boone could think of something. As they walked back toward the picnic site, he didn't force the conversation. Instead he enjoyed the waning daylight, the peaceful scene and the timeless feeling of the moment.

Then the cameraman in front of him tripped.

"Fuck!"

Byron landed hard on his ass and nearly pitched his video camera into Pittance Creek. Clay leaped to grab it and offered a hand to the young man.

"Thanks." Byron got up gingerly and rubbed his lower back. "Damn tree roots."

The ground was smooth as far as Clay could see, but

he'd let the kid have his dignity. "You all right?" he asked as he handed back the camera.

"Yeah." Byron looked over his shoulder. "You better not be filming this," he said to Craig.

Craig chuckled. "Of course I'm filming this. It'll go on the bloopers reel."

"Turn it off." Byron pushed past Clay to confront Craig. "I said, turn it off."

"No way."

Clay moved back to stand by Nora. They exchanged an amused look while the two men were arguing. When she held his gaze, he lifted a brow. She nodded imperceptibly, and he bent down slowly enough to give her a chance to pull away. When Nora held her ground, he kissed her. At first she held still, as if braced to flee, but then she softened and the kiss became real. He cupped the back of her neck and savored the taste of her, running his tongue over the curve of her lips and moving closer when she let him in.

A moment later, Nora pulled back. "Behave," she said quietly in what he supposed was her schoolmarm voice. It was a sexy voice, and it had the opposite effect than the one she was probably hoping for.

"I don't want to." He leaned in for another one.

She didn't stop him, so he slid an arm around her waist. She felt so good in his arms he didn't care if they were being filmed. Nora didn't protest, so he took his time and enjoyed himself, until the sudden quiet told him the cameramen had spotted them.

He broke away from Nora reluctantly. "To be continued later."

"Maybe." But she smiled and his heart lifted.

His mind went back to the puzzle she'd presented him. How could they get to know each other quickly enough to make up their minds about marrying?

It all came down to time, he decided. He was going to spend every moment he could with Nora.

"TALK ABOUT SEX," Renata said, surveying Nora and the other women as they sat at the kitchen table in the manor the next morning, ostensibly to come up with a full proposal for their next B and B guests. "You girls are alone, the talk gets racy, you swap stories. You know the drill."

"You've got to be kidding," Nora said. She definitely didn't intend to take part in some kind of girls gone wild scenario.

"I never kid," Renata shot back. "Start rolling. I'll be back later to check on things."

An uncomfortable silence filled the room after she'd left. Byron, the youngest cameraman, had taken up a position on one side of the room, and Craig had positioned himself on the other side. A third man held a boom over their heads, and several other people waited in the wings to help out where needed.

"Tell us more about your honeymoon, Riley," Avery said in a strained voice.

Riley made a face. "I already told you everything—"

Craig made a rolling motion with his hands—a kind of *start talking* gesture. Riley gave in with a sigh. "It was... wonderful," she said.

"That's what you said last time. We want details." Her tone expressionless, Avery fiddled with the pen and paper she'd brought to the table. A pitcher of lemonade sat sweating nearby. Nora took a sip from her glass, savoring the tartness of the drink.

Riley glared at Avery in exasperation, but then, with a sidelong look at Byron, she dropped a hand to her belly and spoke with an exaggerated Western drawl. "Let's just say if I'm not pregnant, it's not for lack of trying. That cowboy really put me through my paces."

Savannah choked on the sip she had just taken. "TMI! We're being filmed," she hissed.

But something had gotten into Riley, and she continued. "We went at it morning, noon and night."

"Was it romantic?" Avery played along with a grin.

"It was... exhausting. I don't know what got into Boone. I slept through some of it, I think. He just kept on going." Riley waved a hand expressively.

Avery laughed, a giggle that turned into a snort.

"Some men have the courtesy to stop when that happens," Savannah said, so seriously it took Nora a minute to realize she had joined in the game.

"Not Boone." Riley shrugged her shoulders. "The man's a machine. He really ought to have three or four wives."

If Savannah could jump in, so could she, Nora figured. Why the hell shouldn't she kid around? Things had been so serious for so long she could use a laugh. "You can always share him around," she said. "Maybe make a little money on the side. It's not like he's bringing a lot of that to the table, right?"

"Can I borrow him tonight?" Savannah asked. "It's been a while, and I could use a good f—"

"All right, ladies." Craig clapped his hands together so loudly they all jumped. "You've had your fun. And I hope you enjoyed yourselves."

"Renata told us to talk about sex," Avery said sweetly. "We aim to please."

"No, you thought you'd be clever," Craig said. "You thought you'd make it impossible for us to use this segment. Sorry to disappoint you, ladies—this is reality TV. Audiences eat this shit up. We'll probably lead off the next episode with it." He motioned to Byron. "Come on. We've got enough."

The women watched them leave.

"I'd probably better warn Boone about that," Riley said, picking at the fabric of her gown.

"Will he be mad?" Avery asked.

Riley shook his head. "He'll think it's funny. I hope." She straightened with a grin. "Now that they're gone, let's get to work. I've got to get back soon so Boone can screw me silly again."

"I miss you," Savannah said, leaning over and giving her a hug.

"I miss you, too, but you can't borrow my husband." Riley hugged her back. "Now, tell me about this client."

Avery brightened. "She's coming with some friends in just a few weeks. She wants painting lessons and a carriage ride..."

They brainstormed ideas for an hour before deciding they'd better split up and do their usual morning chores. Riley headed back down to Base Camp. It was Nora's turn to do the bedrooms, giving each en suite a quick clean up and sweeping the bedroom floors, along with the hall and staircase. She decided to start with her own room, but when she climbed the two flights of stairs and reached for the knob of her third-floor bedroom, the door swung open. Nora stopped in her tracks.

That was strange; she was sure she'd shut it tightly before she'd gone down to breakfast this morning. She'd heard the click when the latch caught. Uneasiness crept through her before she could ward it off. She bit her lip, hating the way she looked for trouble everywhere these days.

She couldn't bring herself to enter the room, though. What if someone was still in there?

Footsteps pounded up the stairs behind her— Savannah coming to fetch something from her room.

Savannah paused when she saw her standing outside her door. "What's wrong?"

"Someone's been here." Nora reproached herself for blurting it out like that. She didn't know for sure it was true.

"What do you mean?" Savannah crossed to her.

"In my room. I closed the door this morning. Just now it was open."

Savannah hesitated, then turned and called, "Avery!"

Thirty seconds later, a panting Avery joined them. "What is it?"

"Nora thinks someone's been in her room."

Avery's shoulders slumped. "But—"

Nora, unable to stand it anymore, pushed the door open and strode inside. It was empty. Of course.

"What about the bathroom?" Savannah said in a low tone, coming up behind her.

Hating herself for the way her heart was pounding, Nora stalked across the room and pushed the door wide open. A glance told her the en suite was empty, too. "No one's here," she said, relief making her almost giddy.

"You're braver than I am," Avery said, trailing into the room. "What made you think someone was here?"

Nora explained about her door.

"That could have happened at any time, though," Avery said thoughtfully. "Someone could have been and gone."

"We locked the main doors," Savannah reminded her.

"No, we didn't. I let the camera crew come in the front door this morning, and you let Renata in through the back."

"Then both doors are unlocked right now?"

"I'll go check." Avery ran lightly down the stairs.

Savannah turned to Nora. "What about the other bedrooms?"

Nora looked at her in dismay, but there was nothing for it but to search them, too. Just as they had the day before, they walked through the house, starting with the bedrooms and ending in the kitchen. Avery joined them halfway through without needing to be told what they were doing.

"There's no one here," she said out loud when they were done, stating the obvious.

"I'm sorry," Nora said. "I'm just jumpy, I guess."

"What is this really about?" Avery asked her. "Is it the camera crews, or are you worried about that stalker?"

"Have you received any of those awful messages since you've been here?" Savannah added.

"No. Of course not—no one knows my phone number except our families."

"But with the show's website he might know where you are," Avery said. "I understand if you're nervous."

Nora didn't want to talk about it. "I'm going to finish my chores."

"I'll come up with you. I left my apron upstairs," Savannah said.

They walked up together, leaving Avery in the kitchen.

"I'm sorry," Nora said again. "I can't believe I'm being so overwrought about all of this."

"I can't believe you've been so calm. Not with what you've been through this year," Savannah countered. She gave Nora a quick hug before going to fetch her apron. Nora entered her room—and immediately felt that something was wrong. She scanned the bed, the dresser, desk and bookshelves—and sucked in a breath.

There—on the shelf where she'd placed some of her favorite paperbacks and textbooks. One of them had been pulled partway out, its spine jutting an inch or so out past all the others.

She hadn't done that; she'd been reading the same paperback for days.

Nora swiftly crossed the room and tugged it out the rest of the way.

The Teacher as Student.

She dropped it like the book had burned her. It used to be one of her favorites—a treatise on the way children learned when left to themselves and how teachers could study them to learn better teaching methods.

She didn't think she'd ever be able to read it again.

Her stalker was sending a message. She was sure of it. *You think you can teach me anything? Wait until I'm the one in charge.*

"Savannah?"

Savannah came running. "What is it?"

"He... he *was* here," she said, her voice so thin it didn't sound like her own.

"Who? The stalker?" Savannah caught sight of her face. "Nora? What happened?"

"The book... that one..." She couldn't get the words out. Instead, she pointed toward the textbook on the floor.

Savannah went over to examine it. "I don't understand."

"It was sticking out of the bookshelf!" Nora knew

she wasn't making any sense. "I didn't do that. I haven't touched it."

"Are you sure?"

"He was here!" Nora's knees had grown wobbly, and she lurched over to sit on the bed. Wrapping her arms around her middle, she bent over, suddenly dizzy.

"Nora, are you okay?" Savannah crouched on the floor beside her.

"He was in my room," Nora insisted.

"Maybe it wasn't your stalker. Maybe it was someone else." Savannah's face was pale.

"Like who?"

Savannah shrugged. "Renata. A crew member. How far was it pulled out?"

"Just a little. An inch, maybe."

Savannah's brows furrowed. "An inch?"

"Maybe. Maybe a little less."

"But..." Her friend joined her on the bed. "Nora, could you be mistaken? Maybe you didn't push it in all the way. Maybe you didn't notice before and it's only because you're so..." She trailed off.

"I didn't imagine it!" Nora was stung by Savannah's insinuations, but at the same time she'd begun to doubt herself.

Maybe she *was* wrong. Maybe she had been the one to pull it out. Maybe when she'd searched the shelf for the paperback she was reading, she'd dislodged it a little and hadn't noticed.

But in her heart she knew it wasn't true. Her bookshelf had been neat when she left earlier—just the way she liked it.

"Let's go downstairs," Savannah said.

They met Avery in the kitchen. She took one look at Nora and fetched her a glass of water.

"Out in the sunshine," Savannah ordered them. "She's had a shock," she said to Avery. "She needs fresh air and light. And I think it's time you told us everything that happened back in Baltimore, Nora. We need to figure this out."

When they were settled on the back porch, that's what Nora did. At first her words came in broken phrases, but as she spoke, it became easier. All the pent-up fear and worry came spilling out, but no tears. She was damned if she would cry now when she needed all her wits about her.

"I really think he was here," she told them. Her stomach sank when she caught the glance that ran between them. It sounded crazy. She knew it did.

"Whether or not he was, we need to be more careful," Avery declared. "Every time someone comes or goes, we'll lock the doors. Every time."

"We need to tell the men about your stalker, too," Savannah said. "They're all ex-military. They'll know how to protect us."

"No!" Nora struggled for calm. She had to be clear on that point. "Renata will have a field day with it," she explained. "She'll be all over my past, interviewing people, digging up dirt."

"Do you have something to hide?"

Nora blinked at Savannah's question. "Of course

not! But they'll make it look like I do. A student is stalking me. Leaving sexual messages. What'll they make of that? I taught seventeen and eighteen year olds. What will they insinuate?"

Savannah nodded. "You're right." She sounded defeated. "Renata's a pit bull, and the show is more important to her than any of us. She's already run background checks on us. You know that, right?"

"What do you mean?" Nora was aghast.

"Some of my family and friends told me they'd gotten calls from the show. Renata asked them a lot of questions."

"Yep. My family got those calls, too," Avery confirmed.

"I don't have any family." Nora thought about who Renata might call. Her old school? Would the administration let slip about the stalker?

No, she decided. They hadn't wanted to pursue it. They'd been grateful when she'd left. Her old friends didn't know about it, either. She'd let all her close relationships slide during her mother's illness. Renata must be dying to dig up more dirt on her than she'd gotten so far.

"We can't say anything to anyone," she insisted. "Like you said, we'll be careful. There's no way an eighteen-year-old boy can keep running around Chance Creek without being caught. He'll run out of cash. If he's even here."

"A minute ago you were persuading us he'd been in your room," Savannah said.

"Tell Clay," Avery urged. "Tell him everything you've told us and let him know you want to keep it from Renata. He'll know what to do."

"Okay," Nora agreed reluctantly. "I'll tell him."

CHAPTER THIRTEEN

"A MISSION?" BOONE looked thoughtful as he considered Clay's request. "Yeah, I can give you a mission. I can go one better than that, too."

"What do you mean?" Clay stroked the nose of a roan mare. They were standing in the stables, discussing which horse would be the best mount for a novice rider. And where they might find an old-fashioned sidesaddle.

"Renata isn't pleased by the lack of girl boy interaction, as she keeps putting it in that wonderful British accent of hers. She's complained to Fulsom, and he's lowered the boom. All the women have to move to Base Camp by the end of the day."

"Hell." That was going to set off some fireworks. But as long as they didn't pack up and leave, it would work in his favor. He sure wouldn't mind the extra time he'd get to spend with Nora. "Here's to Fulsom."

Boone laughed. "Yeah, well, I hope you're right. I hope those women don't cause too much trouble down here."

"They won't. I don't suppose you can assign Nora

to my tent? That would speed things up a bunch." He stroked the mare's silky flank. She'd do very well for someone like Nora, he decided.

"Sorry. She gets her own. It's up to you to entice her to share yours."

"Working on it."

"I'll make the announcement at lunch. Better go see to your men. Looks like Dell's taking charge." Boone jutted his chin in the direction of the distant building site, where a knot of men stood talking and gesturing to each other instead of working.

"Shit." Clay made tracks to intervene before things got out of hand. He wasn't quick enough, though. When he reached the building site and took in the way Dell was lecturing the other men, he lost his temper.

"What's going on here?" He pushed his way among the men and faced his father.

"We're just discussing the plans. You're crazy if you're going to build something like this. None of this is to code."

"Actually, it is. I've gone over all of it with the county planner, and I've gotten it approved." It had taken a lot of work, but he'd done it—partially thanks to Fulsom's deep pockets.

"This house is three hundred square feet!"

"That's the point. Living lightly on the land, Dad."

"No one's going to live in a house like that."

"We're all going to live in houses like that." He was ready to snap. Didn't his father see that? Or was that what Dell wanted—everyone to be as miserable as he was?

"That's ridiculous. Why build a house at all? Why not buy a trailer? Better yet, you all can live in your cars—at least they move."

Clay noticed the other men edging away. He needed to shut this down, fast. "That's the whole point of this community, Dad. Doing things differently. Using fewer resources—"

"No one wants a house with a single bathroom, either. Not these days. Two bedrooms and two baths—that's the minimum," Dell countered. "Five and three—that's what people really want." His father was getting a stubborn look Clay knew all too well.

"Dad, I've got my orders for the morning; I need to build this house. But if you dislike the way we're doing it so much, you don't have to be here. Why don't you go look for a job? That's why you're here, right? I'll see you at lunch."

Dell glared at him, opened his mouth to speak, closed it again and stalked off, cursing a blue streak. Clay took a breath and turned around. As he'd expected, his men's expressions were mutinous.

"Someone better figure out the chain of command," Curtis said.

"Let's get it figured out right now," Clay growled. "I designed these houses. I'm going to build them. You listen to me, not my father. If he comes around while I'm not here, tell him to bugger off."

"He's scared, you know," Harris said suddenly.

"Scared?" Dell? Not likely. "How do figure that?"

He forced himself to keep his cool. If this went on much longer, he'd end up as hot-tempered as his dad.

"Job outlook isn't great for a man his age."

Clay rubbed a hand over his chin. Yeah, he knew that. He knew, too, that Dell's self-confidence was wrapped up in his work. "Nothing I can do about that."

"Why the hell does he need an employer?" Curtis asked. "He's got plenty of experience. Why isn't he self-employed?"

"That's a damn good question. I think it has to do with my grandparents losing their ranch way back when. He's always said you should let someone else shoulder the risk," Clay answered.

"I guess that didn't work out for him," Curtis said and got back to work.

Clay kept up a running argument with Dell in his mind all morning, so he was too distracted to think much about Boone's plans until hunger pangs warned him lunch was imminent. When Kai rang the gong that signified a meal was ready, his men put away their tools and moved hastily toward the circle and fire pit, where they ate most days when the weather cooperated. As they drew close he smelled chili. His stomach rumbled, and for the first time that morning he relaxed a little.

When he caught sight of the women tramping down the hill from the manor, however, anticipation got the better of him. He knew Nora and the others wouldn't like having to sleep in tents in Base Camp, but he figured it wouldn't change things too much for them. They would work up at the manor in the daytime, and join the men in camp at dinner. Evenings with Nora would give him time to talk to her, woo her—and maybe ultimately change her mind about marrying him.

"Grab your food and gather round," Boone called out when everyone was present. All the camera crews took their positions in the background. Clay knew they'd eat after lunch was over, when everyone was back at work. It took some minutes for the hubbub to subside as people lined up, got their chili and cornbread, and found seats on the logs and stumps around the area.

Clay took the opportunity to move close to Nora. "Sit with me." He gestured to a log, and she did so, but she seemed preoccupied and didn't return his smile.

"Do you know what this is about?" she asked. "We got a summons half an hour ago. Sounds like something big."

It occurred to Clay that it was better to let Boone take the fall for Fulsom's new demands. It was the coward's way out, but there were plenty of obstacles between him and Nora without adding another one. He was saved from having to answer when Boone began to speak.

"Our goal is to demonstrate that a sustainable life is a good life," Boone began. "Everything we're doing here at Base Camp is arranged with that in mind. I don't have to tell any of you how important it is that we succeed. We're not trying to impose some Spartan lifestyle on the rest of the world because of some righteous, holier-than-thou attitude. We're trying to show people that life doesn't have to suck if it's not as grandiose and consumption-driven as it is in America today. People can argue the whys and wherefores of living lightly on the land. Some are going to choose to do so because they think it's right. Others are going to choose to do so when and if conditions change so drastically there isn't any other choice. Regardless of how they get to it, we're here to tell them—hey, it ain't so bad here in sustainability-land."

Clay found himself nodding. Boone had summed things up nicely.

"All of us here have committed to this goal, whether it was our reason for coming here, or we got roped into it after we arrived. So now it's time for us to walk the walk. We've got a lot to accomplish in a very short time. When the rest of you men joined us four founders here at Base Camp, I told you it was going to be a dictatorship for a while. Well, that dictatorship starts today. If you don't think you can follow orders, it's time to leave."

Clay caught the look Nora, Avery and Savannah exchanged. Riley was nervously pleating the fabric of her gown between her fingers. The men, on the other hand, seemed unconcerned; none of them were strangers to taking orders. Win was looking at Angus. Clay wasn't sure she'd heard a word Boone had said.

"As for you women..." For the first time, Boone hesitated. "Here's the thing. Like it or not, you're part of the show, and Renata says they're having a hard time filming interactions between all of us. So as of tonight..." He hesitated again, took a breath and went on.

"You'll need to sleep down in Base Camp. We've got tents and bedding for all of you—"

As he went on, Clay watched Riley watch her friends, her distress plain to see. Riley was already sleeping in Base Camp with Boone, but it was obvious she thought her friends would be angry.

Nora, Avery and Savannah exchanged a look Clay couldn't begin to fathom. Nora nodded slightly, and the others looked thoughtful.

Boone wound down. "Well? What do you say?" He visibly braced himself against their reaction.

"Okay," Savannah said simply when none of the others answered. "We'll move down after lunch. But we'll still run the B and B, and use the manor during the day."

"Of course." Boone looked nonplussed. "You... don't mind?"

"Not if it's for the show," Avery said sweetly.

"The show trumps everything," Nora agreed. "At least for now."

Clay blinked. He wasn't sure what had just happened, but something odd was going on. He told himself not to look a gift horse in the mouth, though. The women had agreed to sleep at Base Camp. That was a start.

But he'd expected a fight. So had Boone. The women's reactions were... weird. Even Riley was regarding her friends strangely.

"Okay... good." Boone looked around. "Right. So there's one more thing. We need help down here. Riley's going to start working with me in the gardens. Savannah, you'll work with Jericho's team on the energy grid. Avery, you're on bison duty with Walker's crew. Nora? You'll join Clay's group and help with the building."

If he expected the women to accept these orders with the same equanimity with which they'd greeted his directive to sleep in Base Camp, he was sadly mistaken.

"Wait…you're joking, right?" Nora said. Her face was slack with shock. "We don't have time for that!"

"Two hours a day, that's all we're asking. From ten to twelve every morning. You'll still have all afternoon for your writing. And of course when there are guests at the B and B, we won't expect you to work at Base Camp—or sleep here."

"But—"

Clay waited for the explosion he knew was coming. This was his fault. He'd asked for a mission and Boone had given him an obvious one. Working two hours a day with him would give Nora a chance to see who he really was. She'd see his skills, the way he led the other men, his dedication to the project. It was a perfect plan… except Nora would hate it.

"Look," Boone said to her. "If we lose this contest, Riley loses the home she loves. The land her forefathers cleared from the wilderness. I don't want that to happen. I don't think you do, either. So how about it? Are you in or out?"

That was the Boone Clay knew. Not the one who hesitated and braced for an attack—the one who told people how things were going to be done. It didn't hurt he'd played the friend card. How could Nora possibly complain now?

"I… Of course, but—" Nora stuttered to a stop. She turned to Clay, obviously wanting his support, and Clay saw her dilemma. She had taken on a part-time job. She had a B and B to run when guests came. She had her work to do around the manor—and she was trying to write a novel.

"We do our chores in the morning." Nora turned back to Boone when Clay didn't come to her aid.

"You'll just have to get up earlier," Boone said reasonably. "Come on, Nora. You'll be working with one of the best. Watching Clay build a house is like watching an artist create a masterpiece. It's different than anything you've done before. You might like it."

Just when Clay thought Nora might lose her cool, Savannah stepped in. "I think it's a good idea," she said firmly. "We're all trying to live together, and we should be able to work together, too. In return, I'm sure that when we have guests at the B and B, all you men will pitch in and help us get ready for them. Right?"

Boone scratched the back of his neck. "Well, that depends—"

"Of course we will." Jericho spoke over him. "That's what we're all about here. Helping each other."

"WHEN I AGREED to come to Westfield I had no idea I was going to live in a tent," Savannah grumbled late that afternoon when they met up at the base of the staircase, each with a suitcase and a roll of bedding.

"You were the one who said it was a good idea," Nora told her.

"I said working together was a good idea. Not sleeping on the ground."

"Well, I feel like this is all my fault," Nora admitted. "If I hadn't kicked up such a fuss over nothing earlier, you guys wouldn't have agreed to move."

"I'm not sure we would have won that war anyway," Avery said. "Besides, it'll kind of be fun. It's not like we're leaving the manor, and this way we'll get to spend more time with Riley."

"And Walker," Savannah teased her.

"There's that, too." Avery grinned.

"Ready?" Nora asked them.

"Let's go." Avery locked the front door, led them through the hall and kitchen and out the back, and locked that one, too. The hike down to Base Camp wasn't long, but Nora was panting when they reached it. Maybe she'd packed a few too many things.

"Let me help you with that," Clay said, coming to greet her when they arrived in camp. "I've got a tent for you. Why don't you set up over here?" He led her to a space next to his own tent. "This is me," Clay said. "That's my dad's." He nodded at another one right beside it.

"Nora! Come set up over here," Win called, striding over from the direction of the big garden the men had dug. "This is the women's side. I don't know about you, but I figure we need some privacy at night." She pointed to her tent and a stack of other ones still in their rolls, a short but significant distance from where the men were camped.

"Be right there," she called to Win.

Clay grunted. "This site is better."

"I think I'd better stick with the women." She headed toward them before he could persuade her otherwise. If she slept that close to Clay, she couldn't answer for the consequences, which was probably why he wanted her there.

"You could just share *my* tent, you know," Clay murmured as he kept pace with her.

"I don't think so." That would be disastrous. He'd have a ring on her finger in no time.

"You said we should spend as much time as possible together. You said you won't marry me until you know me," Clay reminded her with a grin.

She tilted her neck to look up at him. "And you think sleeping together is the answer to that?"

"I don't see why not."

"We're not there yet, Clay." She knew he was teasing, but she refused to lead him on. She didn't think they ever would be. There simply wasn't time. They reached the vicinity of Win's site, and Nora picked a spot near where Avery and Savannah were setting up. "Here's a good place."

Clay pulled the tent from its bag and began to deftly set it up. "Listen. I know this isn't ideal, but working together will give us more time to get to know each other, and even if you won't share my tent, I hope you'll spend your evenings with me." He held up a hand to forestall her. "I know you'll need to write. I'll be making schedules and lists. No reason we can't do that together."

"In a tent?" They looked pretty small to her.

"A tent, or the bunkhouse, or at the fire pit. Wherever you want."

"That depends on how the rest of the day goes." She watched him snap the tent poles together. "Are you going to boss me around when we work together?"

A wolfish grin tugged at his mouth. "Hell, yeah." He laughed at her reaction. "I've got to tell you what to do. I can't leave you to guess."

"We'll be at each other's throats in an hour." When he was done with the tent, she unzipped the fly and stowed her suitcase and bedding inside.

"Why? Can't you take orders?" Clay helped her up when she was done. "I think it'll be fun."

"You think so, huh?"

Maybe she and the others would be safer sleeping down here in Base Camp, but she was pretty sure all kinds of sparks were going to fly between her and Clay.

"Gather up, folks," Boone called out. Nora turned to Clay for an explanation, but Clay shrugged. They joined the rest of the people streaming toward Boone. "I've got a surprise for you. Fulsom's here with the first episode of *Base Camp*. Everyone in the bunkhouse for the showing."

Nora groaned. No one else looked any more excited than she felt.

"Come on, let's get it over with. The first one's the

worst, right?" Boone led the way.

There was nothing to do but follow.

FOR THE FIRST time since he'd been in combat, Clay found himself praying. If only he could persuade himself that Fulsom wasn't about to toss a hand grenade into the mix, he would have found it fascinating to watch a show filmed about his life. He was curious how all the scenes the camera crews had covered would get patched together into a cohesive whole. Nothing had really happened so far, after all. They hadn't even finished a house.

But knowing Fulsom, his people would take bits and pieces and concoct some monstrosity that didn't have any bearing on reality. As Clay took his seat in the bunkhouse and watched Boone get a big screen up and running from his laptop, he couldn't help pleading with God that somehow a miracle would happen and this would turn out better than he feared.

Fulsom paced the front of the room in his usual preening style. "Episode one of *Base Camp* airs tonight, and we expect a tremendous audience tuning in," he announced. "We thought it only fair you get first crack at seeing it. Hope you all like it as much as I do."

Clay doubted it, but he held his tongue.

"Here we go," Boone said, and hit a key on his laptop. The Base Camp logo appeared on the screen, along with a swell of upbeat music. They watched the introduction in silence, although each person in the room shifted a bit when they were introduced on-screen. As on the website, the men all seemed larger than life, and the women hyper-feminine in their Regency outfits. Fulsom's people managed to sum up the situation at Base Camp in a few short sentences, and a voice actor who sounded as posh as Renata explained the goals—and the consequences if the members of Base Camp fell short of them.

The show segued into a string of interviews Renata had done during the first couple of days. They introduced each participant and explained why they were there. Fulsom's crew had spliced those interviews together with recent headlines about climate change, resource degradation, droughts, floods, storms and more. Clay found himself nodding along, and then he straightened when footage flashed by that he could swear was from their mission in Yemen. Clay blinked and looked again, but the images on the screen had jumped back to Base Camp.

"Did you see that?" he asked Jericho in an undertone.

Jericho nodded but kept his gaze on the screen.

"Of course, climate change isn't the only thing on these men's minds," the voice-over said. A flurry of different images passed by. Boone and Riley's return from their honeymoon, Jericho and Savannah talking earnestly, Walker teaching Avery to ride.

So far, so good, Clay thought. When a new shot honed in on the building site, with him and the other men working away on the first tiny house, he was impressed and gratified at how much attention the show paid to the details of his work.

He exchanged an approving glance with Boone. This wasn't so bad, after all.

"Clay's good with a hammer," the voice-over said as the camera focused on him framing up the tiny house. "But how will he fare with the ladies?"

Uh-oh, Clay thought.

A quick montage followed. He and Nora exchanging glances as Fulsom spoke the first day of filming. Outtakes from his interview with Renata as she grilled him about her. More takes from Renata questioning Nora about her feelings for him. And of course, a close-up of him leaning in for a kiss—and Nora whacking him with the paperweight. Just as he'd feared, the sequence was repeated several times for good measure.

Dell's face filled the screen and Clay nearly groaned out loud. "I remember the way you always came running over here back then. I figured you liked that pretty little girl who used to spend her summers here. What was her name? Riley?"

Shit. He couldn't believe they'd included that.

"It was the money I liked, Pops, not Riley. Riley just married Boone Rudman, remember?" he said on-screen.

"I remember Boone. That boy always did end up on top when you two scrapped."

Boone laughed out loud. Clay shot him a dirty look.

"We never scrapped over Riley," on-screen Clay said right on cue.

"Oh, you say that now." Dell turned, caught sight of Nora and made a face. "I mean, well, that's all in the past now, of course."

A shot of Nora's face—from god knew when; it certainly wasn't at the picnic—flashed on-screen. She looked horrified... or disgusted.

Clay turned to look at her now. She was wearing an identical expression as she stared at the screen. He could only guess how she felt. This was excruciating. He breathed a sigh of relief when the show switched to Jericho and caught him staring up at the manor.

"Clay isn't the only one struggling to find a bride," the voice-over intoned. The camera zoomed closer until Savannah's figure became apparent in the manor's backyard. Another shot of Jericho's face, his desire so clear, the room fell silent.

A half-hour later, Boone stopped the video.

"Well? What do you think?" Fulsom asked. He was standing so proudly, Clay wondered if he expected applause. But no one was clapping.

"Didn't know I looked so damn Scottish," Angus finally said.

The laughter that followed broke the spell.

"It's always a shock to see yourself on television for the first time," Renata spoke up. "You all did very well. The reticence you displayed about being filmed is par for the course with people new to the process. I expect from now on there'll be no more squeamishness about it."

Clay snorted. Yeah. He doubted that. He felt like he'd been whacked with a two-by-four. They'd made him look... ridiculous.

"Clay? Do you have something to share with the class?" Renata arched an eyebrow at him.

"Just that this *process*, as you call it, is mighty uncomfortable. Especially to the ego."

"Look. You're human. Our audience is human. When we put your imperfections on display, viewers bond with you." She waited for him to take that in. "You men are larger than life to our audience. Military men who've served with honor. Men willing to give up everything to prove something to the rest of the world. There has to be something about you they can relate to."

"What about us?" Nora spoke up. "We women were supposed to be bit players. None of us signed up for this."

"I did," Win contradicted her. "I like the show. I think it's great."

"That's because they've made you and Angus into the great love story of the twenty-first century."

"Are you kidding?" Win retorted. "People won't be able to take their eyes off you and Clay. Will they or won't they? That's what everyone will be talking about around the watercoolers at work this week."

Clay tried to keep his eyes on his hands. Was Nora thinking about that possibility? He thought about it constantly.

He couldn't help himself. He looked at Nora.

And found her looking back at him.

CHAPTER FOURTEEN

A HALF-HOUR LATER Nora was back at the manor, sitting by the window in the parlor, still reeling from the preview of the show, when a car pulled up and a woman got out. It had to be Walker's grandmother, Nora realized, and she took a deep breath to regain her composure. Seeing herself on the screen, all her statements ripped out of context, made her feel stripped and exposed to the world. But it was Clay who'd borne the brunt of the spotlight, and she'd seen him in a brand-new way—as a man who wanted a woman and had little chance of getting her. It pained her to see him laughed at when anyone with any sense could see that this was a good man. A man who deserved to be happy.

She'd never felt so confused before. The show had infuriated and startled her in equal measures and now she wasn't sure what to do, or how to react to Clay the next time she saw him. As she went to open the door, she decided she couldn't do anything for the moment. Time to switch gears and try to impress Walker's grandmother. She needed this job to save her sanity.

When she opened the front door, she estimated the woman was in her sixties, but it was hard to tell. She had the kind of ageless beauty that defied categorization. Her face was round, her cheekbones prominent and her skin bronzed in a way that set off the white strands in her straight, nearly-black hair. Nora wished she was an artist so she could sketch the woman, but when she took in her no-nonsense expression, that flight of fancy disappeared in a puff of smoke. This wasn't someone who sat around waiting to be sketched. She was a woman who got things done.

"Hello," Nora called out as she approached. "I'm Nora Ridgeway."

"Sue Norton," the woman said in return, her dark brown eyes missing nothing as she surveyed Nora and the house.

"Come on inside. I've got tea brewing—I've set us up at the kitchen table, where we'll have room to work."

"I'll follow you."

Sue's cadence was foreign to Nora, and Nora wondered if she had grown up speaking the Crow language alongside English. There was much about Walker she didn't know, so it was difficult to make any guesses about his grandmother.

"I'm very curious to know what type of curriculum you're working on," she said as she led Sue through the house to the kitchen in back. She was glad she had such a tidy, welcoming place to host the meeting. Though she knew little about Walker's grandmother, she felt like she was hosting a distinguished guest. Maybe it was the woman's almost regal bearing.

"My students learn from books in which they do not appear, except as an afterthought," Sue said. She sat down carefully and cupped her hands around the cup of tea Nora handed her as if she was cold, despite the warmth of the day. "Textbooks superimpose a world on them that does not support our way of seeing things. They feel alien from themselves as they learn. This is damaging in two ways."

Nora waited for her to go on, fascinated, and feeling like she'd found a kindred spirit in Chance Creek for the first time. She loved the philosophy of teaching, and could talk for hours about methods and motivations.

"They either feel separate from what they are trying to learn—as if it has no meaning for them—or they embrace it, and no longer feel like their homes, families and culture have any meaning." Sue took a sip of tea and sat quietly, as if she'd said everything she'd come to say.

"So you want to write a new history textbook that embraces the Crow world view?"

"Not just one." Sue's dark eyes glinted as she studied Nora over her cup.

Nora sat back. "Walker told me it was for seventh graders. I thought this would be a short-term project."

Sue smiled for the first time. "Walker doesn't know what he's talking about. He seldom does."

Surprise stiffened Nora's spine. She wasn't used to people treating Walker lightly. "He always gave me the impression he was a deep thinker."

"Because he's quiet?" Sue nodded. "Stones are quiet, too, and maybe they think deep thoughts. Who's to know unless they speak them?"

Now they were talking in riddles, although Nora had a feeling Sue had just shot a very sharp barb in her grandson's direction. Unfortunately, just like Walker, it was impossible to tell if she was joking, and Nora didn't want to offend her by laughing if she wasn't. She took a sip of her tea to steady her nerves. "What is it you want from me, exactly?"

"It seems to me that a Crow textbook will benefit a Crow student." Sue tapped one finger on the table. "But it also seems to me that if a white man's textbook can untether a Crow from his culture, maybe a Crow textbook can untether a white man from the belief that only his history is important. So maybe there are several different plans here."

Nora smiled, too. "That's sneaky."

"If a white lady writes a textbook, then it can't be just for the Crow." Sue raised an eyebrow. Nora took that as a question. Was she willing to join Sue's plot to undermine the establishment?

Sue seemed to take her hesitation as a negative sign. "Look at the men down there. They understand about the world, the land, how to treat it right, and only one of them is Crow. This land has value, and I don't mean money. It has value to our lives. If we think about that, if we let it govern our actions, we will all benefit. Not just the Crow."

"That's true." Nora hadn't thought about it that

way, but Sue was right. With climate change becoming one of the hottest topics of the age, teachers were scrambling for good resources to use to teach about it. Respecting the land was a concept that crossed all superficial boundaries now. "You think the Crow have something in particular to add to the conversation?"

"I know we do. And we've waited a long time to be heard."

Sue's quiet words held a world of history in them, and Nora had to resist the urge to reach out and take the woman's hand, because she felt it, too—not that the Crow in particular needed to be heard, but that everyone close to the land did. If she and Sue combined their efforts—and leaned on the members of Base Camp for more technical information—they might come up with something truly unique. Something teachers like her hungered for when it came to introducing students to the idea of stewardship of the world.

"That's devious." But Nora found herself smiling. "You still want Crow-centric textbooks for the children in your own school, though?"

Sue nodded. "Our culture foremost in every subject. Math, English, Social Studies... Otherwise we disappear."

"And for the more general ones? Will you reference Crow history and world view in them, or is it more that you want a sense of Crow principles to underlie the information?"

"Walker was right," Sue said. "You're no dummy."

"No." Nora liked this woman—and her guerrilla

tactics. "I'm no dummy. Which is why you'll need to explain very carefully to me what those principles are."

As Sue did so, Nora began to feel there was something to keep her here at Westfield after all—besides her friends and Clay, of course. It was something all hers. A new mandate. An idea so subversive she could get behind it. A project so big it could take years. Writing course material for the kids in Sue's schools would be fascinating enough, but writing a textbook—or several textbooks—based on the principles that land and resources didn't simply exist to be exploited, that the greater good—and long-term repercussions—should be considered before taking any action, and that the world itself is a gift we share with the generations who have gone before us, and those who come after... She could get behind that—because those were ideas she shared.

Other people shared them, too.

"When do we start?"

LATE THAT AFTERNOON, Clay was sitting at a desk in the bunkhouse when Dell walked in. His father had made himself scarce these past couple of days, and Clay hoped Dell had finally gotten a lead on a job, but he knew the minute he saw the plans in his dad's hands that wasn't the case. "Hear me out," Dell said. "If you add ten more square feet to those houses of yours, you can have a real kitchen." He thrust a sketch into Clay's hands. "You'd put the dishwasher here, double ovens there. And look—that way you could fit a full-size refrigerator in there."

"We're not doing double ovens," Clay protested, looking at the plans in dismay. "And we're definitely not doing a full-size refrigerator. Remember the power constraints I showed you? It wasn't easy coming in under them, but I managed to do it, and my design offers plenty of counter space for food preparation."

"No one's going to prepare food when there's no dishwasher to do the dishes. And before you tell me it's more sustainable to do them by hand, I know that's not true. I looked it up." He thrust his phone into Clay's face.

"I've read all of these reports," Clay said. "I know that if a family fills a dishwasher daily then yes, it takes less water to wash them with a machine, but there are ways to handwash using less water, and we will be eating most meals communally cooked in the kitchen in the bunkhouse. We're keeping the houses small, and we don't have the space."

"Women are territorial," Dell argued. "They hate sharing kitchens and they hate being told to do things by hand. You'll see. I'm trying to protect you. I don't want to watch you fail."

"I'm thirty-one, Dad. I don't need protection and I won't fail." He hoped. Even now the first of the houses—the one slated for Boone and Riley to inhabit—was taking shape as he crafted its interior with Curtis's help. All too soon he'd get to see Riley's reaction to her new home. He knew Boone would love it, and Riley had liked the plans he'd shown her. Still, he'd be lying if he said he wasn't concerned she might not like it in real life, so Dell's assertions were hitting home.

And what about Nora? He hadn't shown her the plans yet. Maybe he should, just in case Dell was right and she wanted something different. He couldn't add square footage, though. Not now. Harris was already framing Clay's house in.

"That's what they all say." Dell stalked out. Clay knew he should follow. His dad was still smarting over being fired, and their continual conflicts didn't help, but what about his own self-confidence? He couldn't help but feel Dell was trying to undermine him with his constant fault-finding.

Instead he decided it was time to call his mom. She'd had a break from his father for several days now. Maybe she'd changed her mind and wanted Dell back.

He dialed, stood up and paced the bunkhouse while his phone rang.

"Hello."

"Mom, it's Clay."

"You held out longer than I thought you would." Lizette seemed in good spirits, not at all like a woman who was missing her husband.

"It's about Dad."

"I'm not surprised."

"Can't he come home?"

"Not unless he's found himself a new career."

"I'm not sure there are any jobs for him right now. You know he's—"

"I didn't say *job*, Clay. I said career."

Clay perched on the edge of the desk, wondering what the distinction was. Before he could ask, she went on, "Your father never wanted to be a contractor, and he doesn't want to be one now."

"Could have fooled me; he's all over my projects."

"Because he's bored. Clay, he's been bored for over thirty years. Isn't it time for that to change?"

"Most people are a little bit dissatisfied with their jobs, don't you think?" He stood up again and crossed to look out the window. Dell stood near the empty fire pit, his hands in his pockets, watching the various members of their community busy with their work.

"I'm not talking about dissatisfaction. I'm talking about something far worse. The man needs a change, and I can't make it for him."

"But you can force him to make it for himself? Is that what you mean?" He turned away from the window. He couldn't stand seeing Dell like that, shunted off to one side.

Useless.

"Exactly. I always knew you were a smart boy."

"I'm not a—"

"Which means it's about time for you to find your passion, too, isn't it?" His mom hung up before he could ask her what she meant.

Hell. Why couldn't one single thing be easy? He was working on his passions right now. Hadn't he slaved over his tiny house plans—the ones Dell kept dismissing? Outside, a building was taking shape exactly the way he'd planned it.

Or it would be, if Dell stopped interfering.

Clay turned back to the window. Where had his dad gone now?

WHEN SUE LEFT, Nora hurried down to Base Camp and found everyone already gathered for the meal Kai had cooked. In the early days at Base Camp, Boone had cooked over an open fire, but now that the population was swelling and they were building their community, they'd gotten serious about sustainability in the way it related to cooking.

"The guys are ramping up real solar service for the bunkhouse kitchen," Kai said, when Nora asked how things were going, "but for now these babies will do the trick on a sunny day like today." He pointed out the kitchen door toward a line of solar ovens that made Base Camp look like a hippie haven to Nora. She was amazed at the meal he'd managed to cook in them. Stew, corn bread—and a salad to round things out.

"I saved you a seat," Clay said when she'd been served her meal and approached the logs around the empty fire pit. She liked the tradition of eating outside and happily took a seat next to him before she remembered the awkwardness of seeing themselves on television earlier. Nora found that couldn't compete with her enthusiasm for the project Sue had brought to her, though. After her afternoon's conversation with the principal, she felt energized. For the first time in days, she wasn't worried about Clay, the show, her stalker, her novel or anything else.

"I'm looking forward to our date tonight," he said.

"I didn't realize we had one." Nora had planned to start an outline of the first textbook. She couldn't wait to dive into the project.

"You'd better believe it." Clay kept eating calmly, but the fine lines around his eyes and mouth crinkled with humor as she struggled to formulate a reply. She had work to do, but... when he looked at her that way she wished there were more hours in the evening. Spending a little time with Clay wouldn't be so bad.

She was glad that with the big crowd gathering around the empty fire pit, the cameras had too much to focus on to be filming them. "I've got to work for at least an hour before I can do anything else," she warned him.

"Yes, ma'am."

She bit back a smile at his overdone drawl. "Why do I get the feeling you were a handful back in school?"

"What makes you think I'm not a handful now?"

Her gaze dropped below his belt buckle. "Several handfuls, is my guess." Nora swallowed. Maybe Clay hadn't heard that.

"Did you seriously say that out loud?" Clay cocked his head.

"I think I did." Nora giggled, tried to cover it up and snorted instead. A laugh escaped her tightly compressed lips. She never said things like that. And she never snorted. Another unladylike sound slipped out. The whole textbook thing had made her giddy.

"Handfuls?" he repeated. He set his plate down.

Leaned in. "Handfuls?"

"Several," Nora repeated and giggled again.

"Did Kai slip you something in your salad?"

He must have, because suddenly, perched on a log next to Clay, eating solar-cooked stew, with a project to look forward to, she felt—good.

Clay leaned in and whispered, "We can measure those handfuls later, if you like."

"I've got work to do, remember?" she whispered back primly, his breath in her ear sending shivers down her spine. She wouldn't mind getting Clay out of those jeans, if she was honest with herself. But wasn't there some reason not to? As charged up as she felt, it was hard to remember why.

"We can at least cop a lot of feels while you're writing, right?"

Nora laughed out loud and several heads turned their way. "No, we can't." She was flirting with him, Nora thought. Flirting and joking about sex without a whisper of worry. That damn stalker hadn't gotten to her after all, had he? Heady with triumph, Nora leaned toward Clay. "Handfuls."

Clay shook his head. "That's it. We're going to your tent right now."

"Nope. I'm hungry." She took a bite of stew and slid him a look from under her eyelashes.

"That's just it. I'm hungry, too." The desire in his eyes was so powerful, Nora faltered.

Maybe she wasn't ready for this after all.

She glanced up and spotted Ed focusing his camera

on them. "We're being watched," she said shortly and went back to her meal.

Clay scanned the fire ring, nodded and picked up his plate again. Some of her bravado faded away as they ate. There were lots of good reasons not to get involved with Clay, and those damn cameras represented one of them.

When they finished the meal and brought their dishes back to Kai, however, Clay took her hand. "Your tent or mine?"

"I'm supposed to write," she reminded him. A breeze toyed with a strand of her hair that had come undone from her updo and she tucked it back into her bonnet. She was second-guessing herself. Nerves had kicked in and she wasn't sure she was ready to be alone with Clay, after all. Mostly, she was afraid he'd do something that triggered one of her ridiculous reactions. She didn't think she could stand it if she embarrassed herself again.

She didn't want to feel anxious around Clay. Earlier, their banter had turned her on, but she knew if she went with Clay to his tent—or hers—they'd be well on their way to making love. Could she do that?

She wasn't sure.

She wanted to.

Nora held back a sigh. Taking her stalker and her overreactions out of the equation, there was still the problem of the show and Fulsom's demands. If and when she made love to Clay, it would be hard to pretend she didn't know where their relationship was headed. Or that Fulsom's timeline worked for her.

"Go grab your laptop and come back here. We'll work in the bunkhouse for a while," Clay said. "I'll kick Boone out so you can take the desk."

He must have read her hesitation. He was being a gentleman, which made it all the harder to resist him.

"Seems like Base Camp needs a few more workspaces," she made herself say lightly.

"Base Camp needs more of everything. We'll get there," Clay told her.

Nora hurried to her tent, found her laptop and came back. Some of the men were still gathered around the fire pit, where they'd lit a small fire. She liked the homey feel of the camp, despite her reluctance to move down here. Maybe it wouldn't be so bad to camp out for a while.

Or maybe it would be when she tried to sleep on the ground tonight.

When she entered the bunkhouse again some minutes later, the main room was empty, so she went to set her things on the desk. She heard the deep rumble of male voices in the kitchen and realized the other founders had gathered there with Clay. Kai was still in there, too. She could hear the clink and clatter of dishes as he washed up. Nora sat down, opened her laptop and waited for it to fire up. She didn't mean to listen in to the men's conversation, but it was hard not to.

"Looks like you're making progress," Jericho said.

"With Nora? A little," Clay said. "I've got a lot of convincing to do, though. Fulsom didn't give us enough time to do this right. How's it going with Savannah?"

Progress, huh? She tried to feel grumpy about that, but in reality, her heart ached for him. Clay was trying so hard to be with her and she was working just as hard to resist him—when she wasn't giving in to him. It wasn't fair to him to keep playing this game. She had to break things off once and for all.

But she didn't want to.

Nora's ears perked up at the mention of Savannah's name, and she turned to hear better, grateful for the distraction. Savannah had been cagey about Jericho for weeks.

"She's not too happy right now. I asked if she wanted to help me prepare for tomorrow, but all she wants to do is play piano. She's pissed she's lost so much of her practice time."

"It'll work out," Boone said. Nora rolled her eyes. Riley's husband was a good man, but messing with Savannah's practice time wasn't going to make her more likely to marry Jericho.

"What about you?" Clay said. "We're all screwed if you don't play along with this, you know." At first Nora thought he was talking to Boone, but then she realized he must be addressing Walker.

"Got it covered."

Definitely Walker. No one else was so terse.

"Are you talking about Avery?" Jericho demanded.

Walker grunted.

"Whoever it is, you'd better get moving. I don't plan to draw the short stick next time," Jericho said.

Their conversation turned to other things, and Nora tried to concentrate on the document on her screen, but she had made little progress with her story before Clay came to check on her. He settled down nearby with a clipboard and a sheaf of papers. "Planning," he said when she raised an eyebrow.

Nora got back to work. Kai, joined by Curtis, cleaned up the meal, and although they made quite a bit of noise hauling in dishes and joking around in the kitchen, she found she didn't mind. It was cozy having people around, and she felt... safe. She decided to put off worrying about her future—and Clay's. Rolling her shoulders, she eased the tension from them. The bunkhouse's windows were open, and snatches of conversation from outside drifted in, too. After years of living alone, it felt good to be part of a large group like this.

"You're smiling," Clay said softly.

Was she? Nora hadn't meant to be; there were important problems to face... soon. "I think I'm... happy." In this moment she was, anyway.

He took her hand. "I'm glad. It's good to have you here, Nora."

"It's good to be here," she admitted.

"Are you done?" He nodded to her laptop. "We could take a walk."

"Okay."

What was she doing? Nora chastised herself as she stood up. This was a perfect time to break things off for good. There were no camera crews around. They'd gone to eat the food Renata ordered for them, and wouldn't be back for a few more minutes.

"What about my laptop?"

"Leave it. Come on. This way," Clay said. He waited for her to shut it down, then led her through the kitchen, giving Kai a salute.

"Slipping out the back?" Kai asked.

"Gonna try."

Clay hurried Nora out the kitchen door and around the far side of the bunkhouse.

He took her on a circuitous route that enabled them to remain unseen until they were far from the bunkhouse. Clay walked confidently, and soon they were well beyond the area of the ranch Nora knew.

"Where are we going?"

"There's a great view over here. We used to come here as kids. Boone, Walker, Jericho and I. And Riley, too, most of the time. She loved to do whatever we did."

Nora smiled at the picture he painted, despite her concerns. She tried to conjure up in her mind a vision of the four men as teenagers and Riley, a few years younger than them, tagging along behind the Four Horsemen of the Apocalypse, as she'd called them back then. What a wonderful childhood, Nora thought wistfully. She'd lived in the city all her life.

The walk settled her nerves and soon she'd convinced herself that this was all it was—an innocent way to pass the time.

"What made you join the Navy?" she asked. Pacing

next to him, her dress swishing as she walked, holding hands with a strong, tall man she fancied, she felt almost transported back in time to an era where life wasn't quite so hectic.

"The Navy was Jericho's idea originally. He got hold of the requirements to join, and we trained like crazy so we'd make the cut. None of our families had the money to own their own ranch. We knew none of us would inherit a spread, so we needed to do something. The Navy was a good answer."

"Funny you didn't choose the Army or Air Force—"

"Hell, no. Navy SEALs all the way. That was the goal and that's what we did."

Clay and his friends hadn't changed over the years, had they? They still set goals together and did whatever it took to meet them. She had to admit she found that admirable.

Even if it took them down some crazy paths.

"If you love the SEALs so much, why leave the Navy? Was there something in particular that made you focus on climate change instead?"

"Yeah. You could say that." They'd been walking along a barbed wire fence that defined a pasture, and Clay opened a gate, guided her through it and closed it behind them again. He led her to a rise in ground from which the landscape fell away, laying out a panoramic view.

"Oh, that's beautiful," Nora said, forgetting her question for the moment.

Clay sat on the ground and tugged her down beside

him. She sat carefully, not wanting to damage her dress.

"It all started in Yemen. Or ended there, depending on how you want to look at it. I'm proud of the way I served my country, and I'm proud of the SEALs for the work they do, but you've got to understand by the time we're called in, a situation has gone to shit. There's no fixing it—there's only dealing with some disaster that generally could have been prevented from happening in the first place if the right people had done the right things. Does that make sense? As much as I pride myself on being able to get into a tight spot and save someone's ass, or minimize the damage, or get the bad guy, I'm also a thinking man. I can't help noticing what should have been done about the situation months or years before I was called in. I can't help thinking about the bigger picture."

"What happened in Yemen?" She vaguely knew there was a civil war going on over there.

"A major fuck-up. We went there to rescue four aid workers who couldn't get out when the hostilities flared up. They were in a convoy, trying to bring medical supplies to a civilian hospital. They couldn't go forward, and they couldn't go back, so they holed up in a bombed-out building—and found they weren't alone. Turned out the building was a school. There were children hiding there, too. Their teacher was dead, and they couldn't get home."

"Oh, Clay." Nora couldn't imagine what that had been like. If a war had broken out while she'd been teaching, she would have done anything she could to keep the children safe. "How old were they? The kids?"

"Young." Clay shook his head, and she could tell his thoughts were far from this pasture. She covered his hand with her own. "The aid workers had a satellite phone. Solar charged. We were able to talk to them, even though we couldn't get to them. We took turns, trying to keep up their morale. Usually I talked to a man named Hendrik Fergusen. He used to be a plastic surgeon, but he gave that up to join the aid organization after he split up with his wife. I felt so bad for him. If only they'd stayed together—if only he'd stayed in Beverly Hills, you know? But when I said that to him, he disagreed."

Clay tilted up his head to look at the sky. Nora did, too. Its deep blue was darkening, and a star or two was out. Under its large expanse, Yemen didn't seem so far away. She wondered if there was a woman over there looking up at the sky, wishing for peace.

"Hendrik said, 'I've lived my whole life doing what others thought I should do. My wife wanted the security that wealth would provide. In the end, though, she left me. So much for security.'"

"That poor man," Nora said, angry on his behalf.

"That's not the way he saw it," Clay said, glancing her way. "'It's the most freeing thing that ever happened,' is how he put it. He told me, 'I took a chance and did exactly what I wanted to do. I helped people who really needed it. I may survive this, I may not, but the first time in my life I'm fulfilled.' I'll never forget that," Clay said. "For the first time, I'm fulfilled."

"What happened?" She thought she knew, but she had to ask.

"We didn't save them," Clay said softly. "We tried. Over and over again. We couldn't. Boone was on the phone with a woman named Francine when the school was hit. They all died, every last one of them."

She heard the pain in his voice and wished she could take it away. She doubted you lived through something like that and ever got away from it, though.

"That's when we decided we had to try something else. It's hard to explain how tiny houses in Montana affect civil wars in Yemen—"

"I get it," Nora said. "Of course the two are connected. Everything we do is connected."

"I can't stop fighting for Hendrik. For Francine. For those kids."

Nora understood—more than she wanted to, really. He'd experienced something life-altering and made a vow he had to uphold. How could she complain if that trumped her qualms about a quick marriage?

Especially when she could change the ending to their story by simply saying yes to Clay.

"I didn't mean to ruin a beautiful evening with hard memories." He turned to face her, and Nora wanted to smooth her fingers over the worry lines around his eyes. He was so dear to her, she realized. She ached to make him happy.

And all she had to do was agree to marry him.

"You didn't ruin anything," Nora said, shifting slightly to put more space between them. "If anything, you made me understand something I couldn't before."

"Did you think I'd signed on to Base Camp out of ego?" Clay lifted her hand into his lap and began massaging it gently. She had the feeling he needed to do something. That coiled energy of his again.

"I'm not sure what I thought. I wasn't sure why you let Fulsom boss you around, I guess."

"I do have an ego," he said. "A big enough one to want what I'm doing here to make a real difference. That means people have to know about it. Lots of people. Fulsom's out of his mind, but he's great at generating buzz."

"That he is."

"I only wish it wasn't causing problems between us."

When he looked at her like that, like he was starving and she was the only food for miles, she knew she was in trouble. All that energy he tried to hold in check burned bright in his eyes. He wanted her.

And, God help her, she wanted him, too.

"Nora—"

He didn't finish his sentence. He leaned in and kissed her and she greeted that kiss gratefully, falling into it like she was diving into a cool lake on a hot summer's day. He lifted her onto his lap, and Nora could only cling to him as he deepened the kiss, tasting her, tangling his tongue with hers.

Nora leaned into him, wrapped her arms around his neck and savored the feel of him. His hardness against her bottom made it all too clear what he wanted, and she ached to unzip his jeans and get a good look at those handfuls.

"Your tent? Or mine?" Clay said finally, and Nora blinked, coming back to herself.

"They'll film us," she protested.

Clay thought about it. "We'll enter camp separately. You go to your tent, I'll go to mine. I'll come to you when the coast is clear." He stole another kiss. "We'll be very, very quiet, but we'll make some noise. Know what I mean?"

She knew exactly what he meant, and heat pulsed low inside her at the thought of what was to come. All her earlier fears were gone. Clay was a good man through and through. She wanted him. She might just... love him.

The realization rocked her. When had that happened? She'd worked so hard to keep her distance and keep her common sense about her. Now she was sitting in his lap, sharing memories, kissing him...

Planning to make love.

They walked back together, their arms entwined, stopping now and then for a long, languorous make-out session. Nora was desperate for more by the time they reached the outskirts of camp.

"See you in a minute," Clay said.

"See you."

The walk alone to her tent, and the time she spent finding the things she needed to prepare for bed by flashlight, calmed her racing pulse—a little. She gathered a towel and her toiletries before heading for the bunkhouse to wash up. She hadn't paid much attention to the men coming and going into the bathroom while she'd been working at the desk earlier, but now she did the math. One toilet, fifteen men and women. That didn't seem sustainable at all.

When she went indoors, Clay was already exiting the bathroom, his hair damp and his towel around his neck.

"How'd you beat me?"

"I'm fast when I want to be." He grinned down at her. She scanned the room, but no one else was in here, and the cameras must have been occupied somewhere else.

She reached up and snatched a kiss. "My turn." She hesitated. "Won't it be pretty crowded in here in the morning?"

"The privies will get their share of traffic," he said.

"You dug privies?" She couldn't keep the shock from her voice.

"Composting toilets, actually. We've got five of them set up in little buildings around the place. I'll show you where they are tomorrow."

"Composting toilets?" She didn't even want to know.

"Don't worry about them. Just get ready for bed. And hurry up—I'm not sure how much longer I can wait."

Nora, glad the cameras were busy elsewhere, knew what he meant. She went into the bathroom, brushed her teeth and washed her face—

And then realized she had a problem. She opened

the door a crack. "Clay? I need Avery. Or Savannah."

He disappeared and came back a moment later. "I don't see them anywhere. I think they already went to bed. Anything I can do to help?"

"No." She'd have to get out of these stays herself. But even as she thought it, she knew it was impossible. They laced up her back. It would be like extricating herself from a straitjacket. "Yes," she said. "But you have to promise to behave."

Clay was by her side in an instant. "Behaving is my number one skill."

"Right." Nora allowed him in, shut the bathroom door and turned her back to him. "I need you to get me out of my dress."

"I thought you'd never ask." Clay's fingers went to the ties at the back of her dress and undid them. When he saw the stays beneath her gown, he whistled. "Holy shit, sweetheart, what'd you do to deserve this?"

"It's what one wears under a Regency gown."

"No wonder your breasts look all..." He cupped his hands and held them up to where she could see in the mirror. "Talk about handfuls."

Nora elbowed him. "Hurry up."

"I'm at your service." He got to work on the stays. For a few anxious moments Nora thought he might be tightening the knots rather than loosening them, but finally he figured it out.

"I can take it from here," she said.

"I had a feeling you'd say that." Clay didn't move. Instead, he reached inside her dress, under her chemise, and slid his fingers an inch or so under her stays. His touch felt good. Too good.

Nora sighed.

Clay seemed to take that as an encouragement and slid his hands higher, lifting her loose stays away from her body. When his fingers brushed the underside of her breasts, she sucked in a breath. He was being so gentle. She closed her eyes as he moved them higher still and cupped her breasts the way he'd mimicked in the mirror. When he brushed her sensitive nipples with his thumbs, she melted against him.

He kissed her under her ear and slid his mouth down her neck. When he slid one hand down over her hip and lower, she stopped him. "Clay."

He nodded and released her. She let her stays fall loosely back in place, her chemise and dress hanging over them. She looked bulky, and the back of her dress was undone, but nothing untoward was showing and at least it was dark out. When she passed by the men gathered at the fire, they wouldn't notice anything wrong.

Clay helped her gather her things, left her alone in the bathroom to finish up and waited for her outside. As she opened the bathroom door, Walker was walking into the bunkhouse. He didn't say a word and neither did they. Clay had grabbed her laptop while waiting for her. He ushered Nora past Walker, out of the bunkhouse, and hurried her back to her tent. Once there, he unzipped the zipper and almost pushed her inside.

"Hey!"

"Sorry. Cameras coming." He followed her inside the tent, yanked the zipper closed and collapsed on the ground beside her, pushing her laptop aside. "We made it."

"I thought you were going to your tent and would come later."

"Woman, you're killing me." Clay reached for her and Nora met him halfway. She allowed him to pull her on top of him where he lay sprawled over her bedding. As she moved over him, tugging on her dress to make it come along with her, she wanted nothing more than to lift it over her head and toss it away.

When Clay's hands slid to the back of her dress, and he asked, "How about we get this off?" she acquiesced gladly. Once its voluminous layers were gone, she straddled him in her chemise, panties and stays, but he quickly peeled the stays off her, too.

"I thought we were supposed to take this slow," she said to tease him, although the hard length of him between her legs made her ache with pleasure and wanting.

"I think we need to get to know each other as thoroughly as possible." As if to make good on his position, he reached up to palm her breasts. Nora sucked in a breath, unprepared for the sensation of his fingers caressing her.

His plan sounded much better than hers.

She lifted her chemise up over her head, suddenly desperate for Clay to see her... all of her. The little slip of silk that was her panties hardly counted. Besides—

she had no doubt he'd dispose of it before too long.

"Nora." The sound of her name in his mouth told her how much he wanted her, too. "No fair getting ahead of me," he added. She appreciated his low tone. It was hard to find privacy in a tent, but he was doing his best for her. He shucked off his clothes more quickly than she'd thought possible, lifting his hips with her still on top of him, and nearly bumped her head against the cloth ceiling of the tent as he unbuttoned his jeans and tugged them down and out from under her.

"I like where this is going," he said, when nothing stood between them but her panties, "but I want to be sure I don't scare you off again. Are you sure this is what you want? We could just talk."

She laughed. Was that even possible at this point? She was grateful for the restraint he was trying to exercise, though. She ran her hands over his chest, and Clay closed his eyes. Moving them lower, across his taut belly, she cherished the silky feel of his naked skin.

When he reached up to kiss her, she shut her eyes and drank in the feeling. Clay was the best at making out, hands down. Nora found herself spiraling into his force field as her breasts grazed his chest.

Clay cupped them again, reached up to take one nipple into his mouth, and she arched back, delighting in the sensations. Relaxing under his touch, even as he brought her alive, Nora thought she'd found heaven.

Some minutes later, Clay rolled her over onto her back and lowered himself between her legs, tugging her panties off and tossing them away. She opened for him, ready to let him do as he would. She wasn't disappointed. As he took his time exploring her with his tongue, Nora dug her fingers into the covers beneath her, lifted her hips to give him deeper access and tried to keep from moaning aloud in the pleasure of it all. She wanted to stay like this forever, open to Clay—exposed to him. When Clay slid one hand up her belly, cupped her breast again and squeezed her nipple lightly between his thumb and forefinger, Nora bit back a cry as she went right over the edge. She wasn't afraid to shatter in front of him. Instead, she gloried in it. Collapsing back in a glorious heap, her chest heaving as she caught her breath, all she wanted was to return the favor.

Clay seemed all too pleased to let her.

As she pushed him onto his back and began a slow, sensual exploration of Clay's body, Nora knew she could be free with him. He was comfortable in his body and she wanted to be more intimate with him. She wanted to make love to him.

But not yet.

Tonight was a just a beginning, and she meant to start off right. Every inch of his hard, lean body turned her on, and she allowed her lips to trace over him, enjoying his tight muscles, the strength held in readiness, the hair on his chest and in a line that led below his belt.

When she reached that region, she took her time to kiss and explore him with her mouth. The length of him made her smile, but his girth sent a shiver through her that made her want to be with him all the more.

Not tonight. Soon, she promised herself, growing warm thinking about what it would feel like when he pressed inside her. For now she took him in her mouth, stifling a groan of pleasure that echoed the sound Clay made when she closed her lips around him.

He felt good. So good. She slid her mouth along the length of him, tasting him. Savoring him. She took him deeper. Repeated the motion. Inside her mouth, Clay grew even harder. God, he was going to feel good when they made love.

He made an unintelligible noise that Nora took as a sign she was doing it right. She delighted in the way she could turn him on. When she felt his fingers slide into her hair, sending hairpins flying, she let him move her, knowing her mouth was making him feel so good he would soon lose control.

Even when Clay pressed on her shoulders, warning her he was close, Nora kept her position. She wasn't afraid to take him in. This was Clay. The man who wanted to marry her, even if they'd only met six weeks ago. All she knew was that she wanted to know every inch of this man, and tonight's exploration of his body was only the beginning. She wanted more. Much more.

She slid her hands underneath him, gripped his hips and took him in even deeper. Clay came with a groan, bucking against her and breathing hard. She savored the experience, savored giving this gift to this man. Nora didn't know when she'd lost all her inhibitions, but Clay had this effect on her.

When he was done, he fell back against her pillow.

"That was... amazing."

She worked her way up to lie beside him. "I agree."

"Nora, I didn't mean—"

"I wanted to," she assured him and smiled as his arms wrapped around her. He pulled her into a spooning position.

A few minutes later they were both asleep.

CHAPTER FIFTEEN

"ALL I'M SAYING is those green roofs are going to take constant upkeep, and they absorb water rather than allowing it to run off and be used again. Take a look at these houses," Dell said the next morning at the building site.

"We're going with the green roofs. It's all planned out, Dad."

"But you haven't looked at this." Dell waved a tablet at him. Clay blamed Boone for lending it to his father. Boone probably thought it would distract Dell, but he'd been gravely mistaken.

"Okay, take a break," Clay said to the other men, and turned to his father. "What is it you need me to see?" He took the tablet when his father handed it to him, and realized he was looking at a website that featured a sustainable community in Arizona. "Conditions there are totally different than they are here, Pops."

"But look at the way they run everything off rainwater. We could do that."

Clay's design did share elements of the principles the Arizonans were using, but he'd altered his plans to suit Montana. "Dad, you don't seem to understand the time pressure we're working under. I can't change my mind every two seconds about what we're building. We have the plans. They're done. Finished. I don't have time to debate everything with you."

"I'm just trying to help."

"You keep saying that, but you're not helping—"

"Clay?"

He bit back his angry words and turned to find Nora had approached without him seeing her.

"Is everything all right?" she asked, looking from him to Dell.

"My son is a stubborn mule," Dell told her.

"My father is an interfering old fart," Clay retorted.

"At least I know when I've overstepped myself. Who are you to think you can reinvent the way houses are built? You don't have any real world experience." Dell's chest had puffed out like an angry rooster's.

"You have no idea when you've overstepped yourself! You're slowing me down. You're undercutting my authority in front of my men. You're just... getting in the way."

An awful silence spread out between them.

"Dad, I didn't mean—"

"Sure you did." Dell turned on his heel and left.

Nora had her arms folded over her chest when Clay turned to her. "That wasn't very nice."

"You have no idea how irritating that man is." But

Clay had blown it, and he knew it. "How about you help Harris for now. See those two-by-fours over there? He'll need those next. Bring them over to him. I'm going back to work on Riley's kitchen."

Curtis joined him in the tiny home, but Clay was finding it hard to concentrate. His conversation with his father kept replaying through his mind, and he was all too aware of Nora outside following Harris's curt commands. He'd hoped to impress her with his building skills, but now everything felt off, and it was killing him after the night they'd just had together.

Nora was every bit as sexy as he'd known she'd be, and even though they'd only fooled around, he'd gone to sleep satisfied. The way she'd taken him in her mouth and kept him there, coaxing him to come with her tongue...

Sweet Jesus.

He got hard all over again just thinking about it.

But now nothing was going right. He wanted to re-capture the light, teasing tone they'd used the night before—and this morning—but she seemed bothered by the way he'd spoken to his father, and the presence of the other men meant he couldn't explain to her why he'd been so short with Dell. He and Curtis struggled to plumb the kitchen sink in Boone and Riley's house, while Harris framed up the second house with Nora's help. When her time with him was up, and he said good-bye to her two hours later, she simply nodded and headed back for the manor without a second glance. The good weather they'd been enjoying broke soon afterward and a warm June rain fell steadily until nightfall. After slogging through the afternoon as best he could, when Clay went into the crowded bunkhouse for dinner, he found Nora looking as frustrated as he felt.

"Bad day?"

"I wrote one new sentence in my book this afternoon," she informed him. "And Sue didn't make it—some crisis at the school. Avery decided to dust all the knickknacks in the curio cupboard in the parlor, and ended up breaking one. We spent the rest of the afternoon trying to figure out how to fix it. Meanwhile, our website isn't getting enough hits, so Savannah and Riley went into town to a café where they'd get an Internet connection for their laptops, and one of James's horses threw a shoe, so they're eating with the Russells tonight."

The evening wasn't going to get any better, Clay knew. Nora would want to work more after dinner and with everyone crowded into the bunkhouse, it made for close quarters on this damp night. "Why don't we take a walk after dinner? It'll help clear your head."

"In the rain?"

"I think it's stopping."

"I really need to work."

"Maybe by the time we get back maybe the bunkhouse will have cleared out some."

"Oh, why not? Today's a big, fat waste anyway."

Clay did his best not to take that personally. Dinner was a quiet affair. Everyone seemed out of sorts tonight.

His father hadn't returned from wherever he'd gone, and Clay wondered if he'd finally returned home. He hoped his parents could sort out their difficulties and his dad could find a better career, but he had his doubts. Dell was so angry these days, and it frustrated Clay that he didn't have any answers. It frustrated him, too, that even when his dad had taken an interest in alternative building methods, they still ended up at each other's throats.

When they were done with their meal, Clay and Nora snuck out through the kitchen again. He was grateful the rain had stopped and the stars were beginning to show between the tatters of the clouds, and even more grateful when they managed to slip away without being caught when the crew went off to eat their meal. This time he led her in a long arc that eventually met back with the track that ran down to Pittance Creek. The grass was wet, and soon his feet were soaked, but he didn't care and Nora didn't seem to mind, either. The hem of her long dress was damp, but she strode along beside him without comment.

"Want to play a game?" Clay asked.

"What kind of game?" He liked the feel of her hand in his. It was small and delicate, but Nora was the kind of woman a man could build a true life with. She wasn't changeable or indecisive. She knew her mind and she stood her ground.

"Ice cream or cake?" Clay asked her.

"Ice cream," she answered without a second thought.

"Now it's your turn."

She thought a moment. "Books or movies?"

"Hmm. That's a trick question. You want me to say books, but the truth is movies."

Nora smiled. "You're right about that, but I'll let it slide. As long as they aren't zombie movies."

"My favorite kind." She groaned and he laughed. "Winter or summer?" he asked, tugging at her hand.

"Summer. Hamburgers or hotdogs?"

He chuckled. "Steak." She elbowed him. "Hamburgers." He lowered his voice. "Kissing or cuddling?" He waited for her reaction to that one, and was gratified when she sent him a sidelong look that betrayed her interest.

"Cuddling. Holding hands or looking into each other's eyes?"

"Holding hands." He squeezed hers and lifted it up to press a kiss in her palm. "Skinny dipping or hot tubbing?" Would she rise to the bait?

"Skinny dipping in a hot tub," she declared. Clay's pulse sped up. That sounded like a lot of fun. "Under the stars or in a five-star hotel room?"

Clay thought about that. "Both could be real good," he said after a minute, "but I think I'd like to have you under the stars." He let go of her hand and slid his arm around her waist. They were under the stars now. Was she thinking about making love to him?

He leaned closer. "On top or underneath?" he whispered into her ear, then kissed the top of her head.

She rested against his chest, and he put his arms

around her. When she tilted her head back, he bent down and possessed her mouth with his. Nora met him with a hunger equal to his own, and something caught fire within Clay. He needed this woman, now and forever. Even the worst day got better when she was around.

When she broke away from him and grabbed his hand, he moaned his discontent, but when she started back for the camp, he understood what she wanted. "Not back there. They'll be waiting for us this time."

"Where, then?"

Clay thought about that. When the answer came, he nearly laughed out loud. "I know a place."

NORA WONDERED IF Clay meant to march her all the way to town after they'd walked for about twenty minutes. "Where are we going?"

"It's just a little farther."

They'd crossed the creek, Clay taking off his shoes and carrying her in his arms, and had followed the track away from the water overland toward the west. The sun was setting, its rays casting long shadows across the coarse landscape.

"Around this bend," Clay said finally, just as Nora was ready to give up altogether. The boots she wore under her gown were sturdy, but they weren't meant for this kind of outing. Her feet were beginning to hurt, but she forgot all that when a small white structure came into view.

"Is that—is that a one-room schoolhouse?" she

asked in surprise.

"You got it. Long out of use, of course." Clay led her to the door and opened it. Nora couldn't believe such a thing still existed. "There's another one nearer to town that's been kept up by the historical society, so this one doesn't get much love. We used to come and play here sometimes as kids, though."

"It's amazing." She couldn't believe it wasn't locked up tight. Didn't vandals get in and destroy things? "Is this on Westfield land?"

Clay nodded. "Yep. Years ago, the Westfield children were educated here along with a lot of their neighbors. It's a testament to the construction skills of our forebears that it's still standing after all this time. Montana winters are hard on buildings that aren't heated. Would you have liked to teach at a school like this?"

"I'd have loved it. I still would. Sometimes I daydream about—" She cut off. She couldn't say that out loud. She'd never told anyone about her secret fantasy.

"About what?" He came and placed his hands on her hips. "You can tell me anything, you know. I won't spill your secrets, and there aren't any cameras here."

She was glad of that, and glad of the dim light, too, as the sun set beyond the hills. Clay leaned down to kiss her, and she thought she could stay right here with him forever, no matter if the windows were boarded up and the building rather musty.

"You daydream about…" he prompted when he pulled back.

"Being a teacher again. Having a school like this someday," she whispered. "Filled with all of our children. Boone and Riley's, Savannah and Jericho's, Avery and Walker's."

"Yours and mine?" Clay suggested, tugging her closer. "I'd like nothing better." He kissed her again, a kiss that thrilled her all the way to her toes and seemed to contain promises of everything that could happen in the years ahead. Standing in front of her, his legs braced apart, Clay seemed the epitome of strength and stability, and Nora longed to be part of his vision.

"You'd like that because then you'd win," she said pertly, because wanting what she couldn't have—or shouldn't have—hurt too much.

"*We'd* win," he corrected her. "It doesn't have to be mutually exclusive, does it?"

"Maybe not," she conceded.

"You still haven't answered," Clay said, sliding his hands up to the ties of her dress. He undid them slowly, giving her every opportunity to stop him.

She didn't want to stop him.

When he had them undone, he kicked off his boots, jeans and boxers, and peeled off his shirt as she turned to present him with her stays. As he worked at them, he stood close enough she could feel his arousal bobbing against her back. She reached behind her to wrap her fingers around him. Clay groaned deep in his throat and worked faster to undo her ties, but as she slid her fingers over him, teasing another groan out of him, his fingers slowed and he braced himself, his hands gripping her hips.

There was something so sexy about playing with Clay when she couldn't see him. As the light faded, it grew dark in the schoolroom, but Nora wasn't afraid. She was with Clay.

Knowing he was caught behind her, helpless under her touch, made her feel wanton and powerful. When he slid a hand down between her legs, however, Nora shut her eyes and moaned, unsure who was teasing who. He must have liked that response, because he slid his hand up under her stays and cupped her breast. Nora leaned into his touch, already panting with need. She didn't know what it was about Clay that brought her so quickly to such a state. A few minutes ago they'd been having a conversation. Now they were joined by a state of bliss they could only create together.

But as good as this felt, she wanted more.

Nora pulled off her dress, shift and stays. Clay helped her, peeling them up and over her head. He hesitated. "The floor's in a bad state. Here. I've got an idea."

He laid her dress and underthings carefully over one of the old desks, took her hand and tugged her over. Gently placing her hands palm down on the wooden surface of another one of them, he stood behind her and slid his hands over her hips. Nora understood what he meant. She braced her hands on the desk, and when she looked back over her shoulder at him, just enough starlight filtered through the gaps of the boarded windows for her to see the gleam in his eyes.

Nudging her legs apart, he reached down to touch her. She knew he'd find her hot and wet; she'd been aching for him for hours. The stroke of his fingers quickly brought her to the brink.

"Clay—"

"I want you really ready." His voice was husky, and as he returned to teasing her, Nora thought there was no way she could hold on. Somehow she did, and a few minutes later, tingling all over, vibrating with need, she moaned with pleasure as he kissed her neck and teased her nipples with his free hand. When she thought she couldn't last any longer, he rustled through the clothes he'd dropped on the floor, pulled a condom out of some pocket and sheathed himself.

"Hold on," he said.

She leaned forward and braced herself again, biting her lip when he nudged against her. As he slowly filled her with a strong, sensuous stroke, she felt weak in the knees.

"Okay?" he whispered in her ear. Nora nodded. More than okay.

Amazing.

As he pulled out and pressed in again, the sensation was so overpowering Nora could only try to hang on. The delicious friction made every nerve ending tingle. She pushed back against him as he sank deep inside her again. Her breasts, taut and heavy, swung as they moved together. Clay tangled a hand in her hair, braced his other hand on her hip and sped up, making her moan all over again.

As Clay's pace picked up, Nora's thoughts and feelings merged into a liquid blur of pleasure. It all felt so good, she didn't want it to end, but the crescendo building inside her couldn't be contained for long, not the way he was touching her.

When her orgasm crashed over her, Nora could only ride the wave of sensation. It pulsed through her hard and fast, shaking her in its intensity, until her vision blurred and she bucked against him as hard as he was crashing into her. When it was over and Clay panted behind her, she had the feeling if he shifted an inch, they could start all over again.

She was ready to try.

"You have to," Clay whispered into her hair as he gently pulled out of her, turned her around and held her against his chest where she could hear his heart beating. She realized her hairdo had fallen apart during their lovemaking, but she didn't care.

"Have to what?" she murmured. She was warm and sated and hungry all at the same time.

"Have to marry me. I want that every day. Don't you?" He tilted up her chin and brushed his mouth over hers, gathering her close against him. "Nora, I want you. I want all of you. Forever. Say yes."

God knew she wanted to. No one had ever made her feel like this. She'd never been able to speak her needs so clearly with a man, either. She felt so easy with Clay, even if they hadn't known each other very long.

Maybe he was right.

"Think about it. Living together, loving each other."

He chuckled. "Building houses together."

Nora blinked. There was the problem. Marrying Clay meant marrying a whole lifestyle. One she hadn't chosen for herself.

"I'm not sure about that last part," she said honestly.

"I was kidding. You won't have to help me forever. It would be cool if you did," he admitted, "but not necessary."

She shifted into a more comfortable position. "I don't like being told what to do with my time. I came here for a reason. Doesn't it bother you to be dictated to?"

With a sigh, Clay eased back an inch, although he kept his arms around her. "I've been in the Navy for years. It's second nature to let myself be allocated to the job that needs me most."

"I didn't join the Navy, though. I didn't even join Base Camp. I got pushed into it."

"Don't let that stop us from being together." He touched her face. There was so much love in his voice, it made Nora ache to hear it. "Sometimes you have to give a little to get a little."

"What about my writing?"

Clay was silent for a moment. "You wrote last night. I would have waited for you if you'd asked tonight."

"An hour here, a half hour there. That's not what I came here for. I'm living in a tent. I'm part of a reality television show. Not by choice."

"I guess what you're getting in return for that is

me," he said bluntly. "Only you can decide if that's enough."

It felt like enough—almost. Nora wasn't wet behind the ears, though. She knew the precedents they were setting right now would carry through their relationship.

"I'm not ready to decide that tonight," she said. "I like you a lot. I like the way we feel together. But I have to know for sure. I'm sorry." She held her breath, afraid he'd leave. He'd gone so still she knew instinctively he was thinking about it.

"I guess I can't expect you to rush into anything." He was obviously disappointed, and Nora's heart constricted.

"Clay, be a little patient, okay?" She moved closer and wrapped her arms around him, fitting her body against his. When he kissed her again, she knew all would be well—at least for now. She kissed him back, her hunger for him welling up all over again. "I want you," she whispered in his ear. "I want you all the time."

"Sooner or later you'll realize what we have is worth fighting for. I'll be waiting," he warned her.

She nodded, not daring to speak. She was so close to saying yes, the word was on her lips as he sheathed himself a second time, lifted her onto the desk and pressed into her all over again as she wrapped her legs around his back.

But still she kept silent.

WHEN CLAY WOKE the following morning, alone in his tent, all he could think of was Nora. He hadn't noticed the long march home when they were finally finished with lovemaking. He'd been too drunk on the taste of her—the feel of being inside her.

He'd proposed.

Clay sat up.

She'd turned him down.

But then she'd made love to him, giving herself so wholeheartedly he felt like they were engaged no matter what she said. She'd looked so beautiful in the dim light, Clay had tried to make the moment last as long as he could, but when she'd arched back and cried out, he'd followed her right over the edge. No one made him as hungry as she did. No woman had availed herself of his body so freely, either. Halfway home she'd been ready for another round. He'd obliged her gladly in a good old-fashioned romp under the stars that left both of them out of breath, and his clothes soaked through. He'd tried to spare her beautiful gown, but he wasn't sure how it had fared.

Back in Base Camp, the rest of its inhabitants long asleep, they'd showered together in the freezing water in the bunkhouse, dried each other off with towels and nearly made love all over again. "You'd better go get some sleep," he'd told her.

"I just want you too much," she'd answered.

He wouldn't rest easy until she became his wife, but Clay thought there was no way she could keep her distance when they were so good together. He'd keep close and keep asking, he decided. There wasn't anything else he could do.

A half hour later, they met in the line for breakfast, and he leaned in for a quick kiss.

"Morning, sweetheart," he whispered.

"Cameras."

"I know." He backed off reluctantly.

Nora was cheerful through the meal, however, and Clay felt good about the chances of things turning out. Maybe he just had to keep making love to her to get her to say yes. He didn't mind that one bit.

After breakfast they parted ways. To Clay's surprise, Dell appeared at the building site with the other men, but instead of interfering and offering unwanted opinions, he simply pitched in and did what he was told. They made terrific progress on Boone and Riley's house.

Clay had never seen Dell like this. He imagined his dad must have acted this way at job sites often enough—he'd never been fired until recently, after all—but it wasn't a side of his father he was familiar with. When Boone came by an hour later and mentioned they really needed a shed built near the main gardens, Clay thought it was a chance to throw his dad a bone.

"Dad, do you want to take that on? You wouldn't have to answer to me," Clay said when he'd pulled Dell aside and told him about Boone's request.

To his surprise, Dell shot him a withering look. "Just like I thought. You want to get rid of me."

"I'm trying to give you a project that will interest you," Clay protested.

"A shed? You think I'm interested in sheds? I've

been in this business for thirty-five years. My aspirations run a little higher than that."

His raised voice attracted attention, and Clay lost his patience. "I don't know what you want from me. I've done everything I can to help you out—"

"I don't want your help. I just want a little god-damned respect! Is that so much to ask?"

Out of the corner of his eye, Clay saw Nora approaching, a wary expression on her face. She hesitated a little distance away, and he knew she was waiting for instructions. Dell caught sight of her, too.

"Steer clear of this one," he said to her, indicating Clay. "He'll treat you like he's treating me someday."

"What about how you're treating me?" Stung, Clay forgot to keep his voice down. "You keep railroading right over me like I'm some kid playing a game. This is serious stuff."

"Tiny houses? Reality TV shows? Pardon me if I think it's all a great big joke." Dell stormed away, leaving Clay close to blowing his top. He couldn't blame the man for his frustration. He was right; there weren't any projects here that suited his skills. Clay had no idea why he didn't just go ahead and become an architect like he'd always wanted to.

Something clicked as Nora approached. His father had always wanted to be an architect. Yet here he was after thirty-five years working construction, still no closer to that goal.

"That wasn't fair of him to say," Nora told him, reaching his side. "He's angry at himself, really."

Clay shoved his hands in his pockets and watched his father stride across the fields toward distant pastures. "I think he's angry because he's never really had a chance to pursue his true goals."

"Do you know what those goals are?" She was back in one of her work gowns, with a voluminous apron over it.

"Yeah, I do," Clay admitted. "They're the same as mine. He wants to be an architect."

"I didn't know that about you. I mean, I knew you designed the tiny houses, but I thought you liked the building part best."

"I like both parts," Clay said. "I like to design things and then build them. But my designs won't be taken seriously if I don't have the right qualifications."

"A degree."

"Exactly."

"Does your dad want to go to school?"

Did he? Clay had no idea.

He pulled out his phone and called his mom. Nora watched him. When his mother answered, he launched right into his questions. "It's architecture, right? That's what Dad needs to do? Why hasn't he ever gone back to school?"

She cut him off. "Is your father still living with you?"

"Yeah. Why? Do you want him to—"

"If he's there, talk to him, not me. For God's sake, you two are hopeless."

When the dial tone buzzed in his ear, Clay frowned

and shoved the phone back into his pocket. Nora was biting back a smile. She'd obviously heard.

"Dell's right over there." She nodded toward where Dell could still be seen striding across a meadow.

"I'll be back in a minute. Go ask Harris if you can give him a hand again, all right?"

"Sure. Good luck."

"I swear it gets more interesting than this," he told her. "I wanted to show you so many things."

"You will."

When he caught up with Dell, his dad waved him away. "I don't want to hear any more about sheds. Or is there a dog house you'd like me to build now?"

Clay chuckled. "Neither. I want to talk to you about something else. Something I've wanted to do for a long time."

"What's that?" Dell finally slowed down. "If this is about getting married and having kids, Jericho filled me in. You've got a deadline. Looks like you've found yourself a good woman. Just don't blow it."

"It's not that." Although that was certainly on his mind. "It's school. I think I might go back for my degree."

Dell stopped, but he kept his gaze on the horizon, as if studying something Clay couldn't see. "Isn't it kinda late for that?"

"I don't think so."

"What'll you study?" His carefully casual tone didn't fool Clay one bit.

"You remember what you said to me when I was

sixteen and I wanted to pursue architecture?"

Dell's lips thinned into a line. "This one of those 'poor me, my parents fucked me up' conversations?"

"No. That's not my intention at all. You told me there was no money in it. You said school cost too much. You said I needed a skill, not a fancy degree."

"That's the way of the world for people like you and me." Dell kept his head turned away.

"You said that, too. It stuck with me. What kind of people are we, Dad? People who don't deserve to be happy?"

Dell's chin lowered a fraction of an inch. "I had a good job and a good wife. I raised a family. Don't tell me I didn't do well."

"I didn't say anything about doing well. I said happy. You can't tell me you're happy right now." He wasn't going to give up that easily. He could tell his dad didn't want to have this conversation, but it was about time they had it out. Dell couldn't moon around Base Camp forever.

"No, I can't." Dell finally turned toward him. "Because my son's talking nonsense."

"I'm talking about the future. See, I'm not asking you this time, Dad. I'm telling you. I'm going to go to school. Probably part-time. Maybe I'll even study online. I don't know yet. All I know is I've always wanted to be an architect, and now I'm going to go for it."

"Fine. Do whatever the hell you want to. I'm going to take a nap." Dell headed for his tent while Clay watched him go. Nap? That was a new one.

He had a feeling Dell would be doing a lot more thinking than sleeping.

Maybe that was a good thing.

He returned to work, his mind still buzzing from his conversation with his father, so that he couldn't even enjoy Nora's presence. By the time she left to return to the manor, though, he'd settled down a bit and was able to get on with the job.

"It looks great," Boone said when he stopped by the building site a half-hour later. It was lunch time and the rest of the men had gone to the bunkhouse, but Clay wanted to keep working.

"Want to help me finish up?" They'd let everyone tour the house later in the day, but first he needed to know that Boone approved of it.

"Sure thing. I can't believe it's nearly done."

Clay nodded. "I know." It felt so good to see his creation take shape in front of him. The tiny house looked just like he'd imagined it would. Better, even. They'd left the locally harvested wood raw so no products would off-gas into the small space. The kitchen was tidy and well-designed, and he felt sure Boone and Riley would like the loft bedroom he'd created for them. A second room at one end of the structure was for Riley's studio—or possibly a nursery someday. He knew Boone and Riley were trying for a baby. The green roof would take time to grow in, but the rest of the structure was complete, and it blended in seamlessly with its surroundings. Clay couldn't wait until the hillside was dotted with houses like this one.

"What do we need to do?" Boone asked.

"A couple of touches on the cabinets, and a few other things."

"Riley's so excited to see the house."

Clay nodded. It must have been hard to start a marriage in a tent. He wanted a home to bring Nora to when they married.

If they married.

He decided not to think about that. "Let's get to it then."

CHAPTER SIXTEEN

"WHY ARE YOU walking funny?" Nora asked Avery when she returned to the manor at noon. She began to pull food out of the refrigerator for lunch, and wondered if eventually Fulsom and Boone would make them spend all their time at Base Camp. She hoped not. She still enjoyed afternoons alone with her friends—just the girls.

"Had my first riding lesson yesterday," Avery said. "And another one this morning. They've caught up to me."

"Ugh. That sounds awful."

"Well, I'm not too happy about the way my legs feel right now, but I love being on horseback, and Walker is a wonderful teacher."

"Are you riding sidesaddle?" Nora remembered Clay and his father talking about that.

"Nope. I just pull on a pair of pants under my dress, hitch everything else around my waist and go for it. I figured it was a decent compromise."

"What does Walker think about that?" She supposed if she ever learned to ride that would be a much easier way to accomplish it than sidesaddle.

"What's that about Walker?" Savannah came in, grabbed a glass out of the cupboard and filled it with water. She drained it dry. "Oh, that's good. I needed that. Harnessing the sun is thirsty work."

"He's teaching Avery to ride."

Savannah lifted an eyebrow. "I bet he is."

"Shut up," Avery said good-naturedly. "I wish. He hasn't so much as touched me except to help me get on the horse."

"Watch out; before you know it, you'll be engaged," Nora said, turning back to the pantry.

"Who's engaged?" Riley ducked in the doorway.

"No one's engaged. At least, not yet. A girl can dream," Avery said.

Nora pulled out some salad fixings and got to work chopping up vegetables. Avery grabbed the salad dressing and began to set the table for four.

"How are things going with you and Boone?" Savannah asked Riley.

"Now that we're back, he's pretty stressed out about the show and getting everything done. He's trying to figure out how to find more women."

"Boone the matchmaker. Hard to fathom," Nora said.

"Maybe he'll turn out to be good at it," Riley said.

"Are you two working hard at that pregnancy thing?" Savannah asked. "Morning, noon and night, and all that?"

"We're working at it," Riley said dryly. A shadow clouded her face. "We really are working at it, but I don't feel pregnant."

"It's only been a few days," Savannah exclaimed.

"I know. It's just... there's so much pressure. I feel like I should be doing something."

"I think you're doing what's called for," Savannah said with a grin.

"Is the pressure causing a strain between you two?" Avery asked with concern.

Riley leaned against the counter. "No. Not at all. Boone's pretty happy to keep trying." She grinned, too. "How about you, Nora? Are you or aren't you?"

"Pregnant?" Nora paused in the process of filling a pot with water.

"Not pregnant, doing it—with Clay?"

"That's pretty nosy."

"You *are* doing it with him," Avery exclaimed. "You dog! How on earth are you pulling that off when we're all in tents?"

"That's my little secret. Besides, I have no idea where things between us are going." She peeled a cucumber and began to chop it. "Did you lock the door behind you?" she asked Riley.

"Sorry." Riley rushed to do so. "The last thing I need is another interview with Renata. She got all up close and personal this morning about my family and the ranch. 'Do you blame Boone for losing your inheritance?'" She mimicked Renata's plummy British accent. "Is the front door locked, too?" she asked.

"I think so. We all came in the back," Nora said. The reminder of their need for caution took away some of her pleasure in their little gathering. She hadn't thought about her stalker today, though, and that was progress. Spending most of her time in a group meant she felt safe.

"Where do you see things going with Clay?" Savannah asked cautiously.

"If you mean am I going to marry him, I really don't know," Nora said.

Riley frowned. "Why not? If you're getting close, I mean?"

"You know why not. I hate being rushed. I refuse to marry a man I don't know well. Look what happened to my parents." She finished chopping the cucumber and reached for a carrot.

Riley bit her lip. "Boone's going to bring in other women soon, Nora. Don't wait too long to decide. You know Clay has to marry by July tenth." Riley turned to the others. "That goes for you, too. Boone's serious about matching people up."

A sharp rap on the kitchen door startled them. Avery went to open it, and Win bustled in. Nora was sure she wasn't the only one relieved by the interruption.

"What's going on? Are we planning a coup?" she asked when she got inside.

"Not quite," Nora said. "From the sound of things, the cavalry's coming to help the other side."

"Cavalry?" Win looked from one to the other of

them for an explanation.

"Boone's bringing in more women," Riley told her.

"Competition," Avery said sourly.

"They're only competition if you're in the game." Win shrugged. "I thought you three said you weren't interested."

"It's more complicated than that," Riley said tactfully. Win had proved to be much more friendly and fun than she'd seemed when she first got to Westfield, but none of them had quite relaxed enough around her to let her into their confidences.

"No, it's not," Win said. "When you see something you want, you go for it. At least, that's how I like to do things."

"Has Angus proposed yet?" Avery challenged her.

Nora bit back a smile.

"No, he hasn't. Because I've told him he can't yet. I want a real, old-fashioned courtship. He's taking me on a picnic tonight."

"With his father or without?" Nora asked dryly, mindful of how her picnic with Clay had turned out.

Avery coughed. Win gave Nora a puzzled look. "Without, I expect, since his father passed away last year."

Nora closed her eyes. "I'm sorry. I'm just..." She didn't bother to finish the statement. She didn't know what she was. Annoyed? Discouraged?

Confused?

She didn't like the idea of more women at Base Camp, especially ones who might want to hook up with

Clay. As hesitant as she was to marry him, she didn't want Clay to marry someone else. Not after the last few days.

"Let's eat our lunch and get to our projects," Riley suggested.

"Do you mind if I join you?" Win asked. "Sometimes it's nice to be with other women."

"Not at all," Riley said.

Avery laid another plate on the table. Nora felt a tinge of guilt that they didn't include Win more in their activities, but it had seemed that all she wanted was to be with Angus. She brought the large bowl of salad to the table and set it in the middle. "Dig in. We've got some French bread, too, if anyone needs something more substantial."

They kept the conversation general, and soon the meal was over. The women cleaned up together and then dispersed, Avery and Savannah to the parlor, Win out the back door to return to Base Camp. Riley came to stand near Nora, who was putting the last of the dishes away. She touched Nora's sleeve. "You know I'd never judge you for jumping in head-first with Clay, right? I think you two have a real chance at a wonderful marriage. I've seen the way he looks at you, Nora. That man is in love with you. If you have to marry fast, maybe it's better to do that than to always wonder what might have happened if you don't."

Nora nodded. "Maybe. He wants to go back to school," she added.

"Right away?"

Nora shook her head. "After the show's over, I suppose. I know he wouldn't do anything to disrupt that."

"Clay's a man who wants to make a better future, isn't he?" Riley mused. "Seems to me you could do worse."

CHAPTER SEVENTEEN

A S THE HOUSE neared completion, Clay's thoughts strayed to his father again. It still burned him that Dell had walked away in anger when he'd told him his plans. He never wanted to end up as bitter or frustrated with his career as his dad was, and it worried him a little what would happen after the houses were built. One part of building a sustainable community was that the members of the community needed ways to bring in an income. The bison herd they would establish would help with that; bison was a luxury meat, and the herd Jake Matheson was partnering with Evan Mortimer to run had already found solid markets. Clay didn't mind helping with that business, but it didn't call him the way architecture did. He wanted to bring his flavor of eco-conscious housing to a wider audience. That meant school.

It bothered him now that he'd never made the effort before. Hell, Walker had done just fine when he went for his bachelor's degree, and he'd come from the same kind of working-class background Clay had. Still, every time Clay had thought about taking the Navy up on the options it offered, Dell's voice had always echoed through his mind. *That's not for the likes of us.*

Why did Dell still believe that?

"Did you ever want to go to college?" Clay asked Boone. He passed his friend handles one by one and Boone screwed them into each of the little cabinet doors. He was trying to let Boone do as much as he could to finish off the project. He knew it would mean a lot to Riley to know her husband had worked on some of the final touches.

Boone shook his head. "Not really. You know me—I like to do things, not study them."

"Yeah." But some things required a degree.

"You thinking about school?"

Clay nodded. "I won't screw up anything with Base Camp, but yeah. It's time." He held a piece of edging in place while Boone screwed it in.

"I'll say."

When Clay looked up in surprise, Boone went on. "I always wondered why you stuck with the SEALs so long. You're meant to build things. Anyone who knows you can see that."

Clay positioned another piece of wood. "I think we could all say that. That's why we're here, right?"

"I think every life has more than one story to it, but it's funny how a theme runs through all of them," Boone said. "We walked through our story about serving our country through our military service. Now we're in our story about serving our country through demonstrating a sustainable life."

"That's fucking poetic, Chief."

Boone laughed. "Yeah. Shit, time to install a composting toilet or something, before I start writing sonnets."

"Speaking of composting toilets, want to help me install yours?"

"Hell, yeah."

As he and Boone unboxed the toilet and wrestled it into place in the tiny bathroom, he felt like he'd truly accomplished something. In no time at all, this house would be a real home.

"Looks good," Boone said when they were done.

"Think Riley will be okay with it?"

"She's been using the ones around camp, and she says she'll adapt." He scratched his head. "I wouldn't say she's thrilled about it, but she's being a good sport. I figure I'd better keep her happy in other ways. Some of this sustainability stuff stacks the odds against me, if you know what I mean."

Clay definitely did. It would be far easier to woo Nora with a house like the manor than with a small, eco-conscious building like this one.

"Nora will come around," Boone said, as if reading his thoughts.

"I sure hope so." Clay stood back and nodded. "We're about done. Want to let Riley see the place?"

"Sure do! I'll go get her."

Boone was off in a flash. Clay gathered up their tools and stowed them away, wishing suddenly they'd taken more time to clean up. But the house would speak for itself. Either Riley would love it, or she wouldn't.

He wondered what Nora's reaction would be. Fifteen minutes later, he watched with pride as Boone scooped Riley into his arms and carried her carefully across the threshold into their brand-new tiny home.

Just like his original drawings had shown, the home looked like it was growing straight out of the hillside. There hadn't been enough time for its green roof to sprout, but it would soon, which would only heighten the illusion that it was an organic structure rather than a man-made one. The south-facing exterior wall was an earthy stucco color to absorb sunlight and hold it in colder months. The overhang of the roof and the thick sod on top of it would shelter the structure from the hot days of summer and the bitter cold of winter. Large windows would let in plenty of sunlight, and a gorgeous, hand-hewn door allowed access into the interior.

Inside, the wooden walls and floors gave the house a cabin-like feel. The space was small but built-in shelves and cupboards everywhere provided plenty of storage. Unlike someone living in a typical single family home in suburbia, Boone and Riley didn't need storage for their own lawnmower, power tools, snow blower and the like. They would share larger tools and machines like that with the community and store them in the barns and outbuildings.

Everyone took turns parading through the small house to see the end product, oohing and aahing over it. Even Dell turned up and walked through. Clay wished he knew what his father really thought of the tiny house, but he was a little relieved when Dell didn't say anything.

But when Nora took her turn he found himself pacing until she'd gone in, looked around and finally come back out again.

"Well, what do you think?" Riley asked her excitedly.

"It's beautiful," Nora said. "I think you'll be very happy there."

"I know I will!" Riley threw her arms around Nora's neck.

"It's Clay you should be hugging," Nora told her. "He's the one who built it."

"I had some help. Including your husband," Clay said to Riley.

"I'll hug everyone then!" And Riley did. Clay relaxed. He'd done it. And Nora liked the home he'd built. That meant more to him than anything else.

Jericho clapped him on the shoulder. "Only nine more to go."

"We've already started the next one."

WHEN SUE ARRIVED that afternoon, Nora was happily waiting for her. So far in their planning sessions, they'd worked to define the scope of the project, and Nora knew Sue wanted textbooks for every grade—and in every subject. They'd agreed to start with the seventh grade Social Studies textbook aimed for use on the reservation, and go from there.

"Why seventh grade?" Nora had asked.

"It's a transition year," Sue had said. "Around twelve or thirteen, children make a decision about who they're going to be. I want them thinking about their culture and people then. We'll start small and build." Nora didn't doubt that Sue could move mountains if she wanted to, and she was grateful to be part of the project.

Today, however, it was clear from the start Sue was in a sour mood.

"Just trouble," she said when Nora let her into the manor and led her to the kitchen. "That's what you are, aren't you?" The lines that framed her mouth were cut deeper than usual. "I should have known."

"Known what?" Nora didn't understand what Sue meant. She gestured for her to take a seat at the kitchen table, as usual, but Sue stayed standing.

"That you'd come here and make problems for us. The lot of you."

Nora felt like she'd lost all bearing in their conversation, but before she could protest, Sue continued. "That... Avery." She spit out the name. "She isn't the one for my grandson. He's been promised."

"Avery?" Nora tried to keep up. Was she talking about Avery's crush on Walker? How on earth did she know about that?

Sue clutched the notebooks she held in her arms like a shield against Nora's perfidy. "I heard all about what she'd doing. My nephew saw it with his own eyes."

"Who is your nephew?" Nora felt she owed it to

Avery to get to the bottom of the matter, no matter how awkward this conversation was.

"Tom Norton. He works at the lumberyard in Chance Creek. He brought a delivery to this ranch. He saw." Sue leaned in close to make her point.

A number of trucks had been in and out of Base Camp over the past few weeks. Nora supposed Tom could be one of the men who'd brought supplies. Clay was determined to use locally sourced wood whenever possible, she'd learned from working with him in the mornings. They hadn't had time to cut down trees from their own property and age them, but he'd found local suppliers he'd deemed the best alternative.

"I don't know what Tom saw, and even if I did it wouldn't be my business. Walker is a grown man. He can do what he likes, can't he?" All she wanted was to sit down and talk about curriculum again. She wasn't used to discussing her friends' private lives with strangers. Especially not with someone as fierce as Sue.

"He's promised," Sue reiterated. "So tell her hands off. We won't work today." She retreated as quickly as she'd come, slamming the front door and driving off in her small silver car before Nora could catch up with her. Nora locked the door reflexively and peered out the parlor window after her, watching dust rise along the track with a sinking feeling. Was their project over—when it had only just begun?

She retreated into the parlor and sat on the sofa, flummoxed. What did Sue mean when she said Walker was promised? Was she talking about an arranged marriage?

Did Native Americans do that kind of thing?

Whatever she meant, it spelled trouble for Avery, and that was the last thing her friend needed. Avery wasn't reserved like she was. She wore her heart on her sleeve, and she threw herself headlong into her passions. She'd be too easy to tear down and stomp on. Nora had a feeling Sue was the opposite: tough, no-nonsense and willing to do whatever it took to protect her grandson.

Not that Walker needed protecting.

Walker could take care of himself. It was Avery she was worried about.

As she sat in the parlor by herself, she became aware of how quiet it was. She'd gotten used to the hubbub down in Base Camp, and usually when she came to the manor, the other women were here, too. This afternoon they'd gone to Alice's for a fitting of Savannah's new dress. Nora had stayed behind to meet with Sue. Now she wished she had a car so she could catch up to her friends.

She knew she should get back to work on her novel, but she wasn't making any progress with it, and she found the project she was pursuing with Sue far more interesting. Maybe she should ask Walker for Sue's phone number so she could call and try to work things out.

She could imagine how that would go.

Probably better to wait for Sue to simmer down and come back on her own terms.

Nora gathered up her notebook, thinking that instead of tackling her novel again she'd go over some of the plans she'd made with Sue and keep fleshing out their notes. She had the cell phone today, which meant she could look things up on the Internet if necessary. First she needed a pick-me-up, though. Heading back into the kitchen, she tossed her notebook on the table, grabbed a couple of Avery's homemade cookies, put them on a plate, pulled out a glass from the cupboard and poured herself some lemonade. She put the jug back in the fridge and ran upstairs to fetch a couple of books Sue had let her borrow to gain more background on Crow history and language.

When she came back down, she set them on the table with a thump, and came to a halt with a gasp. On the counter sat two identical glasses of lemonade.

She'd only poured one. Nora was sure of that. She'd poured one and slid the pitcher back onto the top shelf of the refrigerator. Had Avery and Savannah returned while she was upstairs?

Why hadn't she heard them unlock the door? The old-fashioned key made a heck of a racket in the lock.

"Hello?" she called, the hairs on her neck standing on end. She crossed to the fridge, opened it and saw the pitcher right where she'd left it. "Avery? Savannah? Hello!"

There was no answer, but then she'd known there wouldn't be. Nora backed across the kitchen toward the door, relief washing over her when she collided with it. She twisted the door handle and tried to open it.

Locked.

Of course it was. She'd locked it after entering, and she'd let Sue in the front. When Sue had left that way again, she'd locked the front door, too.

She hurriedly twisted the bolt of the kitchen door open, escaped outside and slammed it shut behind her. She fumbled for her key, found it in her pocket and locked it tight.

Even the sunny backyard didn't feel safe, though. Nora clattered down the porch steps and hurried toward Base Camp.

"Nora?"

She slowed down when she spotted Clay coming toward her. "I think there's someone in the manor," she told him as he drew near.

His brows drew together in concern. "Someone like who?"

"I don't know." She quickly related what had happened.

"Sounds like Avery or Savannah playing a trick on you. Are you sure they aren't home?"

"I haven't seen them. James is driving them, so it'd be hard for them to sneak in."

"Okay, let's take a look."

Nora hung back when Clay walked toward the manor, then decided she'd rather be with him than alone. Besides, he didn't have a key.

She let him in reluctantly, and Clay took the lead again. He stepped into the empty kitchen and Nora followed. Both of them halted in the doorway.

"Where's the second glass?" Clay asked.

Words failed her. Where there'd been two glasses, now there was only one. She pointed, her hand trembling. "Th…there," she finally managed to say. "It was right there, by the other one."

Clay moved closer to investigate. "Are you sure? This glass is sweating." He picked it up and indicated the ring left on the counter. "If there was another one and someone moved it, we'd see the ring."

"Unless they wiped up after themselves."

"Maybe. But where did they go?"

"They could be anywhere. That's the thing!" she cried suddenly, pushed to her limit. "Inside, outside. Who knows?"

He looked like he would say something more, but then he nodded. "You really think someone's here?"

"Yes." Would he believe her? Nora didn't know what she'd do if he brushed her off, so when Clay pulled out his phone and placed a call, she breathed a sigh of relief.

"I need everyone up at the manor, stat. Keep a look out as you come for any strangers on the property. Nora says someone was here. No—no description. She didn't see him. I'll explain when you get here."

Her relief came too soon, though. The next hour and a half was a nightmare for Nora. Men in and out of the manor, searching through all of their things. The cameras following them everywhere, recording everything. Her friends arrived partway through and panicked before Nora explained what had happened. Savannah ran upstairs and barred Renata's crew from her room.

"He's not here," Nora heard her yell. "Leave my stuff alone!"

Riley threw away the remaining glass of lemonade and poured Nora a beer.

"Think this will help?" Nora said, taking a long drink.

"I hope so." Riley moved closer. "You don't think Renata uncovered information about your stalker when she looked into our backgrounds, do you? Could she possibly be orchestrating things to make a story?"

Nora hadn't considered that possibility. "If she is, I'm going to strangle her."

"It's all clear. If someone was here, they got away," Boone said finally.

"*If* someone was here?" Nora's voice was sharp. She set the bottle down on the counter. "Someone was here, all right. They poured an extra glass of lemonade, remember?"

All the men in the room shifted, and Nora understood. "You don't believe me!"

"It wasn't there when Clay got here—"

"I checked the front door and it was locked," Clay added. "We came in the back. If someone had been in here, where did they go?"

"That's the whole point. He's trying to drive me insane. He wants me to doubt myself so I'll be more vulnerable."

"Who is?" Boone asked.

"The man who stalked me back in Baltimore."

She caught the look Boone exchanged with Jericho

and her temper flared.

"Where was Sue?" Walker asked before she could say anything. Nora swallowed her fury and answered him. At least he'd asked a reasonable question.

"She walked out on me. She was pissed—about you."

For the first time since she'd known him, Walker looked surprised. "Me?"

"That's right." With a glance at Avery, she subsided into silence. Let him figure it out.

Walker's features schooled themselves into hard lines.

Renata walked into the kitchen. "Nora? Interview time."

"Are you kidding me?" Nora couldn't believe how smug the director looked. No way was she going to be made into a laughingstock on-screen—again. "I bet it was you who did this," she asserted. "One of your crew snuck in, didn't they?"

"No."

"You like to start scenarios and give us little pushes. I wouldn't put it past you."

Renata shook her head. "It wasn't us. And what I'd like to know is how come we've never heard about this stalker of yours? We asked you for details about your lives."

"I didn't feel like sharing that one. Can you blame me? He's only followed me here because your show broadcast my whereabouts."

"We don't know that your stalker *is* here," Clay said

in a placating tone. "There could be other explanations."

"Maybe it's someone who's trying to get a guest appearance on the show," Jericho said. "Some of the people who comment on the website are definitely fringe elements."

"He's right," Renata said, shrugging. "It could very well be a fan."

"If it was someone who wanted to be on the show, they'd make themselves seen," Nora said.

"Maybe they think if they're clever enough they'll get hired on," Boone said.

None of them were taking this seriously. The room was overcrowded, but Nora suddenly felt alone. It didn't matter how many people were around her if no one believed she was in danger.

"It's time for dinner, and I bet everyone's hungry," Riley said reasonably. "Let's lock up the manor and go back to Base Camp. From now on we'll make sure none of us is ever in the house alone."

"We can't rent out rooms as a B and B if we have some man running around breaking in," Nora told her. "He threatened to kill me back in Baltimore, remember?"

That shut everyone up.

"If there's someone sneaking in, they wouldn't come when a crowd was staying here," Savannah ventured.

"You really want to risk it?" Nora stood her ground.

"Let's go eat," Riley said again.

"I want that interview," Renata said.

"Later," Boone told her.

Nora gave up. She opened the back door and ushered everyone outside, including the cameramen, and picked up the notebook and books she'd left on the table earlier, giving the kitchen one last look before walking out and locking the door again.

Someone had been there.

She was sure of it.

CHAPTER EIGHTEEN

DINNER THAT NIGHT was rice and beans, with flatbread and lemon broccoli on the side. Dell turned up, and Clay filled him in on what was happening.

"Sounds like she's working too hard," Dell pronounced.

"She's no dummy, Dad." But Clay wasn't sure what to think of the afternoon's events. On the one hand, he knew Nora was far too level-headed to make something like that up. On the other hand, she'd been stressed out since she got here, and she'd just had an incident with Sue, whom she greatly admired. Couldn't that have caused her to make a mistake? Nora's stalker was definitely on her mind these days.

He joined her and her friends when he'd loaded up his plate, but Nora didn't acknowledge him. Was she angry that he hadn't stood up for her when people cast doubts on her story?

"You never told us why Sue left," Avery said to Nora suddenly.

Nora shrugged. "She's as communicative as Walker is."

Clay sat down next to Nora on a log, but she didn't look his way.

"Walker's not so bad when you get to know him. Our riding lessons have been fun," Avery said.

Nora shook her head.

"What?"

"Maybe you shouldn't spend so much time with him. You don't know him very well."

"Well, if I don't spend time with him, how am I supposed to get to know him?" her friend joked.

"I just don't want you to get hurt if things don't turn out—"

Avery slammed her plate down on the log beside her. "What's this all about?"

Clay, about to take a bite, stopped, his fork in mid-air. He wasn't the only one surprised by Avery's sudden outburst. He spotted a camera crew honing in on them.

Figured.

"You keep assuming Walker won't want me," Avery went on. "Why is that? Boone married Riley, Clay's obviously after you, Jericho's all over Savannah. Why couldn't Walker be interested in me?"

"I never said that. It's just…"

"Just what? That I'm too ugly? Too short? Too boring? What?"

"You're making a scene." Several people were looking their way.

"You're the one who started this. I want an answer!"

Avery demanded.

Nora looked like she wished she'd never brought it up. "I gave you one before—you're too different. All I'm saying is you should guard your heart a little bit more than you normally do. I don't want you to get hurt."

"I—"

"Everything all right here?"

Nora jumped. So did Clay. He hadn't seen Walker approach. That damned trick of his.

"It's fine," Nora said stubbornly.

"No, it's not. Nora's just explaining why no man could ever love me!" Avery said wildly.

Nora wilted under the weight of Walker's gaze. "That's not what I said at all. I told her to be careful. I care about Avery and I don't want to see her hurt."

"Men might be interested," he said in his quiet way. Clay was surprised—that betrayed a lot more of his thoughts than Walker normally shared.

"I never said they couldn't be."

"Then why are you trying so hard to make me feel bad?" Avery was obviously on the verge of tears.

Nora threw up her hands. "Because Walker's spoken for, that's why!"

WALKER WENT SO still Nora thought he'd turned to stone. A silence stretched out between the three of them with nothing but the whir of the cameras to fill it. She would've given anything to take back the words she'd just said. This was none of her business.

Avery turned on him. "What does that mean? You're engaged?" Her eyes widened. "Don't tell me you're married, Walker Norton, or I swear to God—"

"I'm not married." His voice could have sliced through steel. He kept his gaze on Nora. She resisted the urge to take a step back. "Yet."

"Yet?" Avery's voice slid up in an ungainly warble. "Damn it!" She knocked her plate to the ground and strode off toward the cluster of women's tents.

Nora set her plate down and followed her. "Avery."

"Go away." Avery picked up her pace, and when she reached her tent she climbed in and zipped up the fly. "Go away," she shouted again when Nora got there.

"I didn't know how to tell you—"

"Now I know. Are you happy?"

"Of course not! Avery—"

"I love him! Don't you know that? I love him!"

"I know." Nora sat down beside the tent flap. Everyone in camp knew now, if they hadn't before. "I'm so sorry." She listened helplessly to Avery's sobs. Avery was such a kind, caring, open person, without subterfuge. You knew where you stood with her. You didn't worry about what she might be doing behind your back. Exactly the kind of person Fate seemed to single out for its worst betrayals.

There wasn't anything she could do but sit like a guard outside Avery's tent as the sensitive woman inside weathered another blow. The idea of Avery toughening her hide so that the world could carry on in its cynical, cruel way made Nora furious. It was the world that should have to change; not Avery.

"Nora." Avery's hand pressed against the side of the tent some minutes later, long after her sobs had quieted down and a long silence had made Nora wonder if Avery had fallen asleep.

Nora pressed her hand against the dark outline. "I'm here."

"Am I always going to be alone?" Avery whispered.

"No. Of course not," Nora assured her. "Not you. You were made for happiness, Avery." She hoped that was true. "Whatever's going on, Walker cares about you, I know it. I'm not sure what Sue meant when she told me Walker was taken, but he'll figure it out."

"If I can't have him, I don't want anyone," Avery said quietly.

"It's going to be okay," Nora assured her.

But if that was true, why hadn't Walker come to tell Avery himself?

CHAPTER NINETEEN

"**W**HAT THE HELL is this about you being engaged?" Boone asked Walker when Riley, Savannah and Win moved away to the women's side of the camp, huddling together near Savannah's tent, leaving Nora to sit sentry near Avery's.

Clay had never seen Walker look so uncomfortable. "Crow business."

"I don't care if it is. Spill it."

Walker hesitated a long while. "A promise was made. A long time ago."

"Is it a promise you're going to keep?"

After a long moment, Walker shrugged.

"Is she willing to live at Base Camp?"

Walker shrugged again.

"That's not good enough." Boone ran a hand over his short-cropped hair. "Whatever this is about, fix it."

"It'll take time."

"You don't have time! Get it done. Jericho?"

"Yeah?" Jericho sat up when Boone called him out.

"What's the deal with you and Savannah?"

"I'm working on it."

"Work faster!"

"But—"

Boone fixed him with a hard look. "I've had enough of everyone fucking around. I've done my part, but you all are dragging your feet. Pair up and get ready to get hitched. And pass on the message to your crew." Boone stood up and stalked to the bunkhouse. One of the cameramen followed him. The other stayed put, still filming.

"What got into him?" Jericho asked, rising slowly.

"It's got to be Fulsom," Clay said.

"That man better stay out of things," Jericho said. "He's fucked everything up enough."

WHEN AVERY ASKED her to get Riley, Nora got the message and left the two of them alone. She drifted back toward her own tent, anticipating a little quiet time to pull together her thoughts. Her heart ached for Avery. She wasn't sure where Clay had gotten to, but she was grateful not to have to talk to him at the moment. It stung that he didn't fully believe that someone had been in the manor with her earlier. Maybe the scenario stretched credulity, but if he wanted to be her husband, he needed to trust her as much as she'd begun to trust him.

She was so buried in her thoughts she didn't notice Win was coming to intercept her until Win put a hand on her arm.

"Clay loves you," Win said without preamble.

"Whatever's going on—whatever the show's doing to you two, don't let it override how you really feel about him."

"It's not the show." Nora tried to get around her. She wasn't in the mood for this conversation.

Win blocked her again. "Love is special. It's priceless. It doesn't always happen between a man and a woman, no matter how much they wish it would. If what's between you two is real, don't throw it away because of your pride."

"This has nothing to do with pride. I'm being practical."

"Are you?"

Win stepped aside this time. Nora pushed past her and stalked to her tent. Crouching down, she reached to unzip the fly and found it already open. Had she left it that way this morning? If so, her tent would be full of mosquitos. Just what she needed tonight.

Nora crawled through the opening, thoroughly frustrated with the way the day had gone, but her gown caught on the zipper as she turned around to do it up again. She yanked it free, heard the fabric tear and sat down with a thump, ready to scream. The one she'd worn when she'd made love to Clay needed a wash. Now this one was torn. The tent was far too small and stuffy to offer her a comfortable place to nurse her grievances, but where else could she go?

She zipped up the flap brusquely, turned around and settled herself on the bedding she'd left neatly arranged on the floor. The only way to salvage the remainder of the day was to write something. Anything. She reached for her notebook, which she'd stored with her laptop in a canvas bag before going to dinner.

Her laptop was there. So was the little case of pens and pencils she kept with it. The two books Sue had loaned her were there, too.

But her notebook was gone.

She searched the bag again and confirmed her findings. She quickly sorted through the rest of her things, seizing her purse and spilling its contents over her bedclothes. Change, receipts, makeup and her wallet tumbled out. She sighed in relief when she found her cash, credit cards and IDs intact. She hadn't been robbed.

Nora sat back, confused and unnerved all at once. Where was her notebook? Had she left it somewhere?

Up at the manor, she decided. She'd been upset by the time they'd given up on the search. She thought she'd grabbed it when she'd picked up Sue's books, but maybe she hadn't after all.

What about the cell phone?

She patted down her dress and was relieved to find it still in her pocket. Her notebook was probably sitting on the kitchen table.

Unless her stalker had been in her tent, too.

No.

No way he could have been. If she'd brought the notebook down here, it would have been after everyone had searched the manor, which meant ten men, five women and a host of crew members had been scattered through the camp. There was no way anyone could have gotten to her tent without being seen.

Even if everyone had been at dinner, and her tent was one of the farthest from the campfire ring.

Fear prickled down her spine. Nora made herself think hard. She honestly couldn't remember now if she'd had the notebook or not when she'd left the manor, and there was no way she'd go back up there to check—or sound the alarm and make everyone search again. She'd have to wait for daylight and ask her friends to go with her to look for it.

She wouldn't ask Clay.

Nora sat on her pallet and drew up her knees, listening to her surroundings. She could hear the murmur of Avery's and Riley's voices as they talked quietly in Avery's tent. Win's voice came from farther away, with Angus's accented tone answering. She wondered where Savannah had gone. She heard a low murmur of masculine voices probably grouped around the campfire.

She was far from alone, but her tent was on the outskirts of the encampment. Was her stalker watching her even now? Or was she simply losing her mind?

"Nora? Are you in there?"

Clay's voice startled her so badly Nora spun to a crouching position before she realized who it was. Her heart pounding, she unzipped the tent flap and climbed out.

Clay looked tired, and she wondered if he was as frustrated as she was. "I wanted to come by and make sure you're okay. I know you probably want to work," he said.

"I'm all right. Just a little jumpy." She couldn't seem to figure out what to do with her hands. Or what to say to him, either. She was still angry he hadn't seemed to believe her earlier, but she was grateful for his presence now.

"That must have been unnerving up at the manor." He touched her arm.

"And embarrassing," she said frankly, "when no one found anyone."

"Anyone under the stress you've been dealing with could make a mistake." He took her hand.

Nora froze. Surely she couldn't have heard that right.

"If someone was stalking me, I'd see danger every-where." He chuckled. "I do that anyway. After so many years with the SEALs, you get a habit of watching everything."

But she hadn't made a mistake, Nora thought. She tried to tug her hand away, furious that he didn't believe her. Her stalker's tricks were working; everyone thought she was insane.

Maybe she was.

Clay kissed her cheek softly. "How about I stay with you tonight?" he whispered in her ear.

Nora took note of the cameras capturing all this, and reached the limit of her patience. "I don't think so."

"Come on. You'll sleep better with someone else around. Besides, nothing gets past me." Clay brushed his lips over her forehead. Nora blinked at the irony of what he'd just said. How could he think of sex when someone was messing with her sanity? When Walker had as good as admitted he'd been leading Avery on? Could Clay really have such a one-track mind? As if in answer, he added, "I've been thinking about you all day."

"What did Boone want to talk to you about?" she asked aloud to give herself time to settle down. If there had been a paperweight handy, she would have used it, but this wasn't the time or place. There were cameras filming them. The entire camp bustled around them, settling in for the night. Besides, beneath her renewed fury she understood Clay didn't mean to offend her. He was just... being a stupid man.

Clay chuckled again. "He said it's time for us to get a move on and find wives. Nothing new. Anyway, I agree with him. I want to be with you, Nora."

He wanted to be with her, but he thought she was nuts. Just a dumb, delusional woman who saw things because she was stressed out. If she was that fragile, why bother with her? Because he had a deadline to find a wife?

As he bent to press another kiss under her ear, Nora squirmed away from him. "I'm tired, Clay."

He followed her, trying again to pull her into an embrace.

"I said I'm tired!" She shoved him away. The camp went silent, and all eyes turned to look at them. Nora could only growl in frustration, dive back into her tent and close the flap.

"Nora—"

She sat on her pallet and buried her face in her hands. "Go away!" Now she sounded like Avery. She could understand her friend's frustration. If only this day would just end.

After a moment she heard his footsteps move away. Conversations started again all around her, a reassuring murmur that told her she wasn't alone.

But she was alone, wasn't she? Clay didn't believe her.

No one did.

Nora pulled her knees to her chest and rested her forehead on them. Something fundamental had shifted in her life in the month and a half she'd been at Westfield. It had started when she'd lived at the manor with her friends. The ache of loneliness that had resided inside her for so long she hadn't even realized it was there finally let go—replaced by the glow of friendship and togetherness.

These past few days she and Clay had been a couple had dissolved those past hurts even more, until she'd begun to feel like there was hope for a normal life.

Now all that was gone.

Her stalker was ruining her life all over again.

CHAPTER TWENTY

T HE WALK BACK to his tent seemed to stretch for miles. All eyes rested on him as Clay made his way over to it and climbed in.

"Clay? I have a few questions for you." Renata's voice penetrated the thin fabric almost as soon as he'd zipped up the flap.

He just bet she did. "Fuck off, Renata."

"Why don't you believe Nora? Do you think she's unstable? If so, do you worry about any offspring the two of you might have?"

He wanted to burst from the tent, get her in a choke hold and shake her until she gained some sense of dignity and respect, but Clay knew that was exactly the kind of drama Renata was hoping for.

So instead, he dug in his bag, found his cell phone and earbuds and turned his country music up high until she finally went away.

He'd blown it again. Big time.

Renata was right—why had he doubted Nora? Just because something wasn't likely didn't mean it didn't happen.

Another voice finally penetrated the music. Clay turned down the volume on his phone. "What?"

"Let me in." It was Dell.

Clay nearly stuck his earbuds back in, but instead unzipped the fly. "What's wrong?"

Dell pushed his way inside the small tent before Clay could object, and closed it up after him. Clay edged back so Dell could sit, too. As they faced each other, cross-legged, Clay didn't think he'd been this close to his father since he was a boy. A sudden surge of nostalgia for his childhood left him unsettled. All those dinners around the table with his parents and siblings. The times his dad had set them all laughing with an imitation of his boss. The way he'd crowed about their achievements and brought home pizzas to celebrate even though his mom had said a home-cooked meal would be better. Clay realized he'd never told his father how he felt about all of that and the way he appreciated that he'd sacrificed so much to make a good life for his family.

"Dad—"

"Here's the thing," Dell interrupted. "You're going about all this in a completely back-assed way—"

Something within Clay snapped. "For God's sake!" He lunged for the fly, unzipped it and shoved Dell toward the opening.

"What the hell?" Dell struggled to keep his seat.

"Out. Get out, Dad. I don't need any more of your shit. Stop telling me what to do. Stop telling me how I fucked up. Just… get the hell out of here!"

Dell clamped his mouth shut, surged to his feet, stepped out of the tent and stalked away. Clay thought he'd head for his truck, but instead he struck out toward Pittance Creek.

Whatever, Clay thought. He'd had enough. If Dell wasn't gone by morning, he'd throw his dad out.

MANY HOURS LATER, Clay was woken from an uneasy sleep by the sound of shouting. At first he thought it was the glow of the rising sun that traced the shadows on his tent, but when sleep dissipated and he focused on the shouts, a word penetrated the fog still slowing down his mind.

"Fire!"

He was wide awake and out of his tent a second later. He spotted the flames and ran toward them, other members of the community flocking around him.

"Bucket brigade!" someone shouted.

"Get the hose." Another voice pierced the darkness.

Clay dashed to help. He was relieved to see it wasn't Boone and Riley's house in flames, but the second one they'd started to frame in was engulfed in fire.

The house that should have been his and Nora's.

He stumbled with the realization, but caught himself and kept going. Walker already manned a hose—an extension from the bunkhouse. Others were dashing back and forth from the bunkhouse with buckets filled from an outside tap. Even members of the camera crew were helping out. Clay grabbed a shovel and moved close to start throwing dirt on the nearest flames. A short time later he looked up to find Nora doing the same beside him. She bent to the task with a will, never pausing or complaining. She was still dressed, and Clay wondered if she'd slept at all. Regret bit deep for the way he'd left her earlier. He wanted to say something—to apologize—but the fire had to be their first priority. He was still working flat out when trucks from the volunteer fire district came roaring up the lane.

They extinguished the remainder of the flames quickly, while the cameramen raced to film the action for the show. Clay leaned on the handle of his shovel, catching his breath.

"How on earth did it start?" Nora asked, coming to stand next to him.

"I don't know." He scraped the sweat from his brow with the back of his hand. He realized he was barefoot, dressed only in his boxer briefs. He didn't care; everyone else had been roused from bed, too.

"All right, people. Go clean up. Kai, you want to get some coffee going?" Boone called out. "Clay, Jericho, Walker—come with me."

"Nora—"

"You'd better go talk to Boone. Find out how this happened." Her brows were furrowed. "How could the house catch fire all on its own?"

He shrugged. "I'll find you later. In the morning. We have to talk."

Nora nodded and turned away. She moved slowly, probably worn out by the unaccustomed exercise. Even in the dim light he could see her dress was ruined.

"Nora," he called after her. "Thanks."

"For what?" She turned around.

"Helping to put out the fire."

He couldn't read her expression in the dim light. "Of course," she finally said, and kept going.

Clay wanted to go after her. Instead he ducked into his own tent, quickly pulled on some clothes and went to find Boone.

He found him huddled with the local fire chief, Walker and Jericho. Every cameraman in the place was filming something. Renata had cornered Kai on his way to the bunkhouse and was trying to interview him. "What do you know so far?"

"Come and take a look at this," Ed Brookings, the fire chief, said. He led the way to the smoldering ruins of the small house, turned on a bright flashlight and pointed out the damage at several places around what was left of the structure. Cameramen swarmed around to document what he was saying.

"What does that show?" Jericho asked.

"Arson," Walker said. "Multiple start points. Someone used an accelerant."

"That's right," Brookings said. "You boys know someone who wants to shut you down?"

"WOULD YOU HELP me change?" Nora asked Avery when she found her friends talking near the tents.

"Of course. I need to change, too." Avery held up her arms to indicate her filthy nightgown.

"We should just go up to the manor," Riley said in a low voice. "Each of us could take a hot soak and we could wash our clothes, too."

"Renata's people would have a field day with that." Savannah nodded toward Ed, who was even now filming the scene.

"You'd think they'd focus on the fire," Nora said grumpily. A hot bath would be heaven right now. She didn't relish the thought of scrubbing off the soot and sweat in a cold shower in the bunkhouse. "I don't know how I'm ever going to get this dress clean again." She pulled out one of her work gowns. It was in much better shape than either of her nicer ones.

"I heard one of the firemen say the fire was deliberately set," Avery said.

Nora stilled. "It was arson?"

"Who would do that?" Savannah asked.

"That developer, Montague, maybe?" Riley asked. She was pale and knew what Riley must be thinking—their tiny home was a stone's throw from the one that had burned down. What if someone had set it on fire? Would the alarm have roused them in time?

"Maybe," Savannah said. "Or maybe your stalker decided to take things to the next level, Nora."

Nora blinked. "I thought you guys didn't believe he was here." Of course she'd thought the same thing, but after what had happened this afternoon, she'd been afraid to bring it up.

"The glass, the book, the lemonade and now this? I think it's at least time to investigate it," Savannah told her.

"I think so, too," Avery said.

"Something else strange happened earlier." Nora filled them in quickly.

"You definitely had your notebook when you came down here," Riley said. "I saw you carrying it. You'd better go talk to Boone."

"I saw it, too," Savannah said.

Nora wasn't sure why tears stung her eyes, but she blinked them back and swallowed the lump in her throat. She was so stupid; she should have asked her friends earlier if they'd seen her bring her notebook down to Base Camp.

"Okay." She looked down at her soot-smudged dress and decided she'd deal with it later. "I'll be right back."

She wound her way through the tents toward the burnt skeleton of the tiny house, where Clay and the others still stood, talking, a couple of the cameramen still filming them. As she approached the group, she guessed none of them would sleep tonight. Their deep voices rumbled in urgent tones as they talked—the sound of men making a plan. She hung on the outskirts of their circle a little shyly at first, not wanting to interrupt. In the low light, with the smell of smoke still wafting around them, they were more SEALs than civilians, and she wasn't sure if they'd welcome her.

Still, she had a piece of pertinent information they didn't know.

"Kai, I want you and Harris to—" Boone was saying when she took a deep breath and pushed her way through the circle.

"Excuse me."

Boone looked up. "Nora, we've got it under control. Let the women know—"

"I have to tell you something."

He scanned her face. "All right. Shoot."

"Something happened today. After we got back from the manor." She described bringing home the notebook, stowing it with her other things in the tent and zipping up the flap when she left.

"When I came back from dinner the flap was open and the notebook was gone."

"Are you sure you—"

"Riley saw me bring the notebook back. So did Savannah," she said firmly. She was done being doubted.

Done doubting herself, too.

After a long moment, Boone nodded. "Okay. Someone was in your tent. I'm not sure it has any bearing on this, though." He gestured toward the burned down building.

"The thing is… that lemonade glass and the notebook? Those aren't the only strange things that have happened since I've come to Westfield."

"You haven't heard from your stalker since you left Baltimore, right?" Clay said. When she hesitated, his brows drew together. "Nora, are you serious?"

"He hasn't called, if that's what you mean. It's just… there have been a couple of times…" She knew she had to bite the bullet and explain everything, even if it did sound ridiculous. "Once Avery, Savannah and I were in the kitchen up at the manor and a glass fell off the desk and broke in the parlor. I'd left it far from the edge, and there was no water at all on the desk afterward. Someone had to have picked it up and dropped it. We searched the house and didn't find anyone."

"You searched—" Clay shook his head. "Jesus, Nora." The other men looked as concerned as he did, but Nora pressed on. After all, who were they to chastise her for not speaking up? None of them had believed her today, had they?

"Another time I went up to my room and found the door open. I thought I'd shut it. Nothing was missing. Nothing had been touched, except... a book. It was pulled partway out from my bookshelf. I hadn't touched it in weeks."

"What book?" Boone asked. She was grateful they weren't all laughing at her. The incidents sounded so trivial.

"It was a textbook. It's called, *The Teacher as Student.*"

"Does that have any significance?"

Nora didn't want to answer that. Not in this crowd of men forming a circle around her. Their testosterone was palpable—and it made her uncomfortable. "It's something he used to say." She forced the words out. "That I had nothing to teach him. But he had a lot to teach me. He liked to describe... what he'd do to me." She was almost whispering by the time she finished. Saying it out loud made her skin crawl. She wanted to block the memory of the other things he'd said, but she failed.

"Anything else?" Boone prompted.

"That's it."

"Why didn't you say anything sooner?" Clay said.

"Each incident by itself seemed trivial. Impossible to prove. Look at the way you all reacted this afternoon."

"But that's because—"

"None of that matters now," Boone broke in. "The only thing that does is finding the man who set the fire and keeping Nora safe in the meantime. Clay, from now on, you're Nora's bodyguard."

She almost laughed, it sounded so ridiculous, but when she turned to Clay, there wasn't a trace of humor in his face. Instead, he was alert, concerned... focused. Clay nodded to Boone. "I'm on it." He turned to Nora. "Until we catch this motherfucker, wherever you are, I am."

Nora realized he meant it, too. Just like that, he'd take on responsibility for her safety. He'd spend every minute of his day protecting her.

Something clicked in Nora's brain. Something so simple, and yet so important it was hard to put into words. She kept judging Clay as if he were any man—someone like her father, or her stalker, even, but that wasn't who Clay was. He was a man who made a decision and stuck with it. A man dedicated to service—to his fellow citizens, to his country—and, ultimately, to the world.

Earlier she'd laughed at his inability to see what was right in front of his face, as if being a SEAL should have made him infallible. But it wasn't his skills or training—or some superpower he'd gained from his service—that defined who he was. It was his willingness to give his life to protect someone else.

And his willingness to give his heart to one woman for a lifetime.

Someone who maybe didn't deserve his heart.

In a flash she understood that just like his unswerving dedication to service, he'd never deviated from his devotion to her. He'd told her he'd fallen for her the moment he saw her.

And he'd never wavered since.

It had nothing to do with Base Camp or the television show. He already loved her. He was already sure. He was ready to pledge himself to her, build a home for her, protect her—give his life for her if need be. She kept looking for complications and he kept handing her a single, solid truth.

No man had ever cared for her like that before. No wonder she hadn't understood.

"I'll take Nora and the women to the bunkhouse," Clay was saying. "That's the easiest place to monitor."

"Sounds good," Boone said. "We'll start a search and keep a watch for this asshole."

"Copy that."

"Clay," Nora began, needing to tell him about her revelation. "Clay, I—"

But as the group broke apart, the fire chief strode

up again. "Found something. Anyone recognize this?" He held up something white. A T-shirt, maybe?

Clay, who'd been so warrior-like moments ago he'd made her heart race, faltered mid-stride.

"Yeah, I recognize it," he said. He took the shirt from the chief and held it out to read the logo. A high school wrestling team. "It's my dad's."

CHAPTER TWENTY-ONE

CLAY COULDN'T BELIEVE what the fire chief had pulled from the ruins of the blaze. Nor could he believe that Dell was nowhere to be found when they went looking for him. Despite the fact he'd been headed for Pittance Creek the last time Clay saw him, his truck was now gone.

Had he set the fire because of their fight?

Jericho took over as Nora's bodyguard and rounded up the women in the bunkhouse.

"Don't jump to conclusions," Boone told Clay when they were gone. "This is your dad you're talking about."

But what was Clay supposed to think?

"Your father's never broken the law before," Boone said. "Besides, why would he set one of the houses on fire? He wanted to live here, right?"

"Only until Mom took him back." But Boone was right. His mother would never take Dell back if she thought he'd committed a crime. And his father was no criminal.

Although he'd been under a hell of a strain lately.

Over and over again, Clay replayed their last conversation in his mind. He saw himself unzip the tent and tell his father to get out.

Had that been the final straw?

"Are you sure that's his shirt?" Boone asked.

"It's definitely his shirt," Clay confirmed.

"Why would he leave it at the fire as evidence? It doesn't make sense."

"He meant for it to burn, obviously. He didn't think there would be evidence."

"Well, we've set a watch. There's not much more we can do until the sun comes up. Time for everyone to get a little shut-eye. We'll reconvene at first light and figure this out."

There was no way Clay could go to sleep, though. Not until he knew if his father was involved.

He wanted to go to Nora, but what would she say now that it seemed clear his father had set the fire instead of her stalker? Could there really be two men creating mayhem at Westfield?

It seemed so.

Instead of returning to the bunkhouse, he sat on a log near the fire someone had kindled and waited for dawn's gray light to replace the inky darkness of the night. Once they'd found out for sure who'd done it, he'd have to start all over again to build the second house. Just when he thought he'd been getting ahead. Whoever had started the fire had hit him where it hurt.

Which made him doubly suspicious that it could be

Dell.

It was nearly dawn when an engine in the distance roused Clay from a half-slumber. He shook himself awake, and when Dell's truck pulled up, he got to his feet and went to meet his father.

"Where were you?"

Deep lines grooved Dell's face, and he stooped a little as he got out of the truck and closed the door. Clay didn't care if he was tired. He wanted answers.

"I said, where were you?"

Dell frowned. He must have caught a whiff of the charred building because he swung his head around to survey the building site. "What happened?"

"You tell me, old man. Why did you set that fire?"

"I didn't set any fire." When Dell tried to push past him, Clay stepped into his path.

"Tell the truth! Now!"

"I don't know what you're talking about." Dell tried to elbow him aside again.

Clay stood firm. "Are you sure? Because someone set that fire. Took out the house I started. I want to know who did it."

Dell finally seemed to register the severity of the accusation. He looked at the housing site again, took in Boone's house and then the burnt out skeleton nearby. "Shit."

"Yeah, shit. So the question of the hour is, where were you when the fire started?"

For a long, horrible moment, Clay thought Dell would refuse to answer. When he finally did, his head hung low and he couldn't look Clay in the eyes. "I went home. Tried to get your mother to take me back. She refused."

Clay almost felt sorry for him.

Almost.

It could easily be a cover story. If he woke Lizette in the middle of the night and begged her to take him back—or argued with her, more likely—she might get muddled on times when she was questioned later.

Or maybe she'd cover for him no matter what; they were husband and wife.

Dell had been furious that Clay hadn't followed his lead on the house. He'd been even angrier when Clay had assigned him the job of building the tool shed. They'd fought last night. He certainly had a motive.

So did Nora's stalker, though.

"I said, she refused," Dell reiterated.

Clay sniffed the air. Dell didn't smell of alcohol. He'd never been much of a drinker. More his style to drive for miles when he was angry, wasting fuel and polluting the air—

But that didn't matter tonight.

"Dad, the fire chief found your shirt in the wreckage. How do you explain that?"

"My shirt?"

"Your Chance Creek High wrestling shirt. You know the one."

Dell shook his head. "I looked for that shirt last night. I was going to wear it and remind your mother of the past—all the time we spent together. I couldn't find it."

All that T-shirt would remind his mother of is how stubborn Dell could get. "Are you saying someone took it?"

"I had it yesterday."

Clay paced away from him. Was it coincidence that both Dell and Nora were missing items? Was his father being framed? Maybe some of the film footage could clear up some of these mysteries.

"Come on."

"Where?"

"To the fire station. You'd better tell the chief everything you know."

"I'M GLAD YOU told them everything," Avery said to Nora as the women worked to clean up after breakfast. They'd taken over the job from Kai, but kept things simple. Eggs, toast and cereal.

Nora nodded, scrubbing down the battered counter of the bunkhouse kitchen with a dishrag. She felt numb. The events of the past few weeks had taken on a surreal quality in her mind and she didn't know what to think anymore. Had a student—a teenager—actually followed her to Chance Creek? Why not transfer his ire to the new teacher grading him? Had she been wrong all this time? Was it about something other than grades?

"Don't expect sanity from a psychopath," Cab Johnson, the local sheriff, had told her early this morning when he'd come to take her statement. She supposed he was right. Still, even though she'd taught seventeen and eighteen year olds who definitely had the bodies of full grown men, they rarely had much spending money, or cars, or the means to travel all this way and watch her for weeks. It was hard to believe any of it in the light of day.

Still, the tight coil of dread in her belly wouldn't loosen, despite the fact that she and her friends had spent the night together in the bunkhouse with Jericho watching over them, and the knowledge that some of the other men were guarding the ranch outside. Nora wondered how the men could continue to function on so little sleep, but Savannah reminded her that as Navy SEALs they had survived far worse.

Jericho entered the kitchen. Walker came in behind him. "The sheriff and the fire chief are back for another look around. The place is crawling with law enforcement, and some of the men from local ranches are here, too. So the good news is you won't have to spend the day cooped up in here. We're going to reassign people today. Riley and Savannah, you're going to help me out on the solar project. We've got to get it up and running pronto so we can have more lights in camp. Boone and Clay will deal with Cab and the fire chief. Walker, you take Avery and Nora to town. Stock up on everything while you're there. With the extra men hanging around, we'll be feeding a crowd tonight."

"We get to go to town?" Avery echoed. "Thank God. This place is giving me the creeps right now."

"But shouldn't Nora have more people to guard her?" Riley asked. "No offense, Walker."

Walker shrugged.

"We've got that in hand," Jericho said. "You'll have a unit following you to town to see if you pick up a tail."

Nora didn't like the sound of that.

"You're using Nora as bait?" Savannah said.

"Sort of. This guy's M.O. is to be opportunistic. He won't go after Nora in plain sight of other people, but he obviously does his homework and takes chances when he gets them. We're hoping to catch him trailing Nora before he ever gets the chance to attack her. Chance Creek's sheriff's department doesn't have the manpower to watch the ranch on an ongoing basis, and we've got too few men to keep an eye on everything all the time so we'll give this a try and see if we can draw him out. Walker will be in contact with the unit at all times. Don't worry; we've got all our bases covered. This guy, whoever he is, is an amateur. He's going to make a mistake."

Nora realized she wouldn't feel any safer remaining here. Not with the smell of smoke in the air from the charred remains of the second tiny house. She was off-kilter and anxious. "I'll stick to Walker like glue," she assured the others. "Any stalker won't stand a chance."

Jericho answered all of Riley's and Savannah's concerns. Avery helped Nora jot down a quick list of supplies they needed. There were a lot of them, and Nora was too jittery to think straight. She was sure she'd forgotten several things, but when Avery pointed out she'd written down onions twice, she decided it was time to go. They'd simply have to walk up and down all the aisles in the grocery store so they didn't miss anything.

After several rounds of hugs and "be carefuls" from Riley and Savannah, Nora was relieved when they finally got in the truck and left Westfield behind. She settled in happily, feeling safe on the bench seat between Avery and Walker. Renata had insisted they take William, too, and he sat behind them in the extended cab, filming everything.

Avery kept turning around.

"I don't see anyone. I thought a cop car was supposed to follow us."

"The sheriff is following us. If you saw him, so would our mark. He'll hang back," Walker said.

"I don't see anyone else, either. I don't think your stalker is following us, Nora."

"Just because you can't see him doesn't mean he isn't there."

Nora's relief at leaving the ranch disappeared. Walker was right. Whoever it was had managed to sneak into their house several times without them noticing. Into her tent, too.

He'd burned down a house.

It seemed improbable that the sun would rise and shine brightly today after the night they'd been through, but it had done so in a sky so blue it dazzled her. Gradually her anxiety dimmed again and anger took its place. First her stalker had stolen her self-confidence, then he'd stolen her career and now he was stealing Westfield and the life she'd tried to build here.

That stopped right now, she decided. She wasn't going to hand over her future to him. She'd let the fire chief and sheriff do their investigating, and the men of Base Camp keep her safe. Meanwhile, she'd act like she always did.

In the store, she walked purposefully with her shoulders thrown back, refusing to skulk through the aisles looking constantly over her shoulders. When her dress raised the eyebrows of the other customers, she met their gazes head on and refused to be the first one to look away. At all times she was aware of Avery by her side and Walker a pace behind them, his eagle eyes taking everything in. William trailed Walker. Walker ignored him.

She glanced at her list, wondering what she was forgetting.

"There are the beans. Which kind do you need?" Avery interrupted her thoughts.

"Black beans. Lots of them. The way people keep flooding into the ranch, we'd better make enough tacos to feed half the town. We're going to do veggie ones and beef ones, so we'll need a bunch of ground beef, too."

They bent to make their choices, then moved on to pick out tortillas, ground beef and sour cream. Cab met up with them in the dairy aisle.

"No one followed us?" Walker asked him.

The sheriff shook his head. "Not that I saw. I'll stick close, though."

"We've only got a couple more things to find."

Nora scanned the list again. After all they'd gone through to get to the store, so she didn't want to forget anything.

Concentrating, she followed Avery through the rest of the aisles, ticking things off the list as they found them, and pointing to items she hadn't even considered before she saw them. Still, something was nagging at her. Something she'd miss if she went home without it.

"That's it," Avery declared fifteen minutes later. "We've seen everything."

Not everything, Nora thought. Not the thing she was forgetting. It was beginning to drive her crazy. But with three other people waiting for her to declare their trip done, there was nothing for it but to head for the till.

"We'll probably need to come here again in the next few days," Nora told Walker as she pushed the cart toward the front of the store. "I know I've forgotten something. Sorry," she added. "This isn't a good time to be disorganized."

"Oh, Walker's used to it," Avery said with a laugh. "You should see me trying to get ready to help him each morning. I get almost to the barn and then have to turn around and go back for my gloves or my apron. He calls me Avery Latefoot instead of Avery Lightfoot."

Nora turned to Walker in surprise, in time to see him freeze for half a second—the Walker equivalent of embarrassment. He recovered so quickly she would have missed it if she hadn't been looking at him so closely.

"Walker told a joke?" Cab's laugh boomed out. "Didn't know you had it in you, buddy." He slapped Walker on the back.

Avery touched Walker's hand. "He's a very surprising man."

Avery's admiration for the big man was so clear, Nora wanted to reach out and shield her. She was going to get hurt. Sue had said—

A woman's roar of outrage cut across all their chatter and the soft pop music playing in the background of the grocery store. Nora froze. Avery ducked, and both men spun into motion. Walker swept Nora and Avery behind him, and drew a gun Nora hadn't known he was carrying. Cab reached for his sidearm, already breaking into a run toward the sound. William pressed himself up against the shelves and held his camera in front of him like a shield.

Cab didn't have to go far.

Sue Norton stormed forward, all five feet of her quivering with rage. Nora had never seen the Crow woman betray much emotion, so the spectacle in front of her was all the more shocking.

"Walker Norton, you're shaming your family, your ancestors and the very land you dare walk on. How can you do it? How?"

Cab, the closest to her, lifted his hand from his holstered weapon. "Sue, this isn't the time."

"Put that idiotic gun away before I take it away." Sue ignored Cab and confronted her grandson. "You want to end up dead like your father? Or do you think if you kill enough people you'll somehow set things right? Let the dead avenge the dead."

William straightened and pushed forward to capture the argument on film.

Nora exchanged a look with Avery. Her heart still pounding with shock, she straightened, and Avery did, too. She couldn't see Walker's face, but he stood stock-still and let his grandmother's words pour over him.

"Put it away!" Sue swatted at the gun, and Walker yanked it back, then thrust it into a shoulder holster hidden under his light jacket. "Guns. Always guns with you. And now women. White women." She said something in a language Nora couldn't understand.

"Sue, you gotta calm down." Cab moved closer but kept sweeping the store with his gaze, alert for any trouble.

Sue turned and swatted him. "Stay out of Crow business. This isn't your jurisdiction, Sheriff."

"You're not on Crow land," Cab retorted.

If Sue had been angry before, now she was furious. "Not on Crow land? Everywhere you look is Crow land. Everywhere you serve is Crow land—" She struck Cab again.

"Stop it," Avery cried. "Cab's not the one you're mad at!"

Sue turned on Avery. "You got that right. Keep your hands off my grandson. You don't belong here. None of you belong here."

"Grandma." Walker finally found his voice.

"Sue, let's take this outside, shall we?" Cab said.

Taco seasoning.

Nora had no idea why the missing item suddenly popped into her mind, but there it was. Taco seasoning. Without it, the tacos she was supposed to serve tonight to all the people who'd come to help them would be a bust.

Sue hit Walker this time—a hard swat. "Always with the white girls. Always. What's wrong with you men? Why are you turning your back on—"

Nora glanced from the argument in front of her to the ethnic food aisle only steps away. She could see jars of salsa from here. The spice packets had to be just a few feet farther away. She could be there and back before anyone noticed, and with the gathered crowd she'd be perfectly safe.

She edged back, keeping one eye on her friends and the cameraman avidly filming them. Most of the shoppers in the store had been drawn to the front by the argument. They stood peeking out from other aisles, or stood at the tills and gaped at Sue.

"She's something," a white-haired woman told her friend. "Maybe I oughta yell at my grandson like that. Maybe then he'd remember to mow my lawn once in a while."

"Good luck," her companion said. "She's right; they don't make men like they used to."

Nora edged around them and into the ethnic food aisle. There it was. Right there. Just another three feet....two...one—

"Gotcha," said a familiar voice.

The world went dark.

CHAPTER TWENTY-TWO

CLAY SHIFTED AGAIN on the uncomfortable plastic chairs in the waiting room at the Chance Creek sheriff's office, where they'd been sitting for several hours.

"Why are we sitting here if the sheriff is somewhere else?" Dell asked him again. "Waste of time."

"This is where they want us, so this is where we'll stay," Clay said, but he knew what his father meant. He wanted to be back at the ranch—guarding Nora. He told himself there were plenty of men there to do that job, but it didn't help calm his nerves. He couldn't believe how much she'd held back from him. It was his fault, really. He'd assumed from everything she'd said that her stalker was ancient history. He'd never asked if she'd seen anything unusual since she'd come to West-field.

He'd let her down.

"Just a few more minutes," the receptionist said, but she'd been saying that for the last hour, and Clay didn't believe it any more than Dell probably did.

"Waste of time," Dell said again.

Clay fought against the urge to snap at him. That wouldn't accomplish anything, but he wasn't sure how much more of this he could take. He didn't understand how he'd become his father's babysitter. If anything, his mom should be here.

His mom.

Clay pulled out his phone and typed a quick and enigmatic text to her. "At the sheriff's office with Dad." That ought to hook her. He waited, counting the seconds.

"Be right over," she texted back.

Clay bit back a grin. Time to hand over the problem of his father once and for all.

Ten minutes later, Lizette arrived. Five foot five, with short curly hair and a pleasant face, she normally lit up any room she entered, but today she looked like thunder.

"Dell Pickett, what did you do?" She stormed into the waiting room and turned from one to the other of them. Dell stood up. So did Clay.

"I didn't do anything."

"Then it's you?" She turned on Clay.

"Not me. I'm innocent," Clay began, but Lizette snorted.

"Innocent, my ass. When have either of you ever been anything but trouble?"

"Now, Lizette—"

"Don't Lizette me. I've waited for years for you to become the man I wanted to live with. All you've done is put it off and make excuses. I thought kicking you out would bring you to your senses but I was wrong again. I suppose you expect me to bail you out?"

"Mom—"

"Forget it! I've had it—with both of you. How can two intelligent men be so goddamn stupid?"

"I've applied to every damn job in a fifty-mile radius," Dell roared suddenly. "Not just construction, but gas stations, grocery stores, fast-food joints. None of them want me. I'm doing my best!"

Clay held his breath. He'd heard his parents fight before, but not like this. He understood his mother's frustration—and his father's—but he didn't want a bad economy or a lost job to tear his family apart. His father had been far too baffled by the arson for Clay to keep believing he was the perpetrator. Dell wasn't good at subterfuge. Still, he didn't know what to say to diffuse the situation.

"For the last time!" Lizette yelled back. "I don't want you to take another construction job, or a handyman job, and I sure as shootin' don't want to see you bagging groceries when I go to shop!"

"Then what do you want? Because I don't know what to do here!" Dell's voice snagged at the top of his range, and Clay swallowed hard. He couldn't stand to watch his father come undone. He wanted to back away—to get the hell out of there—but there was nowhere to go.

"I don't want to tell you!" Lizette's eyes shone with tears. "I want you to have the guts to look in your heart, see what you're passionate about and make it happen! Jesus, Dell. When are you going to get it?" Without another word she stormed out, leaving Dell and Clay to stare at each other.

"She keeps saying that. I have no idea what she means." Dell turned, too, and walked toward the front door.

"Mr. Pickett." The receptionist, who'd watched everything openmouthed, stood. "Mr. Pickett, you're not supposed to leave."

Dell ignored her and walked out the door. Clay quickly followed him. "Dad? Where are you going?"

"Back to Base Camp. I'm getting my things. I'm getting the hell out of here."

"You can't do that." Clay caught up to him as Dell opened the truck door and climbed into the passenger seat.

"I'm not staying."

Clay decided Cab could find them as easily at Base Camp as he could at the sheriff's office. He got in and backed out, turned the truck around and headed toward the ranch.

"You can't leave Base Camp," he said when they finally pulled in the dusty lane.

"Fine." Dell got out when they parked and slammed the door behind him. He stalked toward the tents past the bunkhouse, where a group of men had gathered. Clay recognized faces from town he hadn't seen in years. Others were more familiar from the weeks he'd been back in Chance Creek. They must have heard about the fire and come to lend a hand with the clean-up. "Get out of my way," Dell said.

"Aren't you the one who started the fire?" one of the ranchers demanded.

"Hell, no," Dell said, starting toward him.

Not another fight. Clay ran to break it up before things got out of hand, but yanked out his cell phone when it buzzed in his pocket.

"Hey, make it quick," he said as Dell and the rancher began to size each other up.

"Walker here. Clay... I lost her."

SOMETHING HARD BENEATH her. Aching head. Dark. A musty smell of aging wood.

As Nora came around, she had no idea how to piece together these clues to form an image of her whereabouts. When she tried to move, she found her hands were bound behind her back. She lay on her side on a wooden floor that hadn't been cleaned in... years, maybe.

She blinked the dust out of her eyes and lifted her head, recognizing the old one-room schoolhouse where she and Clay had made love for the first time. A dull ache blossomed at the back of her head. She didn't think she'd been struck, though. She had a dim memory of a voice. Something sharp.

As if triggered by the memory, a tiny prick of pain in her neck made everything swing into focus. He'd stuck her with something. A needle.

He...

Nora sucked in a breath.

Andrew Pennsley.

Andrew. Why…?

She struggled to a sitting position, an exercise in frustration without the use of her hands. Finally upright, her mouth tasting like chalk and ash, she tried to figure it out. Andrew, a fellow teacher back in Baltimore. What was he doing in Chance Creek?

Why had he…?

In a flash, her stupidity became all too clear. All this time she'd blamed a student for stalking her. She'd spent day after day in her classroom scanning the eyes that looked back at her, looking for guilt. Or hate. Or something to indicate who was tormenting her.

But it had never been a student. It had been a teacher.

Andrew.

She'd never even considered him.

Stupid. Stupid, stupid.

Of course it was Andrew. Two years ago, right after her mother passed away, she'd been asked to team-teach a group of eleventh graders. Dazed with pain and loss, she'd welcomed the chance to share the work with another teacher, and she'd been happy to be paired with a man who took his job as seriously as she did. Andrew, a Social Studies teacher, was known as a man who could control his classroom—as well as hold his students' attention. It had all been a big relief until he asked her out. Nora didn't dislike him. He simply wasn't her type, and she'd been too hurt by her mother's passing to want to be with anyone at the time.

She'd explained all that to him when she turned him down, and thought Andrew had understood. He waved away her apologies, and they'd gone on to teach together for the remainder of the year. The small awkwardness of the situation paled beside losing her mother, and Nora hadn't given it another thought. The following year when they'd been asked to team-teach again, Andrew had agreed, but Nora had declined, and instead had taken over a twelfth grade English position. Andrew paired up with her replacement. He nodded at her when they met in the hall, and she smiled back.

Problem solved.

Except as Nora's eyes adjusted and she took in her surroundings—the dirty floor, the huddle of old-fashioned desks, the boarded up windows—she realized the problem had never been solved after all.

Andrew was still angry.

Furious was a better word. From his point of view she'd turned him down twice. Once as a possible lover. A second time as a teacher.

You think you have so much to teach me. You're wrong.

She'd thought those messages were from a student unhappy with his grades, but it was Andrew who thought he didn't measure up in her eyes.

And he'd taken her prisoner—in the same schoolhouse where she'd made love to Clay for the first time.

Coincidence?

Nora hoped so, because if Andrew had watched them—

Nausea clawed at the back of her throat. Every phone message Andrew had ever left for her crowded into her mind. The threats. The descriptions. The violent, sexual messages.

She had to get out of here.

Now.

Getting to her feet wasn't easy, and the first time she tried she fell flat in the dirt and dust that formed a layer over the old wooden floor. She inched over to the wall, braced herself against it and managed to get up, leaving smears of dirt down the side of her gown.

She was afraid to scream. Afraid Andrew was nearby somewhere, and that she'd lose her chance to escape by calling attention to the fact she was awake.

Chinks of light from gaps in the plywood sheets over the windows let in enough light to see clearly now that the drug Andrew had pumped into her system was wearing off. At one end of the large room was an old-fashioned chalkboard. At the other end of the room was the door. She ran to it, her feet thankfully unbound, and turned to grab the handle with her hands as best she could with them tied behind her back.

It didn't turn. Had Andrew locked it somehow from the outside?

Nora twisted and turned the knob carefully, still afraid to attract Andrew's attention, but the door refused to open. In desperation, she made a quick circuit of the room, looking for another way out, but there wasn't one. The boards across the windows were screwed too tightly into the wooden frames to budge.

She searched in vain for something to cut through the ropes binding her wrists. With mounting panic, Nora returned to the desks that were pushed into the corner and opened them one after another, desperate to find something—anything—to help.

They were all empty.

Finally she had to admit what some part of her had known since she opened her eyes.

When Andrew came back, she'd still be here.

And he'd get his chance to follow through on his threats.

CHAPTER TWENTY-THREE

"**C**LAY, IT'S CAB. Breathe and listen to me."

It was a good thing Walker was off the line, because somehow Clay would have crawled through their cell phone connection and beat his friend to a bloody pulp if he had the chance. How could Walker have lost Nora?

He'd never forgive him. "Tell me you have a plan."

"I've got a plan. We'll have her back within the hour. We're fanning out from ground zero here at the store. I've called in backup from all over the state. We'll have an eye in the sky in a matter of minutes."

"I'll be there sooner than that."

"No—I want you to stay there."

"Like hell—"

"Your man's been watching Nora. Stalking her. For weeks, most likely. He's got a hidey hole nearby; he has to. You've got to find it. If there are any clues as to where he's taken her, they'll be there. I'm counting on you to find them."

That made sense. Clay clutched the phone so hard

he wouldn't have been surprised if it shattered. "I'm on it. Let me know the minute you have news."

"Will do."

Clay cut the line and faced the men who'd only moments before been on the verge of a fight. They must have heard the seriousness of his tone.

"It's Nora. She's gone. Abducted."

Thank God these were men who knew how to get a job done. No lengthy explanations were needed. Within moments he, Boone and Jericho were in a huddle. Seconds later, everyone had been given their orders.

Clay left Savannah and Riley putting the call out for people to join a search party. There were already plenty of men set to fan out and beat the bushes for clues, his father included. With a terse explanation of what they were looking for, he and Boone got everyone in place, and he was finally able to get to the task at hand.

Half the team started at the bunkhouse. The other half started at the manor. They walked in step, examining every square foot of ground they covered. Clay swore under his breath when he thought about the way Nora had kept quiet about her fears. If they'd known more, maybe they'd have caught her attacker before he got to her. But whose fault was that? With cameras filming everything, no wonder she hadn't wanted to talk about her stalker. Hell, the man only knew where she was because of the stupid show.

And then, when she'd finally spoken up, no one believed her.

Of course, the stalker had gotten to Nora even after

they'd known.

If only Dell hadn't distracted him from watching over Nora. All his father had been since he'd arrived was—

Clay forced the thoughts from his mind. *Focus. Scan the ground.* Nothing else mattered now.

His phone buzzed and he answered it quickly. "Clay here."

"It's Boone. We haven't found anything yet, but wanted to let you know we've got a lot more boots on the ground. I think everyone from the Crow reservation just showed up. Walker must have called them in. They've got some trackers. I'm going to work with them myself. Your mom's here, too. She wants to talk to you, so I'm sending a man to take your place."

"Copy that."

Clay burned with impatience, though. If his mother wanted to commiserate with him, this wasn't the time. If she wanted to talk about Dell, he didn't want to hear it.

When his replacement reached him and he made it back to the bunkhouse, his mother, Dell and a cameraman were waiting for them.

"I came to join the search," Lizette said without a greeting. "I'm so sorry—"

"Mom, sorry isn't going to find her." Clay burned to get back to it. Hell, he wanted to be in town with Cab, not here chasing ghost leads.

"Riley told us you're looking for clues about where the man might have stayed."

"We've searched all the obvious places close by,"

Clay said. "The outbuildings, the hunting blinds—"

"I have an idea. You know I love a puzzle."

That was true. Lizette loved riddles, guessing games and anagrams.

"Like I said, we've searched—"

"What about the schoolhouse?" Lizette cut in. "Riley said the messages Nora got were about teaching, students, learning. Have you checked there?"

"I was there the other day. It was empty. No one was hiding there." Fear sliced through Clay as another thought occurred to him. Just because it was empty then didn't mean it was now. If that man had been following them—if he'd seen—

Of course.

He began to run for the lane before he realized he didn't have a vehicle. The members of Base Camp shared several and they were all gone. "Mom—keys!"

"But—"

"Keys!"

She tossed her keyring toward him, and he caught it in mid-air.

"Clay!"

He didn't wait to see who called or what they wanted. It would be much faster to drive to the schoolhouse than run to it overland.

And if Nora was there, he had to get there.

Right now.

He climbed in his mom's truck, started the engine and hit the gas. He was driving down the lane when a thump in back told him someone had just leaped into the box. He glanced over his shoulder.

Dell.

Shit, how had he—?

Clay didn't care. If the man wanted to come along for the ride, so be it. He wouldn't drive any slower for the human cargo back there. He was already putting distance between them and the cameraman running after them.

"Hold on, Pops," he muttered. "This'll be a hell of a ride."

MAYBE ANDREW HAD forgotten her. Maybe he'd been caught.

But Nora wasn't fooling herself. This was all part of his game. Part of the torture. He was making her wait. Making her think about what was to come. She eyed the door, ready to run at it full strength and try to bust it open.

But she didn't.

Andrew was out there. He was waiting for her to lose her cool.

He'd like it if she battered her body against the door in a desperate attempt to get out. It'd get him off if she screamed and cried for help. When he knew she was awake—and desperate—he'd come for her. He'd come anyway, sooner or later, but if she kept quiet she might buy herself some time.

The plywood sheets had irregularities that allowed light in around their edges. Up on the desks again, Nora managed to lean out as far as she dared without her hands to balance her, edged up on tiptoe and just managed to see outside. All that was visible was a sloping hillside dotted with scrub. She craned her neck from side to side to be sure, then edged back until she was standing again.

Leaping carefully down from the old-fashioned desk, Nora scanned the room. She spotted another chink in the boards covering an opposite window. Could she move a desk over that way?

Would Andrew hear?

Time was ticking away. Time she could be using to make her escape. She twisted her wrists in their bindings, the rope burning her skin as she tried to loosen it, but Andrew hadn't been messing around when he tied her up. He meant for her to be helpless when he returned.

She'd have to chance it.

Instead of dragging the desk straight across the room, however, she used her hands to lift and swing first one side and then the other of it around. In this manner she made progress with very little noise. By the time she'd positioned the desk under the window, she was sweating, the fabric of her skirts sticking to her legs. Nora didn't care. She had to know what Andrew was doing.

At first when she looked out the small crack between the plywood boards, she thought she'd struck out again. Like the opposite side, the ground here covered with tough grasses and scrubby brush. But when she looked all the way to the right, her heart caught in her throat. A rough, worn old picnic table was positioned near the front door of the schoolhouse.

And Andrew was sitting on it, smoking a cigarette.

Just as she thought. He was waiting for her to wake up and start screaming.

Well, she wouldn't give him the satisfaction. Not until she was ready for him, anyway.

She stared at the man she'd once regarded as a mild-mannered professional. She'd never heard him lose his temper in the teacher's lounge. Never seen him smoke before, either, but he lit another one off the stub of the first as she watched. As far as she knew, he'd been patient with his students, even if he wasn't beloved by them.

Where had all this aggression and rage come from?

Was it really because she'd turned him down for a date?

Maybe the situation wasn't so dire, she thought. Maybe he truly was mild-mannered and all he wanted to do was scare her. She couldn't imagine Andrew attacking her—

All his messages flooded her mind. The violent acts he'd threatened. The sexually suggestive insinuations.

He'd said he'd kill her.

Slowly.

He'd slid in and out of the manor, playing tricks, messing with her. Had that amped up the anticipation for him? He must have watched them coming and going for days to figure out their patterns.

Nora's heart beat hard in her chest and she let herself down carefully from the desk. She couldn't be fooled by the act Andrew had put on during school hours. The man was sick. He was bigger than her. Stronger. And he might be armed, while her hands were tied behind her back.

That had to change.

Nora searched the room again. If only she had a piece of glass, or a knife—

All she had were some stupid, god-awfully heavy desks.

Heavy.

Nora bent down to examine the desk more closely. It was truly old—made of cast iron with a wood top polished smooth by long use. She was amazed it hadn't been sold along the way. The iron work was lovely, really. But some of the wood was rotted and the desk surface was highly scarred. Maybe that's what had rendered it worthless.

Still…

Crouching down on her knees beside it, Nora turned around so she could feel the metal with her hands. It was cold—almost damp feeling, although it wasn't wet. It was rough, too, sandpapery beneath her fingers. There was a sharp ridge down the front of the leg.

Nora knew it was her only hope. Scooting back until she could reach, she began to rub the rope that bound her wrists against that ridge. It was a long shot, but she had to try.

What else could she do?

Minutes ticked by and her arms and legs ached from the awkward position, but Nora kept on rubbing. She was fighting for her life, and any moment Andrew would come walking through the door. She regretted the time she'd wasted searching for a way out. What was Andrew doing now? Should she check?

No, she had to keep moving.

Her wrists burning and her biceps aching, Nora redoubled her efforts. If she ever got out of here, she'd stop complaining about the tasks she'd had to take on at Base Camp. She'd gladly build houses all day if it meant she got to live.

And Clay. She wanted to see Clay again. She wanted to tell him she'd been wrong about everything. She wanted a chance with him, to see—

Was that a noise?

Footsteps?

Nora hesitated, then rubbed even harder. She had to have an advantage when Andrew walked in—one he didn't expect. Otherwise—

She intensified her efforts, but another noise stopped her in her tracks. Something scraping by the front door. A key in a lock?

Nora rubbed the rope against the rough metal leg even faster, not caring when the metal scraped her wrists, too. She nearly sobbed out loud when she felt a give, and then a snap. Writhing and yanking her wrists apart, she managed to get free of her bonds. She pushed to her feet, staggered as her legs cramped from the unusual position she'd held for so long and searched the room.

She needed a weapon. Something.

The front door bulged as if something heavy was being pushed against it. She heard a muttered curse. Was it stuck? Nora prayed frantically under her breath as she searched for something to arm herself with.

There was nothing. Except—

Nora pulled at one of the rotten desktops, and it came free of its metal undercarriage with a squeak. It wasn't much. Just a rectangle of wood, solid in the middle, soft and splintering away on the sides. She hoped it was enough.

Something banged against the door. Andrew's shoulder? Nora sprinted across to stand beside it where she'd be hidden by the door when it finally swung open. She lifted the wooden desktop over her head and held her breath, her heart beating so fast she thought it might burst from her chest.

Another bang. More swearing.

Andrew burst inside.

He was taller than she remembered. Without his chinos and pressed shirt, he looked rougher, too. His hair had grown out of its neat cut. He wore jeans, tennis shoes and a jacket that looked like he'd salvaged it from a Dumpster. When he turned his head, she saw he had a week's growth of beard, at least.

Nora didn't wait to see more. She bashed the desktop down on his head with all her might. When Andrew staggered a few paces, she ran—

Out the door, down the dirt track and toward the

road beyond.

She'd never run so fast in her life. Her shoes were sensible, but they weren't meant for this kind of activity, and Nora cursed the day she'd ever agreed to wear a Regency gown. Lifting her skirts in both hands, she put her head down and raced like her life depended on it.

It did.

"Nora!"

She sobbed out a garbled plea at the sound of Andrew's voice and sped up. She hadn't hit him hard enough. He was following her. Sprinting even as pain stitched through her side, Nora turned onto the road and hesitated only a fraction of a second. Which way to run? She didn't know where to turn. Where was help? There wasn't a car in sight.

"Nora!"

He was getting closer. Nora dashed to the right, in the direction she thought would lead back to the manor. She ran flat out, gasping for breath, praying for help as she fled down the road.

When a hand clamped down on her shoulder, Nora screamed, lashed out and dislodged it, but Andrew came back a second time. He caught her, hooked an arm around her middle. She tripped, their feet tangled together and they both crashed onto the macadam, knocking the breath out of her lungs. Still, Nora fought with everything she had, kicking and clawing and scrambling to try to stand up again. Andrew caught her arms, pressed them to the pavement and straddled her.

"Shut up. Shut. Up." He let go with one hand, fumbled in his pocket.

Another syringe? Chloroform? Something to knock her out? She didn't wait to find out. She grabbed his arm with her free hand, yanked it toward her mouth and bit him as hard as she could.

"Bitch!" Andrew slapped her, and Nora tasted blood in her mouth. "Fucking bitch. Always screwing things up. Why can't you do what you're supposed to?" He slapped her again. The next time he hit her, his fist was closed.

Pain blossomed in her cheek and Nora sucked in a breath. All her struggles hadn't dislodged him and she was losing strength. Where was everyone? Why hadn't a single car driven down this road?

Suddenly Andrew surged up off her, but Nora's relief was short-lived when he yanked her up with him, ducked down to throw her over his shoulder and headed back the way they'd come. Hanging nearly upside down, it took Nora a minute to orient herself and lash out again, but once she did she fought like a wild thing. He wasn't going to get her back in that school. Because when that door closed—

She turned and twisted, flailing like a fish in his arms until she finally managed to hook her elbow around his neck. She linked it in her other arm and squeezed as hard as she could, trying to choke the life out of him. Andrew clawed at her wrists, but she held tight until he tangled his fingers into her hair and dragged her down by it.

She wasn't sure what happened next. One minute

they were grappling. The next she was down in the dirt at the side of the road. She couldn't breathe. Andrew lifted her up again, and this time half-carried, half-dragged her back to the dirt track that ran to the school. She dug in her heels when she could, made herself as heavy as possible, but to no avail. Andrew, while not a large man, was strong—far stronger than she'd given him credit for.

Finally getting her feet underneath her, she lashed out again, dug her nails into his skin, and when that didn't slow him down she twisted around and bit him again.

"Goddamn it!"

Nora had just thanked her lucky stars that Andrew didn't seem to have a weapon when he dropped her to the ground and kicked her in the head.

He didn't need a weapon.

Nora's head ached and her ears rang. When she tried to sit up, the world spun and the contents of her stomach emptied on the ground.

"Jesus Christ. You bitch. Now look what you've done."

She'd thrown up on his shoe.

Good.

That was something, she thought, but as she fell back in the dirt, she felt the hot tracks of her tears and knew she was losing this fight.

Andrew stood over her, his disgust plain in the twist of his lips.

"Fuck. You," she managed to spit out, the first thing

she'd said since he'd opened the door.

"Yeah. You'd like that, wouldn't you? You always wanted to fuck me, but you couldn't handle it." He moved forward, one foot on either side of her, looming over her like the Colossus of Rhodes. He thought he was as invincible as the stone that had once made up that ancient statue, didn't he? No one was invincible, Nora wanted to tell him. Not even Andrew. "That's why you said no. Well, guess what? You're going to find out what it's like to take me inside you. You're going to beg me—"

In one quick jerk, Nora brought her knees to her chest and kicked with both feet at Andrew's crotch.

He crumpled with a cry, and Nora tried to scramble up. But Andrew had fallen on top of her, and even when she freed her legs, her long skirt was trapped underneath him. He writhed in the dirt, but just as she pulled free, he caught a handful of fabric and yanked her back to the ground.

No way. She wouldn't let him win.

Nora scrabbled and kicked until she was on her hands and knees again, and pulled until the fabric ripped and she came free. Not pausing to look back, she ran, gasping and heaving, toward the street.

She was going to get away. This time she'd get away. There had to be a car—

When the first shot rang out, Nora shrieked and ducked to the side, nearly tripping over the remains of her gown. The next one came to the left, and she raced back the other way. A quick look back told her Andrew was on his feet. He was pursuing her.

Shooting at her.

"Clay!" she screamed as she dashed forward again. "Clay! Please!" She didn't know if she was praying or begging or both. She only knew what she wanted. Clay's arms around her. This nightmare over. To be back at Westfield. At Base Camp.

With Clay.

Nothing else mattered. Not teaching, not writing, not Baltimore—

Just the man she loved. The man who loved her. The one person who made her feel safe and whole.

A third shot buzzed by so close, Nora dropped to the ground, then scrambled forward, half running, half crawling. She couldn't do this anymore. She couldn't—

A crack and a thud and something cold and hot all at once slammed into her shoulder. Nora hit the ground hard enough to black out, but she came to all too soon.

"Crazy bitch." Andrew stood over her. "Playtime's over. Let's get to work."

CHAPTER TWENTY-FOUR

CLAY SLAMMED THE steering wheel with the heel of his hand. Damn it, the turnoff to the school couldn't show up soon enough.

There. There it was.

He barely slowed down as he rounded the corner. Another glance in the mirror told him Dell was still with him. He pulled up in front of the schoolhouse, but Dell leaped from the truck and past him before he could even get the door open. Clay lurched out of the truck behind him, his service weapon heavy in its holster at his hip as he followed Dell to the door. He'd grabbed it from Base Camp's gun safe after the fire the previous evening and was grateful now he had.

Dell pointed to the ground, and Clay saw what he meant. Footsteps and tracks in the dirt. Someone had been here. Several someones.

Dell pointed again.

Clay's heart lurched as he bent closer to look.

Blood.

Nora.

He burst past his father, slammed against the battered door to the schoolhouse and launched himself inside. What he saw would stay with him for years to come. Nora's lifeless body on the floor, a stranger bending over her, fumbling with her gown. Blood staining the shoulder of her pale dress, an enormous, deadly blossom that nearly stopped Clay's heart, before rage started it pounding again triple time.

That rage propelled him forward like a furious bull, his shoulder lowered so when he hit the man, he knocked him flying. He dropped to his knees beside Nora and took in her pale face, her closed eyes and slack muscles.

"He's got a gun!" Dell's shouted warning let Clay duck and cover Nora with his body just in time as a shot rang out, deafening in the enclosed space. A muffled grunt made him turn around to see Dell crumple.

"Dad!"

Time slowed down. Without thought—without awareness—Clay drew his gun, aimed and took his shot, even as the stranger pivoted to put him in his sights.

Clay didn't miss.

The man hit the floor, the neat bullet hole between his eyes already filling with blood.

Clay spun around, looked for another source of danger, saw there was none and scanned the room to assess the damage.

Three bodies. The stalker—at least Clay assumed that's who the man with the gun was.

Dell.

And Nora.

And for one moment—one long moment—something else. A shadow. A ripple. Something he'd seen before on the battlefield.

Death.

Fear ripped through Clay with a jagged knife.

"No." Clay struggled to clear his throat. He had to make noise. Do something to scare it away, because Death didn't appear after someone was gone—it appeared when someone was going. And he'd be damned if he let either his dad or Nora slip away.

"You got one body," he shouted at the empty room as he sprang into action, still feeling that otherworldly presence. "You don't get any more." He tugged his shirt over his head, fell to his knees, pressed it to Nora's wound, then moved awkwardly to get closer to Dell, still keeping pressure on Nora's shoulder. There was so much blood on Dell's clothing he couldn't tell where his father had been hit.

"Neither of them. Do you hear me?" he shouted again.

But Death didn't answer. It never did, though it hovered close.

"Damn it."

Clay fumbled his phone out of his pants. Hit 911.

"I'm at the old schoolhouse—the abandoned one. I've got two down. They're bleeding out. I need an ambulance, now!"

"Sir—"

"This is Clay Pickett, from Westfield. I'm in the

abandoned schoolhouse near the highway. I've got two people shot. I need an ambulance—"

"They're on their way."

He dragged Dell closer to Nora, hating to move him, but unwilling to let him lie where he couldn't tend to him, either. His phone fell to the floor, but he kept one hand pressed on Nora's shoulder and searched Dell for a wound, finally locating it on the side of his neck. He couldn't tell how deep the bullet had gone, but he ripped the tail off the bloodied shirt he pressed to Nora's wound and did the same for his father.

"Nora. Nora, honey, you gotta stay with me." Of the two, he thought she was hurt the worst. Dell's breathing was even, but as he watched, Nora's was getting shallower. "Nora! Do you hear me?"

Her eyes fluttered open, and Clay's breath caught. Thank God.

"Nora? You're safe, honey. You're good. An ambulance is on its way."

"Andrew," she breathed, fear sparking in her eyes.

"Andrew? Is that the man who attacked you? He's dead. He can't hurt you anymore, baby."

She closed her eyes and a tear squeezed out from under her lid. Clay wanted to scoop her into his arms. Wanted to will the life back into her, but he couldn't take his hand from Dell's neck. "Nora. Come on, honey. Stay with me."

Her eyes opened again. "Cold."

Clay swallowed past a lump in his throat. He hadn't frightened Death away, after all. "You'll be warm soon.

You'll be safe and warm, I promise. Just another minute. You can do this."

"He keeps... coming. Keeps... coming."

He hated the pain and fear in her voice. When he spoke again, Clay's throat was raw.

"He's gone now, sweetheart. I swear. It's over."

"Over," she repeated.

"That's right. He's gone. Nora? Nora!"

She'd faded away again. Afraid he was losing her, he shook her gently, wincing because he knew he must be hurting her even more.

"Nora! Stay with me, baby. Come on."

Her eyes opened again. Another tear slid down her cheek.

"I think..." Her voice rasped, and he could tell it was painful for her speak. She moistened her lips and tried again. "I think... I'm ready... to go."

"No!" Clay reared up, then remembered Dell and pressed his palm against his father's neck again. "Nora, no. Please." Clay read the defeat in her eyes and didn't know what to do. She was giving up. That man had harried her out of a job, chased her halfway across the country and nearly killed her. Her ordeal was over, but she couldn't take that in. He had to convince her, but if he took the pressure off Dell's neck, Dell could bleed out in minutes.

Still, Nora was slipping away. He'd seen this too many times to believe otherwise.

"You've got to fight now, Nora. You've got to fight to stay. I need you here."

"I… can't. I'm…sorry." Another tear rolled down her cheek.

Clay clamped his hand on Dell's neck and bent over Nora, dragging Dell even closer. He kissed her, doing the only thing he knew he could do to convince her she hang on. "I love you." He kissed her again. "Baby, I love you. Hang in there. For me. Please."

When he pulled back she searched his face, eyes wide.

But he felt the moment her life left her body.

Clay tilted his head back and howled in rage.

CHAPTER TWENTY-FIVE

"**Y**OU KNOW WHAT I can't understand?" Nora's mother said. "Why you fight so hard for everyone else and not for yourself."

"Mm-mm." Nora couldn't find her voice. Couldn't find her hands for that matter. Or her eyes. She was caught in some kind of gray fog, her mother's words coming from far away and close all at the same time.

Where was she?

"Always a scrapper. Always so fierce. Remember how you kicked Danny Kirkpatrick and made him give Penny Sanders back her sandwich in first grade? They sent you home, but I was so proud of you."

Her mouth tasted like cotton balls.

Her mouth. Where...?

Someone was poking her—hard—in the shoulder. She tried to shift away.

Where was her body?

"But when Vinnie Reins punched you in the stomach, you came home in tears and refused to go back to school until I bribed you with skating lessons. Why didn't you kick him? I always asked myself that."

"Mm… Ow." Nora tried to get away from the pain. *Enough pain.*

Too much.

Too much.

Her mother kept talking. Nora wished she would stop, and dreaded it at the same time.

Her mother—

But—wasn't she…?

"Same thing when Phyllis Reynolds stole your prom date. Didn't say a word. Didn't even badmouth her behind her back. Where was that fighting spirit of yours then? Why don't you fight for yourself, Nora?"

"I… did."

She had fought for herself, hadn't she? Just now? When…

Nora didn't remember when.

"And that job of yours. Those kids. You were a wonderful teacher, Nora. Just wonderful. But then that man—"

That man.

That… Andrew.

Pain stabbed through her again and Nora groaned. *Who…? Why were they hurting her?*

"He took your career," her mother said. "Just… took it! You let him. You let him chase you off."

"Mom." It came out a moan. *She couldn't move. Couldn't feel—*

When the pain sliced through her again it was too much. *She didn't want to—*

"You did. You let him take those kids away from

you. Take your career. Now you're letting him take Clay. And I don't understand it. You never liked to fight for yourself, but you used to fight for those you loved."

Clay. She loved Clay.

"—leaving him behind when you know exactly what that feels like. I thought I raised you better—"

Clay.

"—and if you aren't willing to fight for him, maybe I didn't teach you a thing. Lord knows I tried—"

She'd fight for Clay. She'd—

"If you aren't going to fight for him, then you might as well come with me right now. Crying shame, that's what I say, but if you're ready to leave it all behind— even that nice young man—well then, let go. I've never been able to tell you a thing—"

Nora felt her fingers tense. She wasn't ready. She didn't want to let go. Not of Clay. Not—

"Make a choice, that's all you have to do. It's that simple, like most things in life. Hold on or let go. You know what's right, darling."

For the first time, her mother's voice softened.

"You know what's right," she repeated.

Hold on or let go.

Hold on or—

Nora gasped as air filled her lungs with the scrape of sandpaper. She breathed in, coughed, breathed in again. All around her people worked, paper masks covering their faces, nylon gloves over their hands. Metal instruments, bright lights, the smell of blood.

"Clay," she tried to say, but only her breath rasped

out, hard as stone scraping over stone.

"She's back!" a man in a mask announced triumphantly. "We got her! She's breathing on her own. Someone tell that crazy SEAL before he breaks down the door."

CHAPTER TWENTY-SIX

"T HIS ISN'T GOING to be an easy conversation," Cab warned Clay when they took seats on opposite sides of a table in Linda's Diner in town forty-eight hours after Clay had found Nora in the old schoolhouse. By the time the ambulance had arrived, the camera crews had, too, and he'd followed the gurneys out of the schoolhouse into a crowd of onlookers, cameras, lights and voices all going at once. He'd nearly gone ballistic, but Jericho and Boone had been there. They'd bundled him into the ambulance with Nora, while his father had been carried to the hospital in a second one, and they'd left the crowds behind—for a little while.

The ride had been the stuff of nightmares, the ambulance crew working the defibrillator hard on the way to the hospital. They whisked Nora into one operating room, his father into another, and left him waiting on the other side. He'd tried to follow them, got a little physical when an orderly had restrained him, before finally realizing there was nothing more he could do. He had no idea how long it was before a nurse rushed out to tell him Nora was alive.

Renata and the camera crews had come to the hospital, too, but they'd kept a respectful distance, much to Clay's surprise, and although he knew Renata had interviewed the others about what had happened, she hadn't approached him.

Yet.

It didn't matter. He'd never be able to describe the moment when Nora had died. Or the moment when he'd learned she'd come back to life.

He knew the second episode of the show had come out today, but he didn't give a fuck. Jericho had reported that it was a lot like the first, but that they'd actually filmed quite a bit of the process of building Boone and Avery's house.

"You look like a stud as long as there's a hammer in your hand," Jericho had said. "There's a lot of chatter on the website about the house. People want you to post your building plans."

At any other time, Clay knew that would have gratified him, but today all he could think about was Nora. She had been unconscious but in stable condition since they'd resuscitated her, and Riley, Savannah and Avery were sitting with her—the only reason he'd agreed to leave her side. Her doctor had assured Clay she was out of the woods, even if she hadn't regained consciousness except for that first brief moment.

"She's been through a big shock," the doctor had said. "Sleep is the body's way of dealing with that kind of trauma. She'll wake up when she's ready."

After making the women promise to call him if her condition changed the slightest bit, Clay had visited his father, who had also regained consciousness as soon as the wound in his neck had been tended to. His father had been lucky. The bullet had only grazed his neck. It had pierced his flesh—hence all the blood—but had missed any major arteries. Reassured after checking on him again, Clay had let Cab drive him to the diner. Maybe he was in shock, too. Nothing felt real. He found it hard to breathe most of the time.

"Are you up for hearing this?" Cab asked him as the waitress set down two cups of coffee in front of them. "That's all for now," he told the young woman, and she left, taking the menus with her.

"Yeah." Actually, he wasn't sure at all. But he couldn't go on guessing. He had to know what had happened to Nora. What he kept imagining was bad enough; the truth couldn't be worse.

"It might help for someone she cares about to know what she went through when she wakes up. Understand?" Cab shifted back in his seat.

"Yeah," Clay said again. He did understand that. There was nothing as soul-crushing as having lived through a tragedy that others hadn't, and couldn't imagine. His memories bound him to Boone, Jericho and Walker. They'd served together much of their time in the Navy. They'd shared experiences they didn't speak of, but that haunted all of them.

"We've got the same ghosts," Walker had said once.

That summed it up for Clay. But Nora wouldn't have anyone to share hers. He'd have to do the best he could.

"She fought, Clay." Cab watched him. "She fought like a she-devil. You need to know that. Pennsley might have won in the end, but she made him pay."

Clay had made him pay, too. With his life.

He had no regrets.

"I got the coroner's report. Pennsley had contusions on his head—big enough to suggest he might have suffered a concussion. He had scratch marks on his arms and face. That's to be expected."

Clay nodded, his stomach slipping sideways at the thought of Nora fighting for her life.

"He had several bite marks. Deep bite marks. If he'd come in for treatment, he'd have been given a tetanus shot."

Clay frowned. Bite marks?

"His neck shows signs of bruising. She must have gotten him in a choke hold at some point." Cab's admiration was clear in his voice. Clay's throat thickened, as it had too often in these past forty-eight hours.

"And this is the part I like the best," the sheriff went on, a grin tugging at one corner of his mouth. "His balls showed extensive trauma as well." Cab looked up. "She kicked him so hard she ruptured a testicle."

A sound came out of Clay that might have been a laugh, if it hadn't been so full of pain. It caught in his throat and almost turned into a sob. "Jesus."

"I know."

He fought for control and wished to God they were

anywhere but in a public place. But what would he have done if they weren't?

No. Cab had chosen wisely.

"It's going to take time, Clay. First she's got to heal enough to wake up, and that in itself is a battle. Then she's going to have to decide to stay numb or come back to the land of the living. You've got all this pressure on you to marry."

That he did. He was still being filmed, even now. He turned in his seat, and Ed saluted him from across the restaurant. The man was being as discreet as he could be, but he was still there. At least he was keeping far enough away he wasn't taping their words.

"Fulsom doesn't get to dictate this," Cab told him. "I'll make sure through Boone that he understands that, okay?"

Clay nodded, swallowing hard again. "Yeah. Thanks."

"Remember, she's a fighter. She'll fight her way out of this, too. We're all rooting for you, you know. For both of you."

By the time he made it back to the hospital, Clay felt like he'd fought another war. His mind kept picturing what the struggle between Nora and Andrew must have looked like. Each time he thought about it, he had to fight down nausea and the urge to kill the man all over again.

He stopped short when he entered the waiting room and found his mother there. She sat on the edge of a seat, looking older than she had the last time he saw her.

When she stood to greet him, he noticed her fingers trembling. Had his father taken a turn for the worse?

"Mom?"

"Your father's fine. Your sisters and brothers are with him. He's... fine." She sagged into his arms and began to cry as he crossed the room and crouched before her, thin heaving sobs he'd never heard before. His mother was a pillar of strength. She wasn't an emotional creature. Clay was at a loss for what to do, so he simply held her, patting her on the back as she cried.

"I'm sorry," she wept as the tears kept coming. "But I could have lost him. I sent him away, Clay. I made him leave... and he was shot... and he could have—"

"Shh, Mom—it's okay. He's safe."

"I held it together for all those years while you were in the Navy," she sobbed. "Every time you went overseas, I knew you were in danger. I knew you might not come home. But then you did. You did! And you were safe. Everyone I loved was safe—but then you both went after that monster and left me behind—" Her voice spiraled up, and Clay hugged her tight. He hadn't known how his deployments had affected his mother. He knew she worried, but this pent-up pain—it stabbed him to the core to know how scared she'd been. "He could have shot you. He could have killed both of you. And I sent your father away—"

"Mom." There was nothing he could say. He understood her regrets. "Everyone's okay now." He held her until her tears finally ran out, then stood awkwardly by as she mopped up her face.

"Oh, I'm a mess," she said, blowing her nose into her handkerchief.

"You're fine."

"Don't you tell your father I acted like this. He'd be ashamed of me."

"No, he wouldn't, Mom. He loves you."

She nodded. "I know. God, Clay, I know. I thought I was doing the right thing; forcing him to figure out what would finally make him happy. I was a fool."

"I don't know about that." He patted her arm. "How about we go see him?"

She nodded. "Give me a minute to clean myself up."

Ten minutes later they entered his father's room together, and found Dell and Clay's siblings watching television.

"How are you feeling, Dad?" Clay asked him.

"Fine, just like I was an hour ago when you last asked. I don't know why they're keeping me here. It's just a scratch." Dell's fingers tapped on the remote, and Clay could see there'd be trouble keeping Dell in bed much longer. But his father's restless energy gratified him. It meant Dell was truly recovering already. He itched to go check on Nora.

"I've got something to say," his mother said. She stood by the side of Dell's bed and gripped the metal side rails with both hands. "I was a fool. I should never have—"

Dell made a noise. "I was the fool." He turned off the television and caught sight of Clay, who'd taken a step back toward the door and was motioning to his siblings, thinking this was a conversation his parents would want to have privately. "You stay here, Clay. All of you stay. You need to hear this, too." He set the remote down on the bed. "I'm proud to be a father. Raising you was the best thing that's ever happened to me, except marrying your mother. I've had a good life. But it's no secret we started young, before we had time to make real decisions. One of the things I left behind when I married was my chance to study to be an architect. That was my dream back then."

He sounded like he thought he was issuing a revelation, but all of them knew this. They waited patiently for their father to go on.

Dell nodded finally. "Well, I thought I'd given it up for good. That's where the foolishness comes in. What I forgot is that I'm not in this alone. I have your mother, and I have you. It's time for me to go after that dream. I might need help. I guess I know I can count on getting it. And it's not like I'll be going it alone, right, Clay?"

"No, you won't. I'll be right there with you," Clay said, realizing his dad had finally gotten it—all of it. Knowing Dell would be on his side when he returned to school eased a long-held pain.

"I have another dream," Dell went on. "You all might not know about this one. I always thought... Well, maybe one day...maybe one of my kids might want to work with me. I know I'm a sonofagun, sometimes..." When his children all laughed he looked up. "I guess I'm a sonofagun a lot of the time. Maybe you'll say no, Clay, but this new sustainable nonsense... it's kind of interesting."

Clay reeled back, unprepared for this. "You've disagreed with everything I've done!"

"Not everything. That's what I was trying to tell you the other night in your tent when I said you've gone about it all wrong. You don't have to tell Americans what to do. You have to ask them what they'd do in your position. I don't like being ordered around. No one does. But once I saw what you were after, I started thinking, 'How would I make a house sustainable?' That's why I came up with the way to catch the water running off the roof. But you didn't want to listen."

"You're right. I was so afraid you'd catch a mistake I didn't want to hear it," Clay said slowly. "That's what I've been afraid of all along. I'm no architect. What makes me think I can design a house?"

"You've designed a damn good one. Once you've gone through school, you'll do even better. Who knows what we'll get up to?"

"Sounds like a plan, Dad."

"Good. Now you go check on your girl."

"Yes, sir. Dad—"

"Yeah?"

"Thanks for being with me when I went to get Nora. You saved my life."

"Yeah, well... I think you and your mother helped save mine."

"NORA? EVERYONE'S READY." Several weeks later,

Avery came to sit beside her on the bench Clay had built for her between the tent camp and the bunkhouse. The view wasn't as spectacular as it would have been up near the manor or down near Pittance Creek, but Nora felt safe here among all the activity, and safe was what she needed to feel now.

The doctor had explained that her nightmares would fade, and so would the sudden bouts of tears that overtook her no matter how hard she guarded against them. Her gunshot wound ached, and would for some time, but her fear drained her far more than her physical pain did.

She'd spent several days in the hospital before being allowed to come home. In the weeks since then, she'd alternated between resting on the thick air mattress Clay had bought for her tent and sitting on this bench, soaking in the sunshine and trying to convince herself she was still alive.

She hadn't told anyone about her experience on the operating table. It was just a dream, she'd decided. Her mother couldn't have nagged her back to life from beyond the grave. Every time she thought about it she had to smile a little, though, which inevitably ushered in a new storm of tears. Caught between numbness and anguish, she wasn't sure how to go on.

"All right," she finally said, although she was having a hard time focusing even now. There was a cotton batting barrier between her and life these days. Clay stood on the other side of it, keeping his distance, watching her warily. She knew he was afraid to touch her—to hurt her. She wished he knew that the distance between them hurt more than anything else.

At her worst moments, Nora wondered if he had stopped wanting her. She thought maybe Andrew's attack had changed the way he felt about her. Other times, when her confusion cleared, she knew he was waiting for a sign that she was ready to receive attentions from a man.

The problem was, she didn't know if she was ready, and the more time passed, the harder it got to reach out to him at all.

"Do you want me to help you up?"

She wanted Clay to help her up, but he wasn't here. He was never here—never close enough to touch, anyway.

"The new house," Avery prompted her gently. "The second one's all done. We're going to celebrate."

Of course. And she had to come, too, even though all she really wanted to do was slide back into sleep and dream of Clay. Dream of the days he used to hold her.

Except those weren't the dreams that came when she went to sleep. Instead, nightmares haunted her, in which she fought and fought and Andrew kept coming—

"Put your arm over my shoulder," Avery said. "That's right."

Nora gritted her teeth against the pain as she moved. Avery was on her good side, but every time Nora shifted—or breathed, for that matter—her shoulder ached. She'd been warned she might lose some of the range of motion in her left arm.

She couldn't find it in herself to care.

She was alive—even if nothing seemed real. Sometimes in the morning the sunlight glistened on dew dotting the surrounding pastures, and Nora's heart felt like it would break. The world was so beautiful—and peace so fragile. Was this what Clay had learned from Yemen? She would have to ask him someday.

Avery helped her walk to the building site, an arm around Nora's waist, even though Nora was perfectly capable of walking. She appreciated the gesture, though. Sometimes she felt so insubstantial she thought if she closed her eyes she might drift away. Still, she wished it was Clay's arm around her waist.

All of Base Camp had gathered around the beautiful home Clay had built. The small crowd parted to let them through. Nora took in Clay's satisfaction and the happy faces all around her. She wanted to feel happy, too—reached for it, but fell short. The numbness encircling her was too thick to penetrate. The hum of voices and Renata's low commands to the cameraman all seemed to be coming from far away. Nora wavered a little, but Avery was there. "Can you stand for a minute or two?" she asked.

Nora nodded, blinking to bring the scene in focus again.

Just like Boone and Riley's house, the new little home was built into the side of the hill. Large, south-facing windows lined the front of the structure, and the roof was angled to let in plenty of light while shading the front rooms from the summer glare. What Nora could see through the windows looked lovely, and for one short second something sparked to life inside her— a longing she couldn't name. It was extinguished as fast as it flared, leaving her confused and almost bereft.

Clay, who stood near the door to the house, was watching her. He did that a lot lately. He was afraid to hurt her, Riley said. Afraid to scare her, Savannah had added.

Nora knew they were right, but she wanted him so badly to take her in his arms and press her close so she could hear his heartbeat and know she was alive. Because what she had learned on the operating table that day was that Clay was her life. Not in a possessive way. Not in a helpless way. In the same way the sun set the droplets of dew on the pastures afire.

She wanted to feel that again, and Clay was the key to it.

If only she could put words to her longing.

If only he would come close enough to hear.

A cheer went up from the crowd as Clay opened the door and ushered the first of the onlookers in.

"How about I ask everyone to hold off and give you a turn?" Avery said.

"No." Nora composed her thoughts. "Let's wait. I want to take my time when I go in."

Avery hesitated. "Okay. If you're sure."

They waited until the rest of the crowd had walked through and oohed and aahed over the new building. When the last of them had left and were trailing back toward the fire ring, where Kai was serving a celebratory dinner, Clay turned to them.

"Want to come see?"

His deep voice beckoned to her, and Nora blinked back the tears that stung her eyes. She cried too easily these days. She nodded.

Avery helped her over, but when they reached the door, Nora said, "Clay will take me through." She caught the look he exchanged with Avery.

"I'd... love to." His voice was husky. Avery nodded swiftly. "I'll be at the fire ring. Let me know if you need anything. Stay with her, Clay. She's unsteady."

"Of course. You ready?" Clay said. He slipped a hand under her good elbow. Nora entered the small house and stopped, tears filming her eyes again. It was beautiful. A work of art. While it was built from the same plans as Boone and Riley's home, Clay had used raw wood and hand-carved pieces to personalize it. He'd eschewed corners and angles for rounded lines, and the effect was to make the little home appear as if it had grown out of the ground itself. Every spare inch was utilized for storage, with tiny doors opening to cupboards under the stairs and in nooks and crannies like a fairy's house. There was nothing feminine about it, though. It was evident from the moment she stepped in that this was Clay's home.

She wanted it to be hers.

"Nora," Clay said. "I..." It seemed like he couldn't finish his sentence. "I'm sorry. I screwed up."

She didn't understand.

"I didn't get there. I didn't find you—" His voice broke. "I think about it all the time. How I should have been there. How I should have stopped him—"

How could he think he'd fallen short in any way? Nora put a hand on his chest to cut off the flow of his words. "You saved my life."

He placed his own hand over hers, and lifted it up to press a kiss into her palm. Just as quickly he let go, and backed away. "Sorry."

"For what?" She couldn't keep the frustration out of her voice. Didn't he know what she wanted?

"I'll hurt you."

"No, you won't." She begged him with her eyes to know what she needed. "Clay—"

"Your shoulder—"

"It's fine."

"But—"

"I'm stronger than you think." She didn't sound strong. She couldn't blame him for holding back. "Please, Clay."

He came toward her slowly, and he put his arms around her so tentatively she wanted to scream. Instead she pressed herself against him, tucking herself into the circle of his arms.

"Is this okay?" he asked as he cradled her gently.

"It's not enough," she whispered into the hollow at the base of his neck.

He tightened his embrace a fraction.

"More. Please."

He did as she asked.

"Don't leave," she whispered. She didn't mean for him to hear.

But he did.

"Never." He pressed a kiss to the top of her head. "I will never leave you. Not for the rest of my life. I promise."

She let out a breath that was more like a sob and twisted the fabric of his shirt in her fingers, clinging to him. She wanted to make him promise over and over again, because without him she didn't know how she'd go on.

"I'm here," Clay said, holding her tight. "I will always be here."

"Kiss me." She'd never had the courage to demand such a thing from a man before, but Clay wasn't just any man. He was hers; the one she wanted to share her life with.

He'd been right; once you'd shared a mission and faced death with someone, you got to know them through and through. When she'd needed him, Clay had come as fast as he could. She now knew she could trust him with her heart—and her life.

She knew she loved him so much she'd never let him go.

As he bent to do so, she rose up on tiptoe and met him halfway, and knew they'd finally found the answer together. Neither one of them had to sacrifice to be with the other, or rather, they both did, equally. As long as he bent to satisfy her needs, she could rise to meet his. They could make their way through life's obstacles together.

"I love you," Clay told her when they finally pulled apart.

"I love you, too."

HE WOULD HOLD her until the end of time, Clay decided. Nothing would pry Nora out of his arms. Not while she needed him. If only he'd realized sooner she wanted him close, he would never have left her side from the moment she was wheeled out of the operating room.

No matter. Nora was in his arms where she belonged again. Her stalker was gone. Together they could build the life he always dreamed of. Her reaction to the house he'd built was more than gratifying, but if she wanted to leave it behind, he would in a heartbeat, because nothing mattered except being with her.

"Clay?"

"Yes?"

"The deadline. It must be close."

He nodded.

"When?" she demanded.

"Tomorrow."

"Clay—"

He hated that she even had to worry about that. "It's okay."

She pulled back. "You found someone else?"

The pain in her eyes made him rush to assure her. "No. The others drew straws and Curtis got the short one. He's agreed to marry... the woman Boone found for him. She's coming tomorrow." He hoped she didn't ask more questions. Curtis was sacrificing far too much for him. Boone had waited as long as he could to give Clay a chance with Nora, and then they'd all scrambled in these final days to come up with another solution. Fulsom had backed off his threat to cancel the show over Clay blowing his deadline, given the circumstances, but demanded they draw straws to see who would take his place. When Curtis realized he'd be the one to take the fall, he didn't even want to see the backup bride Boone had originally found for Clay.

"It's not like I can refuse if I don't like the looks of her," he'd said. "Why bother suffering ahead of time?" He'd been a bear ever since, keeping to his tent most of the time. At least he hadn't left.

It killed Clay to think the other man was taking a bullet for him this way, but they'd all discussed it at length and everyone had agreed that Nora deserved the chance to turn Clay down when she was ready—or to decide to marry him—rather than lose him to one of Fulsom's deadlines.

Nora didn't say anything. He didn't know how long they stood that way, but when he became aware that she was trembling in his arms, he knew she'd pushed herself too far. Still keeping an arm around her, he led her to the bedroom at one end of the house, closed the door behind them and untucked the new covers with which he'd made the bed.

"Go on. It's a lot more comfortable than your air mattress." He sat her on the edge of the bed, undid her shoes and helped her under the covers. He had plenty of pillows to prop her up, and though the day was warm, he arranged soft blankets around her until she nodded, letting him know she was comfortable. "How about some dinner?"

"Don't leave yet."

He sat down on the bed beside her and took her hand. He was all too aware of a certain compartment within arms' distance, in which sat a tiny, velvet box. This wasn't the time. Nora was still too weak, too overwhelmed by what had happened. But someday...

"Ask me."

Clay turned to her. "What—?"

"Ask me. Now."

"But—"

"Do it!"

Clay wasn't sure if he was interpreting the situation correctly, but his hand traveled to the door of the compartment as if of its own accord. He opened it, pulled out the little box.

"You're still healing. You don't have to—" he began.

"Yes."

His heart lurched, then warmed. "I haven't even—"

"Yes." Her voice hadn't been so strong since before the attack. Nora reached out as if to take the box from his hands.

He caught her hand in his and held it. "I'm going to do this right," he told her, but joy flooded him, making it hard to speak. "Nora Ridgeway, I've loved you since the moment I laid eyes on you, but you spent the first two months we knew each other running as hard as you could in the other direction. I don't know if I'm the man you deserve. I don't know if I can make you happy, but I do know I'm going to try. Every day for the rest of my life, if you'll let me. Nora, will you be my wife?"

She nodded, tears overflowing her eyes. His hands were shaking as he threaded the engagement ring over her finger, but Clay had never felt so sure of anything. "We'll take all the time you need. This can be the longest engagement in history. I don't care—"

Nora shook her head. "Now."

"But—"

"Now. This minute."

He looked around. "We don't have a preacher, honey."

"Get one." Her face was pale, but a wash of color stained her cheeks. Her eyes were fever-bright. "Anything can happen," she said. "Anything—in a split second. I don't want to wait."

"Neither do I." But it wasn't like he could—

"Clay, I mean it."

She wasn't kidding. Clay didn't know what to do. He'd marry her—hell, he'd marry her right here, in their bedroom, if he could, but—

"Riley. Avery. Savannah. They'll handle everything." She slid down a little, pulling the covers higher. She was overtired. Still in pain. He knew that. Knew, too, he'd do anything to make her happy.

"Okay. I'll talk to them. You get some sleep."

Tucked in among the covers, she was so luminous, for one moment he was afraid he would lose her again, but when he reached for her hand again, her grip was strong. "Tell them what I said," she insisted.

"Nora." Her eyes clouded over as if she knew he was going to let her down. "Are you sure?" he finally said.

She nodded. "I want to marry you when I wake up. Promise?"

"I promise." If he had to kidnap the minister himself he'd get it done. "I won't be far."

"I know." Her eyes were shutting already. Clay pressed a kiss to her mouth.

Then he got to work.

NORA DIDN'T KNOW how they'd done it. She didn't care. To her friends' credit, not one of them tried to persuade her to wait, or change her mind. When she woke up from the most refreshing nap she'd had since the attack, she found Riley, Avery and Savannah seated on the bed with her. Alice stood in the doorway, holding the most beautiful white wedding gown Nora had ever seen. Styled like one of her Regency gowns, it was delicate and wonderful, with simple lines and an elegant train.

"I made it myself. I hope it's what you were dreaming of," Alice said.

"It is. How did you make it so fast?"

"Once there was one wedding at Westfield, I knew there'd be more. I had it in reserve."

Avery helped Nora out of bed, and they all took turns helping her into her gown. Riley did her hair in a chignon. Savannah did her makeup, and Avery put her veil on her head. When someone knocked on the front door to the tiny house, Riley hurried to answer it. She came back with a bouquet of early wildflowers. "Someone's here to see you, Nora. Is that okay?"

"Of course."

She thought Riley meant Clay—that he'd knocked because he knew he wasn't supposed to see her before the wedding. Instead, Sue appeared in the doorway to the bedroom.

"We'll wait for you in the living room," Avery said, and the others withdrew. Uncertainty rippled through Nora. Sue had been so angry the last time she'd seen her. What had she come to say?

Sue clasped her purse before her with both hands. She took her time to compose her thoughts, but Nora understood that was her way.

"PTSD." Sue pronounced each letter distinctly. "My son had it. Walker's father."

It wasn't what Nora had expected to hear. But she'd grown used to Sue's roundabout way of getting to the heart of the matter. She could wait. "I thought he was killed overseas."

"He was." Sue was silent for so long, Nora thought that was the end of it. "Shot himself."

Nora's breath whooshed out of her. "Shot... Why?"

"It's a bad disease. It's a killing disease, if you let it. That feeling gets inside you—like you're already gone.

That's what he used to say to me. 'Mom, I'm already gone.'" She rubbed the fingers on her left hand. Played with her wedding ring. "I tried to tell him otherwise. Tried to show him all the reasons to live. 'Look at your boy,' I'd say." She shook her head. "Wasn't enough to hold him here." She peered at Nora, as if making sure she understood. "What my son never understood was that when he went, he took us with him. He took our hearts."

Nora nodded. She understood that. Understood, too, how close she'd come to leaving Clay and everyone else she loved behind. If it hadn't been for her mother's lecture when she'd woken up in that dreamscape between life and death, she would have left them behind. When Sue spoke again, it took Nora a moment to catch up.

"I distracted my grandson," Sue said, her fingers tightening on her bag. "Walker was supposed to be watching you in that store, and I——"

"It's not your fault," Nora hastened to tell her. She couldn't stand to see the woman hurting like this. If there was one thing she'd learned, it was that the world contained enough pain for everyone without dwelling on the bad things that didn't happen, or were already done.

"I should have come before." Sue nodded vehemently. "That mother of yours. While you were in the hospital, she told me, 'You go to my girl. You tell her to stay alive.' I didn't listen. I was too ashamed."

Nora stilled. "My mother? But——"

"She's a noisy one," Sue said emphatically. "Day and night. 'You tell my girl to stay.' She thinks you've found a good man."

"I don't understand—" But it was so good to hear someone else talk about her mother. It made her seem not so far away. Nora had thought more than once about what her mother had said, that if she wasn't going to fight, maybe she should accompany her right then. Instead she'd returned to her body—to life.

Which meant she wouldn't see her mother again for a long, long time.

"That's because you're thinking like a white girl. We're going to work on that." Sue nodded again. "Work on that with all of you. Especially that Lightfoot one."

"Avery?" Nora's heart lifted. "You won't stop her and Walker—"

"We'll work on her," Sue repeated. "See what's what. There's always another answer, just when you think you've gotten to the end of the answers." She nodded toward the door. "It's time."

Nora took a deep breath. "Thank you. For coming and... telling me about my mother."

"I like her," Sue pronounced. "She and I, we get along."

A tear slipped down Nora's cheek. She had a feeling her mother was close, agreeing with Sue. "I'm glad. Sue—when I'm stronger... when I heal... The curriculum. I'd like to get back to work." She hadn't thought once about her novel, Nora realized, and the reason why was crystal clear. She was meant to write something else—and teach when the time came. While she waited for the children of Base Camp to be born and grow old enough to need a teacher, she was going to write a curriculum for them—for the next generation. She wanted Sue's help.

Sue pulled a handkerchief from her purse and handed it to her. "Something borrowed. The work will be ready when you are. A lifetime of work." She smiled, a rare gift that made Nora's heart throb with gratitude. "Tidy up. Your man's waiting."

Nora did as she was told. When she looked up again, she was alone.

CHAPTER TWENTY-SEVEN

"WE'VE HAD SOME fast weddings in Chance Creek," Mia Matheson, Chance Creek's one and only wedding planner, said as she climbed out of a truck driven by her husband, Luke, "but this takes the cake."

"Thanks for coming on such short notice," Clay said, taking a number of bags from her hands. "What's all this?"

"Hors d'oeuvers. Chips and dip, mainly. I grabbed them from the store on the way over."

"Sounds fantastic."

"We've got folding tables and dinnerware in the back. Ned will be here soon with another load. Everyone's bringing something for the potluck dinner, so that's taken care of. Do you have music?"

"We brought our digital playlists and a set of speakers." Ella Hall bustled up, followed by her sisters-in-law, Regan, Sunshine and Heather. "Should we set things up here? Or will you use the barn again?"

"Here," Clay told her. "I don't think the party will

go too late. We need to keep Nora close to home, so she can rest when she needs to."

"Will do. We've got fairy lights. We'll figure a way to string them up."

Their husbands followed, laden down with more folding chairs and tables. Clay directed them where to drop them off. More trucks and cars were pulling up with each passing minute. When Boone and Jericho came to find him a little later, Clay had stopped setting up tables to watch.

"Looks like all of Chance Creek is going to be here," Boone said.

"Pretty amazing, given they had barely an hour's notice," Jericho said.

"People around here know when something's worth celebrating. Hey, I think that's Reverend Halpern arriving right now."

"I'll go greet him." Clay looked from Boone to Jericho. "Thanks for pitching in and making this possible."

"I've known from the day you landed here you and Nora belonged together," Boone said. "I'm going to go help the women with those lights."

"I agree with Boone," Jericho said when he had gone.

Curtis walked up, his arms full of folding chairs. He dropped them at Clay's feet and clapped him on the back. "Here's the man of the hour. I don't know how you did it, but I'm forever in your debt." He clapped his hand on Clay's shoulder again and shook it. Tipping his head back, he yelled, "Drinks are on me tonight, everyone!"

A ragged cheer went up from everyone who was busy working to set up for the wedding.

"The drinks are on me, actually," Clay said. "What are you going on about?"

"You saved my ass, man. I was due at the altar to marry some loser Boone caught trolling the Internet. But you beat the deadline. I've got forty more days. And I'm going to put them to good use. Starting tonight."

He gathered up the chairs he'd dropped and staggered off.

"He's happy," Clay said.

"Come on," Jericho said. "Those chairs aren't going to set themselves up."

"So what's it going to take for Savannah to realize what she's got in you?" Clay asked him.

"After what it took for Nora to see the light about you? I'm not sure I want to know."

IT GAVE NORA peace to think that her mother was here somewhere, watching over her as she took this important step, but as Nora left the tiny house flanked by her friends, she was all too aware of her father's absence from her life.

She was just deciding that she was okay to walk down the aisle on her own since she'd come this far without a father, when Walker stepped forward from where he'd been leaning against the front of the house.

He crooked his arm and held it out to her. "Don't know if you want me...after everything." His deep voice rumbled with sincerity even as his sentence trailed off. Nora's heart filled all over again. She knew Walker held himself responsible for what had happened to her. So many people did. She hoped that would fade in time, because the truth was Andrew was the only one responsible, and who knew what demons drove him? He was gone, and she was safe. That was all that mattered.

"I'm the one who would be honored," she repeated truthfully. She was soon grateful for the large man's solid presence by her side as Riley, Avery and Savannah took their places in front of her, dressed in their best gowns, to act as her bridesmaids. They led the way toward the crowd—the enormous crowd—assembled on folding chairs in the closest pasture.

Someone had rigged an arch of flowers, under which Reverend Halpern stood. Clay stood in front of the makeshift altar, with Boone and Jericho beside him. Her husband-to-be's handsome face was serious as he watched her step along the aisle left between the seats, leaning heavily on Walker's arm, but when Walker handed her over to Clay, he smiled, and the happiness in Nora's heart nearly overflowed.

"Thank you," she mouthed to Walker, who took his place next to Jericho. Then she faced the reverend, clinging tightly to Clay. She trembled, but not from fear or any kind of trepidation about the life she was agreeing to. It was joy that filled her. Joy to be alive. Joy to be marrying the man she loved.

And joy to be cherished and nurtured by a community like the one that waited behind her for her to say her vows.

"Dearly Beloved," Halpern began. "We are gathered here today…"

Clay squeezed her hand, telling her what she already knew. That he loved her.

That they would be together forever.

That she'd never be alone again.

"SHOULD I TELL our guests to go home?" Clay asked Nora several hours later, when he led her into their new home. Renata had stuck to the bargain he'd struck with her and kept her cameramen focused on the celebration when he and Nora slipped away. In return he agreed they'd do an in-depth interview about their relationship sometime soon. It was worth it to be alone with Nora now.

"No. I'm glad they're here. I like knowing we're surrounded by people who care about us," Nora said, drawing off her gloves and placing them on the small kitchen table. It was possible to hear music and the murmur of voices through the open windows. Nora was right, it was a comforting sound. As long as no one bothered them, Clay didn't mind if they partied on forever outside. Even Curtis's raucous celebrating made him smile. The man would have a hell of a hangover tomorrow.

He led her to the bedroom. All night he'd been anticipating this moment, but now that it was here, he wondered if it was possible to make love to Nora without hurting her shoulder. And what if their lovemaking brought up fears or bad memories of being attacked? He wished they'd had time to talk about it before.

"I'm fine," she told him, as if reading his thoughts.

"You'll have to tell me what to do. I don't want to hurt you," he said, pulling her gently to him.

"I will and you won't," she assured him. "You'll have to help me undress, though."

"Gladly." Clay turned her around. He took his time undoing the ties of her dress and peeling it off her. Dressed in her stays and chemise, she looked so sexy, he allowed himself the pleasure of drinking in the sight of her until she squirmed in his arms.

"Undo my stays," she directed him.

"Yes, ma'am." He made short work of them, moving carefully when he took them off. He laid them in a drawer, shut it and returned to Nora, bunching the fabric of her shift in his hands.

"I want to be naked with you," Nora said. Her desire for him was plain in her voice, filling him with pride, but Clay didn't speed up. He wanted to start off right. He wanted his wife to want him desperately when he filled her tonight.

So he kissed her with her chemise still on, despite her protests, exploring her mouth with his tongue until she kissed him back, clinging to him and pressing herself against him. When he couldn't stand it anymore, he leaned back, lifted the garment gingerly over her head and tossed it away.

"What about you?" She reached up to undo his shirt, but flinched when she raised her arm. Clay took over, making short work of getting undressed, until he was as naked as she was.

"Come on." He led the way to the bed, climbed in and lay on his back. "Hop up on me. That way you can call the shots and I won't hurt you."

But she didn't straddle him right away. Instead, Nora perched on the side of the bed and bent down to take the length of him in her mouth.

"Oh, God—Nora."

She seemed to have taken his words to heart and decided to run the show. As she slid him in and out of her mouth, Clay could only lay back and surrender to her touch. She stroked him with her tongue, circling and playing with him, until his fingers clutched the bed-clothes and twisted them. Now she was the one taking her time, until Clay didn't think he could hold back anymore.

When she finally climbed on top of him, Nora bent forward to trail her nipples over his chest, making him catch his breath.

"Do you want me to wear a condom?"

"No. I'm ready to start our family."

"I'm ready for that, too." She was so beautiful, the swells of her breasts beckoning him to touch, the rock of her hips as she lowered herself onto him enough to send pulses of ecstasy through him.

He'd let her have her fun, but once she slid herself over him and he was pressed deep inside her, Clay took over. His hands on her hips, he pushed in and out until she matched his rhythm, moving above him.

Catching one of her nipples in his mouth, he laved and tugged as he made love to her, the soft fullness of her breast pressing against his lips only fueling the hunger inside him. He stroked in harder, pulled out and stroked in again. Nora bobbed with his motions, arching her back, presenting her breasts to his touch and moaning with delight when he thrust inside her again.

Soon their rhythm was beyond both their control, and Clay, no longer afraid of hurting her, let his need guide him, speeding up his thrusts until they both were panting, close to the edge.

When Nora went over with a cry, Clay chased her into ecstasy, his own grunts shattering the silence of the small room. Knowing she was open to him, that no barrier stood between them, made him come with a ferocity that drained him to the core.

When it was over, they lay in a tangled heap, breathing as one.

"Are you okay?" Clay asked, suddenly worried.

"More than okay."

"Do you think you're pregnant yet?" he joked.

She nodded. "I think I am." Then she smiled a mischievous smile that made his breath catch in his throat. "But just to be sure, we'd better do that again. A lot." She rolled over gingerly onto her back and spread her legs. "Like right now."

"Give me a minute," he growled, but he was already hardening again. He'd never grow tired of being intimate with Nora. As he bent to press a kiss to her thigh, he knew he was finally right where he belonged.

To find out more about Boone, Riley, Clay, Jericho, Walker and the other inhabitants of Westfield, look for *A SEAL's Pledge*, Volume 3 in the *SEALs of Chance Creek* series.

Be the first to know about Cora Seton's new releases! Sign up for her newsletter here!
www.coraseton.com/sign-up-for-my-newsletter

Other books in the SEALs of Chance Creek Series:

A SEAL's Oath
A SEAL's Pledge
A SEAL's Consent

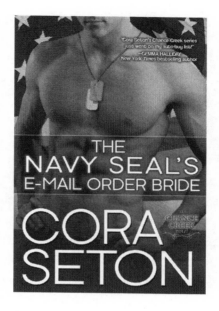

Read on for an excerpt of Volume 1 of
The Heroes of Chance Creek series –
The Navy SEAL's E-Mail Order Bride.

"**B**OYS," LIEUTENANT COMMANDER Mason Hall said, "we're going home."

He sat back in his folding chair and waited for a reaction from his brothers. The recreation hall at Bagram Airfield was as busy as always with men hunched over laptops, watching the widescreen television, or lounging in groups of three or four shooting the breeze. His brothers—three tall, broad shouldered men in uniform—stared back at him from his computer screen, the feeds from their four-way video conversation all relaying a similar reaction to his words.

Utter confusion.

"Home?" Austin was the first to speak. A Special Forces officer just a year younger than Mason, he was currently in Kabul.

"Home," Mason confirmed. "I got a letter from Great Aunt Heloise. Uncle Zeke passed away over the weekend without designating an heir. That means the ranch reverts back to her. She thinks we'll do a better job running it than Darren will." Darren, their first cousin, wasn't known for his responsible behavior and he hated ranching. Mason, on the other hand, loved it. He had missed the ranch, the cattle, the Montana sky and his family's home ever since they'd left it twelve years ago.

"She's giving Crescent Hall to us?" That was Zane, Austin's twin, a Marine currently in Kandahar. The excitement in his tone told Mason all he needed to know—Zane stilled loved the old place as much as he did. When Mason had gotten Heloise's letter, he'd had to read it more than once before he believed it. The Hall would belong to them once more—when he'd thought they'd lost it for good. Suddenly he'd felt like he could breathe fully again after so many years of holding in his anger and frustration over his uncle's behavior. The timing was perfect, too. He was due to ship stateside any day now. By April he'd be a civilian again.

Except it wasn't as easy as all that. Mason took a deep breath. "There are a few conditions."

Colt, his youngest brother, snorted. "Of course—

we're talking about Heloise, aren't we? What's she up to this time?" He was an Air Force combat controller who had served both in Afghanistan and as part of the relief effort a few years back after the massive earthquake which devastated Haiti. He was currently back on United States soil in Florida, training with his unit.

Mason knew what he meant. Calling Heloise eccentric would be an understatement. In her eighties, she had definite opinions and brooked no opposition to her plans and schemes. She meant well, but as his father had always said, she was capable of leaving a swath of destruction in family affairs that rivaled Sherman's march to Atlanta.

"The first condition is that we have to stock the ranch with one hundred pair of cattle within twelve months of taking possession."

"We should be able to do that," Austin said.

"It's going to take some doing to get that ranch up and running again," Zane countered. "Zeke was already letting the place go years ago."

"You have something better to do than fix the place up when you get out?" Mason asked him. He hoped Zane understood the real question: was he in or out?

"I'm in; I'm just saying," Zane said.

Mason suppressed a smile. Zane always knew what he was thinking.

"Good luck with all that," Colt said.

"Thanks," Mason told him. He'd anticipated that inheriting the Hall wouldn't change Colt's mind about staying in the Air Force. He focused on the other two who were both already in the process of winding down their military careers. "If we're going to do this, it'll take a commitment. We're going to have to pool our funds and put our shoulders to the wheel for as long as it takes. Are you up for that?"

"I'll join you there as soon as I'm able to in June," Austin said. "It'll just be like another year in the service. I can handle that."

"I already said I'm in," Zane said. "I'll have boots on the ground in September."

Here's where it got tricky. "There's just one other thing," Mason said. "Aunt Heloise has one more requirement of each of us."

"What's that?" Austin asked when he didn't go on.

"She's worried about the lack of heirs on our side of the family. Darren has children. We don't."

"Plenty of time for that," Zane said. "We're still young, right?"

"Not according to Heloise." Mason decided to get it over and done with. "She's decided that in order for us to inherit the Hall free and clear, we each have to be married within the year. One of us has to have a child."

Stunned silence met this announcement until Colt started to laugh. "Staying in the Air Force doesn't look so bad now, does it?"

"That means you, too," Mason said.

"What? Hold up, now." Colt was startled into soberness. "I won't even live on the ranch. Why do I have to get hitched?"

"Because Heloise says it's time to stop screwing

around. And she controls the land. And you know Heloise."

"How are we going to get around that?" Austin asked.

"We're not." Mason got right to the point. "We're going to find ourselves some women and we're going to marry them."

"In Afghanistan?" Zane's tone made it clear what he thought about that idea.

Tension tightened Mason's jaw. He'd known this was going to be a messy conversation. "Online. I created an online personal ad for all of us. Each of us has a photo, a description and a reply address. A woman can get in touch with whichever of us she chooses and start a conversation. Just weed through your replies until you find the one you want."

"Are you out of your mind?" Zane peered at him through the video screen.

"I don't see what you're upset about. I'm the one who has to have a child. None of you will be out of the service in time."

"Wait a minute—I thought you just got the letter from Heloise." As usual, Austin zeroed in on the inconsistency.

"The letter came about a week ago. I didn't want to get anyone's hopes up until I checked a few things out." Mason shifted in his seat. "Heloise said the place is in rougher shape than we thought. Sounds like Zeke sold off the last of his cattle last year. We're going to have to start from scratch, and we're going to have to move fast to meet her deadline—on both counts. I did all the leg work on the online ad. All you need to do is read some e-mails, look at some photos and pick one. How hard can that be?"

"I'm beginning to think there's a reason you've been single all these years, Straightshot," Austin said. Mason winced at the use of his nickname. The men in his unit had christened him with it during his early days in the service, but as Colt said when his brothers had first heard about it, it made perfect sense. The name had little to do with his accuracy with a rifle, and everything to do with his tendency to find the shortest route from here to done on any mission he was tasked with. Regardless of what obstacles stood in his way.

Colt snickered. "Told you two it was safer to stay in the military. Mason's Matchmaking Service. It has a ring to it. I guess you've found yourself a new career, Mase."

"Stow it." Mason tapped a finger on the table. "Just because I've put the ad up doesn't mean that any of you have to make contact with the women who write you. If it doesn't work, it doesn't work. But you need to marry within the year. If you don't find a wife for yourself, I'll find one for you."

"He would, too," Austin said to the others. "You know he would."

"When does the ad go live?" Zane asked.

"It went live five days ago. You've each got several hundred responses so far. I'll forward them to you as soon as we break the call."

Austin must have leaned toward his webcam because suddenly he filled the screen. "Several hundred?"

"That's right."

Colt's laughter rang out over the line.

"Don't know what you're finding so funny, Colton," Mason said in his best imitation of their late father's voice. "You've got several hundred responses, too."

"What? I told you I was staying..."

"Read through them and answer all the likely ones. I'll be in touch in a few days to check your progress." Mason cut the call.

REGAN ANDERSON WANTED a baby. Right now. Not five years from now. Not even next year.

Right now.

And since she'd just quit her stuffy loan officer job, moved out of her overpriced one bedroom New York City apartment, and completed all her preliminary appointments, she was going to get one via the modern technology of artificial insemination.

As she raced up the three flights of steps to her tiny new studio, she took the pins out of her severe updo and let her thick, auburn hair swirl around her shoulders. By the time she reached the door, she was breathing hard. Inside, she shut and locked it behind her, tossed her briefcase and blazer on the bed which took up the lion's share of the living space, and kicked off her high heels. Her blouse and pencil skirt came next, and thirty seconds later she was down to her skivvies.

Thank God.

She was done with Town and Country Bank. Done with originating loans for people who would scrape and slave away for the next thirty years just to cling to a lousy flat near a subway stop. She was done, done, done being a cog in the wheel of a financial system she couldn't stand to be a part of anymore.

She was starting a new business. Starting a new life.

And she was starting a family, too.

Alone.

After years of looking for Mr. Right, she'd decided he simply didn't exist in New York City. So after several medical exams and consultations, she had scheduled her first round of artificial insemination for the end of April. She couldn't wait.

Meanwhile, she'd throw herself into the task of building her consulting business. She would make it her job to help non-profits assist regular people start new stores and services, buy homes that made sense, and manage their money so that they could get ahead. It might not be as lucrative as being a loan officer, but at least she'd be able to sleep at night.

She wasn't going to think about any of that right now, though. She'd survived her last day at work, survived her exit interview, survived her boss, Jack Richey, pretending to care that she was leaving. Now she was giving herself the weekend off. No work, no nothing—just forty-eight hours of rest and relaxation.

Having grabbed takeout from her favorite Thai restaurant on the way home, Regan spooned it out onto a plate and carried it to her bed. Lined with pillows, it doubled as her couch during waking hours. She sat cross-legged on top of the duvet and savored her food and her freedom. She had bought herself a nice bottle of wine to drink this weekend, figuring it might be her last for an awfully long time. She was all too aware her Chardonnay-sipping days were coming to an end. As soon as her weekend break from reality was over, she planned to spend the next ten months starting her business, while scrimping and saving every penny she could. She would have to move to a bigger apartment right before the baby was born, but given the cost of renting in the city, the temporary downgrade was worth it. She pushed all thoughts of business and the future out of her mind. Rest and relax—that was her job for now.

Two hours and two glasses of wine later, however, rest and relaxation was beginning to feel a lot like loneliness and boredom. In truth, she'd been fighting loneliness for months. She'd broken up with her last boyfriend before Christmas. Here it was March and she was still single. Two of her closest friends had gotten married and moved away in the past twelve months, Laurel to New Hampshire and Rita to New Jersey. They rarely saw each other now and when she'd jokingly mentioned the idea of going ahead and having a child without a husband the last time they'd gotten together, both women had scoffed.

"No way could I have gotten through this pregnancy without Ryan." Laurel ran a hand over her large belly.

"I've felt awful the whole time."

"No way I'm going back to work." Rita's baby was six weeks old. "Thank God Alan brings in enough cash to see us through."

Regan decided not to tell them about her plans until the pregnancy was a done deal. She knew what she was getting into—she didn't need them to tell her how hard it might be. If there'd been any way for her to have a baby normally—with a man she loved—she'd have chosen that path in a heartbeat. But there didn't seem to be a man for her to love in New York. Unfortunately, keeping her secret meant it was hard to call either Rita or Laurel just to chat, and she needed someone to chat with tonight. As dusk descended on the city, Regan felt fear for the first time since making her decision to go ahead with having a child.

What if she'd made a mistake? What if her consultancy business failed? What if she became a welfare mother? What if she had to move back home?

When the thoughts and worries circling her mind grew overwhelming, she topped up her wine, opened up her laptop and clicked on a YouTube video of a cat stuck headfirst in a cereal box. Thank goodness she'd hooked up wi-fi the minute she secured the studio. Simultaneously scanning her Facebook feed, she read an update from an acquaintance named Susan who was exhibiting her art in one of the local galleries. She'd have to stop by this weekend.

She watched a couple more videos—the latest installment in a travel series she loved, and one about over-the-top weddings that made her sad. Determined to cheer up, she hopped onto Pinterest and added more images to her nursery pinboard. Sipping her wine, she checked the news, posted a question on the single parents' forum she frequented, checked her e-mail again, and then tapped a finger on the keys, wondering what to do next. The evening stretched out before her, vacant even of the work she normally took home to do over the weekend. She hadn't felt at such loose ends in years.

Pacing her tiny apartment didn't help. Nor did an attempt at unpacking more of her things. She had finished moving in just last night and boxes still lined one wall. She opened one to reveal books, took a look at her limited shelf space and packed them up again. A second box revealed her collection of vintage fans. No room for them here, either.

She stuck her iTouch into a docking station and turned up some tunes, then drained her glass, poured herself another, and flopped onto her bed. The wine was beginning to take effect—giving her a nice, soft, fuzzy feeling. It hadn't done away with her loneliness, but when she turned back to Facebook on her laptop, the images and YouTube links seemed funnier this time.

Heartened, she scrolled further down her feed until she spotted another post one of her friends had shared. It was an image of a handsome man standing ramrod straight in combat fatigues. *Hello.* He was cute. In fact, he looked like exactly the kind of man she'd always hoped she'd meet. He wasn't thin and arrogant like the up-and-coming Wall Street crowd, or paunchy and cynical like the upper-management men who hung around the bars near work. Instead he looked healthy, muscle-bound, clear-sighted, and vital. What was the post about? She clicked the link underneath it. Maybe there'd be more fantasy-fodder like this man wherever it took her.

There *was* more fantasy fodder. Regan wriggled happily. She had landed on a page that showcased four men. Brothers, she saw, looking more closely—two of them identical twins. Each one seemed to represent a different branch of the United States military. Were they models? Was this some kind of recruitment ploy?

Practical Wives Wanted read the heading at the top. Regan nearly spit out a sip of her wine. Wives Wanted? Practical ones? She considered the men again, then read more.

Looking for a change? the text went on. *Ready for a real challenge? Join four hardworking, clean living men and help bring our family's ranch back to life.*

Skills required—any or all of the following: Riding, roping, construction, animal care, roofing, farming, market gardening, cooking, cleaning, metalworking, small motor repair…

The list went on and on. Regan bit back at a laugh which quickly dissolved into giggles. Small engine repair? How very romantic. Was this supposed to be satire or was it real? It was certainly one of the most intriguing things she'd seen online in a long, long time.

Must be willing to commit to a man and the project. No weekends/no holidays/no sick days. Weaklings need not apply.

Regan snorted. It was beginning to sound like an employment ad. Good luck finding a woman to fill those conditions. She'd tried to find a suitable man for years and came up with Erik—the perennial mooch who'd finally admitted just before Christmas that he liked her old Village apartment more than he liked her. That's why she planned to get pregnant all by herself. There wasn't anyone worth marrying in the whole city. Probably the whole state. And if the men were all worthless, the women probably were, too. She reached for her wine without turning from the screen, missed, and nearly knocked over her glass. She tried again, secured the wine, drained the glass a third time and set it down again.

What she would give to find a real partner. Someone strong, both physically and emotionally. An equal in intelligence and heart. A real man.

But those didn't exist.

If you're sick of wasting your time in a dead-end job, tired of tearing things down instead of building something up, or just ready to get your hands dirty with clean, honest work, write and tell us why you'd make a worthy wife for a man who has spent the last decade in uniform.

There wasn't much to laugh at in this paragraph. Regan read it again, then got up and wandered to the kitchen to top up her glass. She'd never seen a singles ad like this one. She could see why it was going viral. If it was real, these men were something special. Who wanted to do clean, honest work these days? What kind of man was selfless enough to serve in the military instead of sponging off their girlfriends? If she'd known there were guys like this in the world, she might not have been so quick to schedule the artificial insemination appointment.

She wouldn't cancel it, though, because these guys couldn't be for real, and she wasn't waiting another minute to start her family. She had dreamed of having children ever since she was a child herself and organized pretend schools in her backyard for the neighborhood little ones. Babies loved her. Toddlers thought she was the next best thing to teddy bears. Her co-workers at the bank had never appreciated her as much as the average five-year-old did.

Further down the page there were photographs of the ranch the brothers meant to bring back to life. The land was beautiful, if overgrown, but its toppled fences and sagging buildings were a testament to its neglect. The photograph of the main house caught her eye and kept her riveted, though. A large gothic structure, it could be beautiful with the proper care. She could see why these men would dedicate themselves to returning it to its former glory. She tried to imagine what it would be like to live on the ranch with one of them, and immediately her body craved an open sunny sky—the kind you were hard pressed to see in the city. She sunk into the daydream, picturing herself sitting on a back porch sipping lemonade while her cowboy worked and the baby napped. Her husband would have his shirt off while he chopped wood, or mended a fence or whatever it was ranchers did. At the end of the day they'd fall into bed and make love until morning.

Regan sighed. It was a wonderful daydream, but it had no bearing on her life. Disgruntled, she switched over to Netflix and set up a foreign film. She fetched the bottle of wine back to bed with her and leaned against her many pillows. She'd managed to hang her small flatscreen on the opposite wall. In an apartment this tiny, every piece of furniture needed to serve double-duty.

As the movie started, Regan found herself composing messages to the military men in the Wife Wanted ad, in which she described herself as trim and petite, or lithe and strong, or horny and good-enough-looking to do the trick.

An hour later, when the film failed to hold her attention, she grabbed her laptop again. She pulled up the Wife Wanted page and reread it, keeping an eye on the foreign couple on the television screen who alternately argued and kissed.

Crazy what some people did. What was wrong with these men that they needed to advertise for wives instead of going out and meeting them like normal people?

She thought of the online dating sites she'd tried in the past. She'd had some awkward experiences, some horrible first dates, and finally one relationship that lasted for a couple of months before the man was transferred to Tucson and it fizzled out. It hadn't worked for her, but she supposed lots of people found love online these days. They might not advertise directly for spouses, but that was their ultimate intention, right? So maybe this ad wasn't all that unusual.

Most men who posted singles ads weren't as hot as these men were, though. Definitely not the ones she'd met. She poured herself another glass. A small twinge of her conscience told her she'd already had far too much wine for a single night.

To hell with that, Regan thought. As soon as she got pregnant she'd have to stay sober and sane for the next eighteen years. She wouldn't have a husband to trade off with—she'd always be the designated driver, the adult in charge, the sober, wise mother who made sure nothing bad ever happened to her child. Just this one last time she was allowed to blow off steam.

But even as she thought it, a twinge of fear wormed through her belly.

What if she wasn't good enough?

She stood up, strode the two steps to the kitchenette and made herself a bowl of popcorn. She drowned it in butter and salt, returned to the bed in time for the ending credits of the movie, and lined up *Pride and Prejudice* with Colin Firth. Time for comfort food and a comfort movie. *Pride and Prejudice* always did the trick when she felt blue. She checked the Wife Wanted page again on her laptop. If she was going to pick one of the men—which she wasn't—who would she choose?

Mason, the oldest, due to leave the Navy in a matter of weeks, drew her eye first. With his dark crew cut, hard jaw and uncompromising blue eyes he looked like the epitome of a military man. He stated his interests as ranching—of course—history, natural sciences and tactical operations, whatever the hell that was. That left her little more informed than before she'd read it, and she wondered what the man was really like. Did he read the newspaper in bed on Sunday mornings? Did he prefer lasagna or spaghetti? Would he listen to country music in his truck or talk radio? She stared at his photo, willing him to answer.

The next two brothers, Austin and Zane, were less fierce, but looked no less intelligent and determined. Still, they didn't draw her eye the way the way Mason did. Colt, the youngest, was blond with a grin she bet drew women like flies. That one was trouble, and she didn't need trouble.

She read Mason's description again and decided he was the leader of this endeavor. If she was going to pick one, it would be him.

But she wasn't going to pick one. She had given up all that. She'd made a promise to her imaginary child that she would not allow any chaos into its life. No dating until her baby wore a graduation gown, at the very least. She felt another twinge. Was she ready to give up men for nearly two decades? That was a long time.

It's worth it, she told herself. She had no doubt about her desire to be a mother. She had no doubt she'd be a great mom. She was smart, capable and had a good head on her shoulders. She was funny, silly and patient, too. She loved children.

She was just lousy with men.

But that didn't matter anymore. She pushed the laptop aside and returned her attention to *Pride and Prejudice*, quickly falling into an old drinking game she and Laurel had devised one night that required taking a swig of wine each time one of the actresses lifted her eyebrows in polite surprise. When she finished the bottle, she headed to the tiny kitchenette to track down another one, trilling, "Jane! Elizabeth!" at the top of her voice along with Mrs. Bennett in the film. There was no more wine, so she switched to tequila.

By the time Elizabeth Bennett discovered the miracle of Mr. Darcy's palace-sized mansion, and decided she'd been too hasty in turning down his offer of marriage, Regan had decided she too needed to cast off her prejudices and find herself a man. A hot hunk of a military man. She grabbed the laptop, fumbled with the link that would let her leave Mason Hall a message and drafted a brilliant missive worthy of Jane Austen herself.

Dear Lt. Cmdr. Hall,

In her mind she pronounced lieutenant with an "f" like the Brits in the movie onscreen.

It is a truth universally acknowledged, that a single man in possession of a good ranch, must be in want of a wife. Furthermore, it must be self-evident that the wife in question should possess certain qualities numbering amongst them riding, roping, construction, roofing, farming, market gardening, cooking, cleaning, metalworking, animal care, and—most importantly, by Heaven—small motor repair.

Seeing as I am in possession of all these qualities,

not to mention many others you can only have left out through unavoidable oversight or sheer obtuseness—such as glassblowing, cheesemaking, towel origami, heraldry, hovercraft piloting, and an uncanny sense of what cats are thinking—I feel almost forced to catapult myself into your purview.

You will see from my photograph that I am most eminently and majestically suitable for your wife.

She inserted a digital photo of her foot.

In fact, one might wonder why such a paragon of virtue such as I should deign to answer such a peculiar advertisement. The truth is, sir, that I long for adventure. To get my hands dirty with clean, hard work. To build something up instead of tearing it down.

In short, you are really hot. I'd like to lick you.

Yours,

Regan Anderson

On screen, Elizabeth Bennett lifted an eyebrow. Regan knocked back another shot of Jose Cuervo and passed out.

End of Excerpt

The Cowboys of Chance Creek Series:

The Cowboy Inherits a Bride (Volume 0)
The Cowboy's E-Mail Order Bride (Volume 1)
The Cowboy Wins a Bride (Volume 2)
The Cowboy Imports a Bride (Volume 3)
The Cowgirl Ropes a Billionaire (Volume 4)
The Sheriff Catches a Bride (Volume 5)
The Cowboy Lassos a Bride (Volume 6)
The Cowboy Rescues a Bride (Volume 7)
The Cowboy Earns a Bride (Volume 8)
The Cowboy's Christmas Bride (Volume 9)

The Heroes of Chance Creek Series:

The Navy SEAL's E-Mail Order Bride (Volume 1)
The Soldier's E-Mail Order Bride (Volume 2)
The Marine's E-Mail Order Bride (Volume 3)
The Navy SEAL's Christmas Bride (Volume 4)
The Airman's E-Mail Order Bride (Volume 5)

The SEALs of Chance Creek Series:

A SEAL's Oath
A SEAL's Vow
A SEAL's Pledge
A SEAL's Consent